"DROP THE FORCEFIELD," KIRK ORDERED.

The blue sheen disappeared, along with the faint tang of ions in the air.

Kirk put his hand phaser on his belt as he went to the comm. It was already tied into the *Barataria*'s frequency. "This is James Kirk of the Federation *Starship Enterprise*. Please open your hatch and come out."

"This is Commander Teral of the Barataria." The voice was flattened and distorted with hissing feedback. *"I demand that you release my ship."*

"I'm afraid I can't do that until you come out and answer some questions."

There was silence from the comm—only the hissing and popping of the *Barataria*'s open channel.

Kirk turned to Spock. "Well, now what? Do we blow the door open?"

"A most difficult decision," Spock commented.

"I'd hate to ruin such a fine ship," Kirk said speculatively, knowing full well the channel was still open. "But if there's no other way . . ."

Spock caught on fast, as always. "We are currently outside Federation territory. Free-space codes include the rights of salvage—"

"Salvage!" the intercom shrieked.

There was a puff of vacuum breaking, and the seal of the hatch split. The door slid open with a smooth whir.

STAR TREK®

The BADLANDS

BOOK ONE OF TWO

SUSAN WRIGHT

POCKET BOOKS
New York   London   Toronto   Sydney   Singapore

This book is a work of fiction. Names, characters, places and incidents are products of the author's imagination or are used fictitiously. Any resemblance to actual events or locales or persons, living or dead, is entirely coincidental.

An *Original* Publication of POCKET BOOKS

POCKET BOOKS, a division of Simon & Schuster Inc.
1230 Avenue of the Americas, New York, NY 10020

STAR TREK is a Registered Trademark of Paramount Pictures.

A VIACOM COMPANY

This book is published by Pocket Books, a division of Simon & Schuster Inc., under exclusive license from Paramount Pictures.

ISBN: 0-671-03957-1

First Pocket Books printing December 1999

10 9 8 7 6 5 4 3 2 1

POCKET and colophon are registered trademarks of Simon & Schuster Inc.

Printed in the U.S.A.

For Kelly Beaton,
my supportive and loving husband.

Thanks again to Willie Gonzales
for the use of his extensive *Star Trek* video collection.

PART 1

STAR TREK®

Stardate 5650.1
Year 2268

Several months after "The *Enterprise* Incident"

PART I.

Chapter One

THE *ENTERPRISE* dropped out of warp and slowed to full-impulse speed. As the warp field collapsed, the streaks on the viewscreen turned to twinkling lights. A blur of red and orange obscured the majority of the starfield on the screen.

James T. Kirk, captain of the Federation *Starship Enterprise,* sat forward. He had never seen anything quite like this before. Layer upon layer of red, orange, and opaque white clouds.

"What is it, Spock?" Kirk asked.

"Enhancing sensors." Spock bent over his monitor and viewed the phenomenon through the computer readouts. The monitor reflected a green light into Spock's face, accenting his pallor and his upswept Vulcan brows. "It appears to be a plasma storm, Captain."

"I've never seen one this big before," Kirk murmured.

"There is no record in our database of such a phenomenon," Spock agreed.

The image grew larger, and now the individual ribbons of color could be seen, twisting and wrapping around one another. The storms glistened with an inner light, which meant only one thing to Kirk—power. Power enough to cause disruptions in their warp field and make them drop from warp six to three, then to one as they approached the rendezvous coordinates provided by Starfleet Command. The *Enterprise* had left Federation territory days ago.

"The plasma mass is approximately eighty-four parsecs in width." Spock's voice was slightly muffled, as he was absorbed in reading the scanner. "It is roughly spherical in shape, and exerts a strong gravitational pull."

"Approximately eighty-four parsecs...," Kirk repeated in wonder.

"Most curious." Spock turned to examine the viewscreen. As usual, his expression was impassive. "I cannot obtain a precise measurement of the phenomenon. There appears to be a disruption in the scanner readings caused by the plasma emissions at this proximity to the storms."

Kirk stepped down from the captain's chair to get a closer look. Images appearing on a viewscreen were notoriously deceptive. Eighty-four parsecs ... that was nearly one-third of this entire sector—a vast region of space filled with active plasma.

At Spock's announcement, Ensign Chekov glanced at Lieutenant Sulu. Chekov's shoulders hunched as if to brace himself for what lay ahead. His shaggy hair concealed his face from Kirk's view, but the captain didn't have to see Chekov's expression to know the navigator was uneasy.

"Go to one-half impulse," Kirk ordered. That would give them some time to examine the phenomenon.

Sulu was unruffled, as usual, maintaining his crisp posture and tone as he concentrated on the helm data. "Aye, sir."

Turning, Kirk noticed Lieutenant Uhura watching the screen, the ear-receiver in her hand resting gracefully on her lap. Her mouth was slightly open in wonder, and her expressive eyes were shining.

Kirk thought he saw a faint blush as she dropped her head, embarrassed that he had seen her lost in open admiration. Turning back to her console, she said wistfully under her breath, "It's beautiful."

Kirk gave the screen another look. The colored masses moved and shifted together sinuously. "Yes, I suppose it is," he agreed.

Uhura quickly smiled before inserting her ear receiver.

"Any sign of Starfleet transmissions?" Kirk asked.

"None, sir," Uhura reported. "But I'm reading a clear signal from the communications relay."

"Keep me informed," Kirk ordered.

Starfleet had sent them to this distant and unexplored space several weeks ago. In an encoded transmission directly from Admiral Komack, Kirk had been ordered to keep their mission top secret. They had been given the coordinates of each location where the *Enter-*

prise was ordered to anchor a subspace communications relay. After launching each relay, they would then use it to receive the set of coordinates for the next location at which a relay probe was to be placed.

But Kirk had not been told that they would find a large and dangerous plasma storm near the final set of coordinates.

The red turbolift door swished open, and Dr. McCoy stepped onto the bridge. Kirk hid a smile, knowing McCoy was here to see "Why, in blue blazes, Starfleet has dragged us to the end of nowhere!" The doctor had probably felt the ship drop out of warp and hurried up from sickbay.

McCoy started to say something, but his blue eyes looked past Kirk and widened at the sight of the viewscreen. He took a few steps forward, unable to look away. Like Uhura, he seemed enthralled by the shifting orange and white clouds of plasma.

Kirk went over to Spock's science station and placed his hands on the wide red railing around the command center. Spock had one arm bent behind his waist as he leaned over the scanner monitor. His other hand swiftly adjusted the computer controls.

"Prepare a relay," Kirk ordered.

"The plasma may disrupt our readings, Captain," Spock informed him. "The region is unusually turbulent, with electric and magnetic fields interacting. Photons are continuously being produced and absorbed, creating ionic oscillations off the scale."

"Is there any way we can shield the relay?" Kirk asked.

"I will endeavor to do so, sir," Spock assured him. "I suggest we move closer to the storms to heighten telemetry retrieval."

"Proceed," Kirk ordered Chekov at the helm. He returned to his command chair, sat down and ran one hand through his hair.

Dr. McCoy moved closer to the back of Kirk's chair. "So Starfleet sent us out to the middle of nowhere to gawk at a completely natural phenomenon," the doctor muttered under his breath.

Kirk wasn't ready to comment on that. Chekov had sharp ears. He shook his head slightly, knowing the doctor wouldn't press it in their current uncertain situation.

"What in blazes is wrong with the viewscreen?" McCoy added irritably.

Kirk had noticed that the closer they got to the plasma storms, the more static lines appeared on the viewscreen.

Spock replied from the science station. "The plasma discharge is interfering with our sensors."

For the next few minutes, the only sounds on the bridge were the dings and whirs of the computer consoles. Lights flashed rapidly on the science monitors, marking Spock's progress.

Spock finally straightened up from his console. "The science lab has prepared a class-four probe with enhanced telemetry and transponder capacity. The probe should return data up to and immediately following its entry into the area of plasma activity. After that, it is uncertain whether we shall be able to maintain contact."

Kirk nodded. "Very well, Mister Spock. Launch the probe."

Spock pressed a button. "Probe launched, Captain."

On screen, a speck of light arched away from the *Enterprise,* heading directly towards the growing expanse of plasma streamers.

"Gravity and ionized radiation increasing exponentially," Spock announced, monitoring the probe's progress. "X-ray energy off the scale. Kiloelectron voltages exceeding the eighth power. Variability in frequency and intensity in optical and radio pulsations by ten thousand times."

"Volatile place," Kirk muttered.

Dr. McCoy agreed, "I hope you weren't planning to build a vacation home nearby."

"Contact with probe has terminated." Spock was detached and scientifically precise. "Contact was maintained for 2.2 seconds after entry."

Chekov whistled low, then stopped when he realized what he was doing.

"Like a raging tornado," McCoy said with some respect. "We're not going in there . . . are we?"

Kirk didn't know what Starfleet had in mind for them, and that annoyed him. He was the captain of the *Enterprise,* he was supposed to be in the loop about anything that concerned his ship. But he couldn't let the crew know how he felt.

"Spock?" Kirk asked. "Could the *Enterprise* survive in there?"

"It will take me a moment to analyze the data, Captain."

McCoy leaned in closer, his voice dropping. "It makes sense that Starfleet would want to investigate this phenomenon. But why the secrecy? They could hardly keep other people from finding something this big."

"It *is* far from the normal transport lines," Kirk replied speculatively. He didn't want to mention that they were relatively near one end of Romulan territory in the neighboring Beta Quadrant. Perhaps that accounted for the excessive secrecy.

The usual point of contact between Romulans and the Federation was along the Neutral Zone, light years away. Kirk's initial encounter with the Romulans had been the first official contact between the Federation and their ancient foes in over one hundred years. Kirk had won that battle, if you could call it winning. He had never learned the Romulan commander's name, but his resourcefulness, his *humanity*, and his utter ruthlessness in destroying his own starship and killing his entire crew . . . years later Kirk was still haunted by it.

Spock approached the captain's chair. Kirk noticed that the science officer's eyes didn't move to acknowledge Dr. McCoy. Spock had never said anything about it, but Kirk knew that his science officer believed that the doctor tended to get unnecessarily involved in command decisions. Kirk could feel McCoy lean in closer to hear Spock's report.

"Captain, this region of space is in a constant state of energized flux. There appear to be concentrations of activity within the region consisting of hundreds of discrete plasma storms."

Kirk remembered their last layover on Starbase 4 after their encounter with a plasma storm. It had taken weeks to realign their antimatter flow regulators.

"I would not recommend entering the region," Spock finished, lifting one brow in emphasis. "If we do enter the region, the warp engines must be off-line or our plasma exhaust could start an explosive chain reaction."

"I understand." Kirk tightened his hand into a fist. They weren't going anywhere until he received their orders.

Spock returned to the science console to resume his analysis of the plasma storms.

"Approaching the rendezvous coordinates," Sulu reported.

"There is a high level of gravitational pull in this area," Mister Spock warned.

"Captain!" Uhura said, then hesitated.

"Yes, Lieutenant?" he prompted. "Incoming message?"

"Negative. But the plasma storms are interfering with the comm link to the relay station." She tried to adjust the feed, then shook her head in frustration. "I'm not getting a clear signal. It's as if the plasma mass is casting a shadow that the telemetry can't penetrate."

"Scanners are similarly affected," Spock confirmed.

"Understood. Back off, Mister Sulu. Put some distance between us and the plasma storms," Kirk ordered. Consulting with the command console in the arm of his chair, Kirk gave Sulu the coordinates. He intended to place the plasma storms between the *Enterprise* and the Romulan Star Empire, just in case his hunch was correct.

McCoy settled in, as if prepared to wait as long as it took to solve the mystery. "It is pretty," he commented. "It's like watching a sunset."

"Mmm . . . yes," Kirk agreed absently. He replayed Admiral Komak's original orders, hoping that in light of their discovery of the plasma storms it would make more sense. But he was distracted by the flickering lights caused by the enormous energy being released within the plasma storms. "It reminds me of the Badlands."

"What's that?" McCoy asked.

Spock half-turned from his science station. "The Badlands are a region on Earth known for their distinctive erosional formations." His tone became more conversational. "However, Captain, I do not see a correlation between this phenomenon and a geophysical structure."

"The Badlands are in southwestern South Dakota, not far from where I grew up in Iowa," Kirk explained. "The erosion produces strange formations—spires, and flat-topped buttes. Gullies cut straight down, exposing rock that's layered in colors. It's immense and isolated, like these storms. And it's incredibly beautiful."

"Yes," Uhura agreed, startling all of them. "That's exactly what this is. Something mysterious and compelling."

"The Badlands," McCoy said, as if testing it out.

"That's fine by me. Just as long as we don't have to go in there."

McCoy was ready to call it quits and return to sickbay. Nearly an hour of waiting, and still no word from Starfleet. Surely they wouldn't be left out here in the middle of nowhere for days, waiting for their orders.

He sighed, and was irritated by Kirk's amused look. At least *he* was sitting down. McCoy sighed again, and decided that a strategic retreat was called for. "Let me know when you hear—" he started to tell Kirk.

"Sir!" Lieutenant Uhura announced. "There's an incoming transmission from Starfleet. It's encoded."

Kirk turned his chair, expectantly leaning towards Uhura. McCoy raised one corner of his mouth. He knew Kirk's appearance of casual relaxation had just been an act—reclining back in the command chair, his legs stretched out as if he had nothing better to do than to wait at the beck and call of Starfleet Command. McCoy had known it was an act because of Kirk's eyes, narrowed and darting from the viewscreen to Spock's bustling activity at the science station.

"Decoding the message, sir," Uhura informed the captain. "It's from Admiral Komack, marked as an unsecured transmission."

Kirk ordered, "On screen."

McCoy was ready to finally get some hard answers after all the cloak-and-dagger secrecy. He figured the Admiral's message was unsecured because there was no one around. Who could the crew tell?

All of the bridge officers were focused on the

viewscreen. McCoy couldn't blame them. Usually they were briefed about their missions. Yet this time they had been in the dark for weeks. McCoy judged they were near the edge of their tolerance, noting the tension in Chekov's shoulders and the way Scotty sat forward on the edge of his seat.

They were practically quivering with anticipation. Except for Kirk. And Spock, of course. Spock acted like he could hardly tear himself away from his scanner.

"Not interested in finding out what brought us out here, eh Spock?" McCoy couldn't resist prodding.

"On the contrary," Spock said calmly, which just irritated McCoy more.

"Don't get *too* excited," McCoy muttered.

Admiral Komack appeared on the viewscreen. He was an older human who had been a deep-space captain in his younger days. "Captain Kirk, I congratulate you on reaching the rendezvous point. I'm sorry we had to send you on this mission without a proper briefing, but you'll understand in a moment. We knew the *Enterprise* was the only starship for this job." The admiral's expression momentarily eased with a smile, then he was all business again. "We've gotten word that a smuggler will be meeting a transport near your present coordinates. We don't know who is purchasing the information, so you'll have to watch your back. We want you to intercept and apprehend the smuggler before he can transfer the data." He glanced down, his brows drawing together. "We believe it will include technical information on the Romulan plasma-energy weapon. The same weapon that destroyed four Earth Outposts along the Neutral Zone two years ago."

McCoy remembered the staggering loss of life that had resulted from those attacks. During their battle with the wily Romulan ship, which had an unfair advantage because of its cloak, Specialist Robert Tomlinson had been killed. Even worse, Tomlinson had been in the middle of marrying Angela Martine when Earth Outpost 4 was attacked. The *Enterprise* had not been able to prevent the Romulan ship from pulverizing the outposts with their plasma-energy weapon.

The *Enterprise* had barely survived that encounter; afterwards, morale on the ship had suffered. Some began to believe it would be impossible to make a family on board the *Enterprise* while furthering their careers. Many of the younger crewmembers were particularly shaken—they had wanted adventure, but this was their first encounter with mass death.

McCoy felt ancient next to the lot of them. All these baby-faced junior officers should be sent back to the Academy to ripen a bit before they underwent another trial by fire.

Admiral Komack finished providing the specs on the type of vessel the smuggler was using. "I don't need to tell you how important this is to the Federation, Captain. Good luck."

The message faded to the Federation symbol. Then the starfield appeared again with the Badlands swirling in the top half of the viewscreen.

Thoughtfully, Kirk said, "He didn't mention the plasma activity."

"Doubtless, the Admiral is not aware of this phenomenon," Spock said calmly.

"Well, we can use the storms to our advantage." Kirk sat forward. "Move in closer to the Badlands, Mister Sulu. Take us to within 200,000 kilometers."

"Aye, sir!" Sulu agreed.

"Good idea," McCoy told him. "If the plasma storms disrupt our scanners, they're bound to disrupt the smuggler's instruments, too."

"Exactly." Kirk lowered his head and smiled. "We can wait in the sensor shadow and ambush him when he arrives."

"Let's just hope we get to him before he passes along the information," Chekov said.

"We will," Sulu assured him.

Kirk seemed much more reserved than the other bridge officers at the news. "Signal this to all decks, Lieutenant Uhura."

"All decks standing by, sir," Uhura said.

"This is the captain speaking," Kirk said, pausing to be sure he had their attention. "It is of utmost importance that we complete our next mission. You all know we were ordered to leave Federation territory and come to this remote spot. What you don't know, and now must be told, is that we were sent here to intercept important weapons data that is being smuggled out of Romulan territory." He paused to let that sink in. "I want all hands standing by, yellow alert. Captain out."

The mood became more somber, yet everyone was still eager to take on the mission. Smugglers were apparently much more exciting than natural galactic phenomenon. Even McCoy was perfectly ready to admit that he too was relieved they weren't being sent into the Badlands.

As he moved toward the turbolift to go back down to sickbay, McCoy turned for one more look at the swirling plasma clouds as the *Enterprise* moved in closer. The plasma now filled the viewscreen, with only a thin line of friendly star-sprinkled blackness along the bottom. The static increased on the viewscreen.

Sure it was pretty, but the place made him uneasy. And when you'd been a doctor as long as McCoy had, you trusted your instincts.

Chapter Two

MISTER SPOCK didn't need to look at the buttons to punch in commands, reading the lights of his console as easily as he read his monitor. His station integrated the ship's sensor array with the computer core of the *Enterprise*. He slipped a disc in the slot to send the data and his preliminary analysis to the science lab on deck 2, just below the bridge. He issued his orders through the small triangular port.

There were two operations underway. His primary mission was to monitor the remote sensor relay the *Enterprise* had sent to the edge of the sector. It was aimed at Romulan territory, and it enabled them to stay hidden within the sensor blackout that surrounded the plasma storms while monitoring what occurred in the rest of the sector.

Spock had chosen to conceal the powerful sensor relay next to a small diffuse nebula. It gave him the opportunity to gather scientific readings on the nebula while he kept watch for approaching vessels. Spock theorized that the nearby plasma storms had created the conditions that had formed the corkscrew nebula, an ionized mass they were watching as it slowly moved through the sector. The captain had named the blue-and-white clouds the Kamiat Nebula, in honor of the senior astrophysicist at Starfleet Academy.

"Report, Mister Spock," the captain requested.

"Still no sign of vessels on long-range sensors, sir," he reported.

Spock waited a moment to be sure that was all the captain wanted, then he returned to his secondary mission—gathering data on the plasma storms. A remarkable galactic phenomenon.

Spock determined that the plasma storms had fairly stable borders and moved in galactic relative motion, while typical plasma storms crossed against the galactic particulate movement. Spock decided that if circumstances were favorable upon the completion of their primary mission, he would request a shuttle expedition into the plasma storms.

A light blinked red at the top of his console.

Spock instantly accessed the long-range scanners. "The remote sensor relay has been activated, Captain. There is a starship approaching from bearing two-one-two mark four-fifteen."

"On screen," Kirk ordered.

The remote relay had difficulty relaying a visual image through the sensor shadow. But through the static they could make out the shape of a blunt-nosed cylindrical vessel, twice as large as a standard Starfleet shuttlecraft.

Spock magnified the image, bringing the shiny silver hull into sharper focus. They could see the indentations of the warp nacelles built right into the sides of the vessel. An unusual design.

As the vessel passed the remote relay, scores of black along the rear were visible.

"What's that?" Kirk asked, sitting forward.

Spock was already working on it. "It appears the ship has been damaged by a plasma-energy weapon. It is currently moving toward the coordinates provided by Starfleet."

"Let it approach." Kirk narrowed his eyes. "Weapons, Mister Spock?"

"Lasers," Spock confirmed. "Inadequate against our shields. The majority of the energy output is diverted to speed."

"All legs and no teeth," Kirk muttered. "Can they see us?"

"Apparently not while we are within the sensor shadow," Spock informed him. "There is no change in trajectory."

"Prepare tractor beam," Kirk ordered. He turned to Montgomery Scott, the chief engineer, as he entered the bridge. "Scotty, are the engines ready? We'll intercept the vessel at the last possible moment and catch it in the tractor beam. We can't afford to let it break free."

"Aye, it'll hold, sir!" the engineer assured him with a cheery voice. He took the bridge station from his assistant. "The wee lass isna' goin' anywhere."

Spock raised one brow, but he forebore adding that while the vessel might be small, she had a powerful engine. The chief engineer had undoubtedly verified his calculations.

"The vessel is closing on our position, sir," Sulu announced.

Spock hadn't taken his eyes off the scanner. A blip from the sensor relay alerted him. "Captain! Another vessel is approaching. Same trajectory, bearing two-one-two mark four-fifteen."

Kirk started up, instantly on his feet. "Romulan?"

Spock's sensitive ears picked up the faint sounds of human distress from the bridge crew. "Uncertain, sir. The vessel is uncloaked."

"I wonder why it isn't cloaked . . . ," Kirk said speculatively.

"Sir, the propulsion system is one I am not familiar with," Spock informed him. "I am reading unusual neutrino signatures. However, it appears to be a Romulan bird-of-prey."

Kirk nodded decisively. "All hands to battle stations."

"Battle stations, all hands to battle stations," Uhura announced. "Battle stations, all decks acknowledge."

After a moment, Uhura said, "All decks acknowledge, sir."

"All weapons to full power," Kirk ordered.

Spock approved of the captain's bold maneuver. He prepared his station to give maximum scanner feed to weapons stations and the tractor beam. It appeared that pinpoint accuracy would be necessary.

Kirk warned, "Scotty, I'm going to need everything you can give me." Kirk glanced over at the engineering station for Scotty's acknowledgment. "Helm, prepare to move away from the Badlands. But keep us within the sensor shadow as long as possible to hide our presence."

"Aye, sir!" Sulu and Chekov said at once.

The Badlands shifted from the viewscreen as the *Enterprise* veered away, retreating out of the sensor shadow at full impulse power. They couldn't go to warp speed until they were clear, and they would need warp speed in order to cut off the smuggling ship.

Readings from the remote sensor relay indicated that neither of the oncoming vessels had altered course. The plasma storms were effectively masking the presence of the *Enterprise*.

Spock noted the high tension among the bridge officers during this phase of their mission. They anticipated intercepting the smuggler vessel and the difficulty of getting away from the Romulan bird-of-prey.

"We are clearing the sensor shadow of the plasma storms," Spock announced.

"Intercept course, Mister Sulu," Kirk ordered. "Maximum warp."

"Aye, sir!"

The starfield blurred as they entered warp, but Spock was focused on the growing form of the smuggling vessel.

"The vessel is changing course," Sulu announced.

"Verified, Captain," Spock said.

"Adjust course," Kirk ordered.

"Our speed is now at maximum," Sulu reported.

"Sixty seconds to interception," Spock told the captain. "The Romulan bird-of-prey will intercept in eight minutes at their current velocity."

"You've got five minutes to get a tractor beam on that ship and take it into our shuttlebay," Kirk told Scott. "Then I want to be back at top speed, ahead of that bird-of-prey."

"Aye, Captain . . . ," the engineer agreed, though not as eagerly this time.

The timing would be very close. "Entering tractor beam range," Spock said calmly.

"Security detachment to shuttle bay," Kirk ordered through the comm.

The *Enterprise* subtly shifted as they cut in front of the smaller vessel, forcing it to drop out of warp. At the same moment, they too dropped out of warp, activating the tractor beam.

"Tractor locked on," Spock reported.

"She's holding, sir!" the chief engineer called out.

"Bring the ship in, Scotty, and be quick about it."

Spock bent closer to his scanner. Now that the smaller vessel was under control, he turned his attention to the Romulan bird-of-prey. Though he had never seen propulsion readings like these before, he believed he detected irregular spikes in the energy output.

Spock stood up and turned to the captain to emphasize his discovery. "Sir, the antimatter containment field in the Romulan bird-of-prey is fluctuating."

Kirk looked sharply at Spock. "Overloading their engines?"

"It is possible, sir."

"Make challenge," Kirk ordered Lieutenant Uhura. "Warn that ship off."

"I'm trying to, sir," Uhura confirmed, manipulating her console. "They don't acknowledge."

"Tie me in, Lieutenant," Kirk ordered.

"Tying in, sir."

Kirk raised his voice to be sure his words were clear. "Commander, stand down. Our instruments show you're pushing your engines too hard." He paused, but there was no response. "Do you read me, Romulan bird-of-prey? Stand down your engines!"

The second-in-command turned to his commander. "Centurion? Shall you reply?"

The Romulan commander shook his head slightly, motioning for the subcommander to cut off the transmission. He would not waste time talking.

The centurion paced around the perimeter of the spherical bridge, its red slanted walls more familiar than home. He always kept one eye on the round console in the center of the bridge. His men were gathered around the three monitors, running the bird-of-prey through the sensitive controls.

The centurion stayed back, letting them work while he watched their progress. The gold helms of his men gleamed, and their eyes were serious. They knew their honor rested on completing this mission successfully.

His subcommander detached himself from the others, and carefully approached. "Centurion, it is our judgment that the articulation frame cannot withstand the stress—"

"We *will* prevail. We *must*." The centurion knew he had to hold absolute power over his men or they would turn on him, and another would rise to his rank. He did not wish to be assigned patrol duty in some dusty outlying province.

But his ship, his precious ship, was groaning at the bulkheads, strained to its limits. It wasn't built to ride such power. He was proud of this vessel; she had held together when everyone else said she would fail under the prototype engine.

"Divert all power to engines," he ordered. The subcommander nodded curtly and pivoted, returning to his station.

The lights dimmed, indicating that life support had been compromised.

The commander fingered the red sash over his metal-link tunic. The mesh hung heavy and comforting on his body, protecting him. One got used to constant war. It had become natural to sleep with a knife in his hand . . . though at one time he remembered sleeping in his father's house on Romulus, the cool evening breeze coming through the open windows. Once when he was very young, he had been awakened by a burst of white light. He had run to the window as a glorious silver space ship lifted into the sky. Its plumage was as brilliantly painted as a bird in flight, its tail dimming to a ruddy glow as it disappeared. He felt a compelling urge to go with it to exotic places. Ah, the things he had seen in his years of service. . . .

The ship shuddered, and he reached out a gloved hand to hold onto the bulkheads. He could feel the constant stress vibration growing stronger.

His subcommander didn't bother to approach this time. "Sir, we are losing our containment field! We must power down—"

"Maintain speed." The centurion's eyes stopped the subcommander from coming as step closer. "I remind you of your duty."

The subcommander's voice sounded as if he were being strangled, "By your command."

"Ready weapons!" the commander ordered. They didn't have enough energy for the plasma-energy weapon, but they still had torpedoes. He would destroy the traitor who had led him such a long way from his homeland. And he would destroy the Starfleet vessel that dared to interfere. "We shall be victorious. . . ."

Captain Kirk pressed the comm button again, "Romulans, stand down your engines!"

There was no response. That gave him no choice. "Sulu, plot a course back to the Federation."

"Course laid in, sir."

Scotty confirmed, "We've got her, Captain! Snug as a bug in the shuttlebay."

"Ahead, warp 8!" Kirk ordered.

"Aye, sir," Chekov acknowledged.

The strain on the bridge eased slightly. As the *Enterprise* reached warp 8, the trailing edge of the Badlands shifted between them and the Romulan bird-of-prey.

"I've already talked to the engine room, sir," Scott added. "We'll soon be able to get more out of her."

Kirk was watching as the Romulan bird-of-prey disappeared behind the plasma storms. "Perhaps now they'll give up."

"The remote sensor relay indicates the bird-of-prey is continuing to pursue," Spock said.

"Let's see it," Kirk ordered.

The image from the remote sensor relay appeared on the screen. Kirk was tempted to try again to reason with the Romulans, but the martial philosophy of their people prevented them from showing any sign of weakness.

Even their ships were a fierce sight, the upswept wings supporting the warp nacelles, the nose blunted and deadly. The giant stylized bird-of-prey painted on the underhull was intended to evoke an instinctive fear response. Kirk had recognized it instantly, and he felt the same chill every time he encountered a Romulan bird-of-prey.

Suddenly a jagged white flame cut through the back of the bird-of-prey, ripping away in a ball of fire. For a moment the proud beak of the bird flew onward, then it too was consumed in a second, larger explosion.

Kirk squinted against the white-hot flash, flinching as it blossomed even brighter. Red spots were seared into his vision, and he blinked to clear his eyes.

Then he saw a wave of distortion punch through the trailing edge of the plasma storms. "All power to—"

The *Enterprise* was pitched out of the warp field by

the powerful energy wave. Kirk was thrown from his chair as the shockwave tossed the ship.

He expected to hit the floor and was prepared to roll on impact. But instead, his stomach lurched, and he continued to fly through the air. Kirk hit the viewscreen with his back. The concussion knocked the wind out of him.

The lights failed completely, leaving only the red glare from the flashing alert signals.

But still Kirk didn't fall. He hung against the viewscreen, feeling disoriented. Then he abruptly dropped to the deck. He could feel the strain as the artificial gravity system tried vainly to compensate for the unusual conditions.

The *Enterprise* pitched again beneath him, then settled as the failsafes kicked in. Kirk pushed himself up as the emergency lights flickered on.

Spock was the first one to report. "According to the remote sensor relay, the bird-of-prey has been destroyed. Ship's sensors are currently off-line, sir."

Kirk stiffly climbed into his seat, noting the flashing lights as his crew reported in. He kept remembering what the first Romulan commander had told him: *"We are creatures of duty."* Was that reason enough to die?

"Damage, Mister Spock?" Kirk asked.

"Warp and impulse engines are off-line. There are overloads and burnouts in the electroplasma circuits throughout the ship," Spock said. "Minimum auxiliary power. Damage repair crews are already underway."

"How long before we get impulse power back on line?"

Scotty stood up, ready to leave the bridge. "I'll have to see, Captain. Dependin' on how many circuits were blown, it could take some time."

"Do what you can," Kirk told Scott, as the engineer stepped into the turbolift. "Mister Chekov, use thrusters to retreat toward the sensor shadow of the Badlands. Keep us just inside, out of range of the strongest gravitational pull." Weapons would be limited to photon torpedoes while they were on auxiliary power, so Kirk intended to use the plasma storms as cover in case another Romulan vessel showed up. "All decks maintain security alert."

"Acknowledged, sir," Sulu confirmed.

The view shifted away from the last fading spangles of light and spinning debris from the bird-of-prey. Kirk felt a pang of regret. Twice now, his encounters with the Romulans had ended in total destruction.

Kirk punched the comm. "Captain to sickbay. Report."

"McCoy here." The doctor sounded strained. *"Sixteen casualties so far. Mainly impact fractures and contusions."*

Kirk acknowledged, "Could be worse."

"It is worse, Jim. I'm reading high levels of multiflux radiation onboard the ship. It could take an hour for the full effects to manifest."

Kirk asked, "Spock? Why weren't we alerted by the medical program?"

Spock nodded, "Internal sensors are off-line, Captain."

"What will that do to the crew, Doctor?" Kirk asked McCoy.

"I'm not sure yet, Jim. Multiflux radiation is highly erratic. It may simply pass through the ship without affecting anyone."

Kirk told both Spock and Dr. McCoy, "Keep me informed."

For a moment, Kirk considered their distance from Federation territory. If anything went wrong—and it certainly had—they were on their own. As usual, it was best to focus on his primary duty and complete his mission.

Kirk signaled the shuttle bay. "Captain to shuttle bay. Report."

"Sir, the vessel is in our custody." The chief of security's deep voice was unruffled by the disruption in gravity and power. "The forcefield is holding and the hatch has not yet opened."

"Maintain position," Kirk told her. "I'm on my way." He gestured to Spock. "Let's go see what our guest has to say."

Chapter Three

THE ROMULAN VESSEL was in the middle of the shuttle bay, isolated by the blue shimmer of a forcefield. Security personnel were stationed around the walls, their phaser rifles held ready.

Kirk acknowledged Security Chief Kelley. Kelley, a human from the Palazian colony, had recently been assigned duty on board the *Enterprise*. The strong gravity on Palazian created strong, muscular colonists.

Soon after Kelley had joined the crew, Kirk had competed against her in a strenuous new game called parrises squares. Kirk enjoyed playing, but he wasn't sure the sport would catch on with the rest of the crew. McCoy was already complaining about the anticipated increase in minor injuries if it did.

Kelley nodded smartly to the captain as he entered. "There's been no answer to our hails, sir."

Kirk nodded, eyeing the vessel. She was a beauty, sleek and fast. Similar to the finest private cruisers to be found in the Federation. The nose flared at the bottom, curving up to a point, and the warp nacelles bulged out slightly from the sides. The condition of the exterior hull indicated that the ship had been used hard. Yet her design was innovative, so she must have been launched from dry dock within the past few years.

The black scoring along the rear section was unmistakable. It nearly covered the name etched on the starboard panel—*Barataria*. Kirk could see where the plasma beam had licked close to the nacelles on the underside. Obviously the *Barataria* had come within a hair's breadth of being destroyed.

"Drop the forcefield," Kirk ordered. The blue sheen disappeared, along with the faint tang of ions in the air.

Kirk put his hand phaser on his belt as he went to the comm. It was already tied into the *Barataria's* frequency. "This is Captain James Kirk of the Federation *Starship Enterprise*. Please open your hatch and come out."

There was a pause, during which only the hushed breathing of twenty-four security personnel disturbed the silence of the shuttle bay.

"*This is Commander Teral of the Barataria.*" The voice was flattened and distorted with hissing feedback. "*I demand that you release my ship.*"

Kirk glanced at Spock before answering, "Why don't you come out so we can discuss this?"

"*The time for discussion is past,*" Teral noted. "*You took my ship by force.*"

Kirk gestured for the security team to stand down.

They folded their arms, holding their phaser rifles at rest. Kelley remained alert, standing where she could see both Captain Kirk and the vessel.

"You can be assured of your safety," Kirk told the captain. "We acted in haste because you were being pursued by the Romulan bird-of-prey."

"Thank you, but the situation was under control," Teral informed him. *"Am I free to go now?"*

"I'm afraid I can't let you do that until you come out and answer some questions."

There was silence from the comm, only the hissing and popping of the *Barataria*'s open channel.

Kirk turned to Spock. "Well, now what? Do we blow the door open?"

"A most difficult decision," Spock commented.

"I'd hate to ruin such a fine ship," Kirk said speculatively, knowing full well the channel was still open. "But if there's no other way. . . ."

Spock caught on fast, as always. "We are currently outside Federation territory. Free-space codes include the rights of salvage—"

"Salvage!" the intercom shrieked.

There was a puff of vacuum breaking, and the seal of the hatch split. The door slid aside with a smooth whir.

"You cut across my bow!" Commander Teral declared.

She jumped down from her vessel, ignoring the steps in her outrage. Planting both feet wide and folding her arms, she took up a proud stance in front of her ship. "Salvage, indeed!"

"That was the general idea. . . ." Kirk was thoroughly amazed. He had been picturing some renegade alien from one of the planets the Romulan empire had subjugated. Even the name—*Barataria*—was not Romulan.

He hadn't imagined Commander Teral would be a Romulan Amazon, her eyes snapping with fire as she faced down an entire security platoon. She wore linked-mesh body armor, but it wasn't military in style. Her high boots had silver plates covering her shins, and her gauntlets had sliver plates over her forearms. A belt encircled her hips, and a disruptor swung low on the left side, tied to her thigh. Kirk noted that in case it came to a fight.

He hardly wondered that he considered the possibility. Even though she was drastically outnumbered, the Romulan seemed ready and willing to fight.

Kirk walked towards her, with Spock and Kelley half a step behind him. As she came closer, he noted she was as tall as Spock. He stopped well back, warned by the hand shifting to her disruptor. The security platoon tensed, and Kelley made a warning sound low in her throat.

Kirk figured they were close enough. "I'm Captain James Kirk."

"Commander Teral," she replied cautiously. Her dark hair was pulled up tightly, twisted into a knot on top of her head. It showed off her small pointed ears and slanted brows. She shifted to look at the security platoon, and Kirk could see a long tail of hair hanging down from the knot on top, curling slightly at the ends.

"Where's the rest of your crew?" Kirk asked.

"Crew?" She crossed her arms again. "I work alone."

"What sort of work is it that you do?" Spock politely inquired.

"Transport services." She turned and paced to the back of her ship. She bent down, examining the scoring and the bulkheads. "Your tractor beam was gauged too high."

Kirk joined her. "It looks like you were damaged in a recent battle. Is that why the Romulan bird-of-prey was chasing you?"

"I suppose they didn't want to give up once they found a likely target." She bent over to rub at the scoring, then checked the nacelles. Her gloved hands moved over the ship with familiarity.

Kirk waited impatiently until she stood up and faced him again. "Your ship matches the description of one carrying vital data on Romulan plasma weapons systems."

Her eyes opened wide. "Plasma weapons? Ah . . . now I understand. That would be reason enough for you to snatch me from space."

"Do you have this information?" Kirk bluntly asked.

"No, you stopped the wrong ship." Teral smiled. "Maybe it was that Romulan bird-of-prey you destroyed."

"*We* didn't destroy it," Kirk said sharply.

"Ah . . . yes," she repeated noncommittally. "It must have been an engine overload. . . ."

Her bland expression made her look like Spock, but maybe it was just the similar facial characteristics.

"Then you don't mind if we search your ship?" Kirk asked her.

"On the contrary," she replied, "I do mind."

Spock stood with both his hands clasped behind his back, clearly reserving judgment as Kirk and Teral stared at one another. "It would appear you have as little choice in this matter as we," Spock offered.

"Just as I had little choice about being taken hostage?" she asked.

Kirk realized Spock was right—they also had no choice. Starfleet orders were specific. "If you give us the information, you will be free to go."

Exasperated, Teral's voice filled with scorn. "I have nothing to give you."

Kirk tightened his lips, wishing she had not forced him to this. "Spock, search the computer database and scan this ship. I want every circuit checked."

"Aye, sir," Spock acknowledged.

Kirk waited until Spock, Kelley, and two security guards had entered the ship. Commander Teral fumed silently, refusing to meet his eyes. Kelley finally emerged and reported that there were no other crew members on board.

A portable scanner was brought into the shuttle bay. "This will take a while. We'll assign you to secured quarters," Kirk told Teral.

"Am I under arrest?" Commander Teral asked.

"Not if you cooperate," Kirk replied. His instinct was to be gracious with the captain, but he kept reminding himself that any display of weakness would earn contempt from a Romulan. "Otherwise I'll have you taken to the brig."

She hesitated. "I need my tricorder."

"We'll bring you whatever you request," Kirk told her smoothly. Those items would be scanned even more thoroughly than the others.

He held out his hand. "I'll need your weapon. It will be returned to you when you leave."

He faced her down, hoping that he wouldn't have to fight her now, not when things finally seemed to have settled down. He quickly judged the angle, figuring at this distance he could leap forward and grab her arm before she could fire.

She obviously considered it. Then she unfolded her arms, holding her palms out. A few of the security guards raised their rifles in instinctive response.

Teral slowly hooked the disruptor from her belt. There was an instant when he thought she would turn it on him, but instead, she lightly held it out to him.

Kirk took it from her. It was heavier than he expected, with a well-worn grip. He bet she was a good shot.

"This way," he told her.

Several of the security guards fell in, but one of them abruptly stopped in his tracks, making a gasping noise. He bent over, his arms clutching his stomach, his phaser rifle clattering to the floor of the shuttle bay.

Kirk kept his eyes on Commander Teral, who was looking with interest at the fallen man. But she didn't take the opportunity to make a threatening move.

One of the other guards helped him get up. It was

Ensign Matheson. His sweating face had turned an alarming shade of red.

Kelley came up behind Kirk, alerted by the security team. "It's the radiation sickness," she told Kirk. "This is the third one from security. Get him to sickbay," she ordered.

Kirk gestured for the others to follow him and Commander Teral. She was silent as they strode through the corridors. He decided against trying to engage her in conversation. He had the upper hand at the moment, and he intended to retain it.

He took her to quarters on deck 6, in the saucer section of the *Enterprise,* far away from the shuttle bay. At the door, he gestured for the security guards to remain outside.

The commander sauntered inside, taking in the mellow lighting and artistic flower arrangement in the nook by the door. "Nice brig," she told him sarcastically.

"I hope you enjoy it." Kirk gestured to the food slot. "You can order food and drink here. Let me know if there is anything else you need."

Kirk was at the door when she called out, "I need medical attention."

Kirk instantly turned back. "Are you injured?"

Her expression didn't change, but she nodded, holding her head high. "The radiation levels spiked inside the *Barataria* after the Romulan bird-of-prey exploded."

Kirk considered it. "I'll send a medical technician to assist you."

She didn't thank him, but he hadn't really expected she would.

The door closed behind him, and he noted the careful placement of the three security guards. "Remain here." He hesitated, but he had to trust his gut instinct. "No one is to go in alone."

"Aye, sir," the senior guard acknowledged.

At the next comm panel he paused to access sickbay. "Kirk to Dr. McCoy."

There was too long a pause before McCoy answered, *"McCoy here."*

"Doctor, a very unusual patient has just arrived. A Commander Teral."

"Is it an emergency, Jim? Sickbay is overflowing. Twenty-one crew members so far and more every minute."

Kirk was immediately concerned, remembering the way the security guard had doubled over. "What is it, Bones?"

"Near as I can tell, it's an unusual form of multiflux radiation poisoning." McCoy recited the list of symptoms, as if that would help Kirk: nausea, dizziness, skin rash, fever.

"Is it life-threatening?" Kirk asked.

"As long as we don't get another dose, the crew should be fine," McCoy admitted. *"But there's only so much I can do to treat these people. Very little is known about multiflux radiation and what effects it has on humanoids."*

"Acknowledged. Tend to Commander Teral when you can." He paused. "Give her a thorough scan, look for any genetic anomalies or cybernetic implants."

"I heard the smuggler was a Romulan," McCoy said, sounding more interested. *"You think she may not be what she appears?"*

"You tell me, Doctor," Kirk told him. "Kirk out."

The captain considered the corridors. There were fewer people about than usual. Perhaps the crew were at their stations because of the caution alert, yet he was used to seeing people rushing around even during the worst of situations. Thirty-one crew members out of commission.

He pushed the comm button again. "Kirk to Spock."

"Spock here."

"How's the search going?" Kirk asked.

"Nothing to report as of yet, Captain."

Kirk carefully considered his next order. Their mission was to find the information on the plasma weapon, but there was a mystery here he couldn't ignore. If his crew kept dropping like meteorites, they wouldn't be able to get anything done.

"When you get a chance, Spock, we need to find out more about that multiflux radiation that hit us. It's affecting the crew."

"Aye, Captain, another security guard has taken ill since you left."

"See what you can find out," Kirk told him. "I'll be in engineering."

Spock correctly interpreted the captain's order, "when you have a chance," to mean he was to complete the initial phase of the search of the *Barataria*. The scanning team was currently sweeping the inside of the ship micrometer by micrometer. The *Enterprise's* internal scanners were engaged in an exterior sweep of the ship.

Using the computer in the shuttle bay, Spock completed and set on hold a computer program that would compare the scans. They needed to determine if any mass was missing, which would indicate a cavity they had overlooked.

He had already linked a portable diagnostic device into the *Barataria's* systems, and a level-one diagnostic was running. Any additional or isolated information bytes would be detected among the system programs.

Simultaneously, the *Enterprise* computer was downloading the *Barataria's* computer core. The files would have to be searched one at a time for the target data.

Spock had already performed a preliminary analysis of the ship's logs with the help of the universal translator. The *Barataria* had been in port at a busy Romulan space station used by both military and civilian craft. Commander Teral had cryptically informed her log that she had been "forced to jump port without paying the docking fees." A Romulan bird-of-prey had pursued her, and as she went into warp, a plasma beam weapon had been fired. According to her terse log entries, the bird-of-prey had pursued her for several days at top speed.

Spock was interested to note that Teral had thoroughly analyzed the propulsion system of the Romulan bird-of-prey while it pursued her. Though the logs and data entries revealed her superior mental capabilities, she had been unable to determine the structure of the power system. The captain had theorized it was a prototype engine that rumor had said was being constructed by the military.

The *Barataria*'s cargo appeared to be a load of contraband Romulan ale.

Kelley's eyes had lit up when they'd found it in a cleverly concealed bulkhead storage bin. "Now that's what I call contraband!" she said approvingly.

Spock had noted the bottles of blue ale in his report, a desirable commodity on the Federation black market. Yet it hardly seemed worth sending a bird-of-prey to apprehend a smuggler of intoxicants that were legal in the Romulan Star Empire.

"Exterior scan completed," the ship's computer announced.

Spock downloaded the data to await comparison with the scanning team's interior scan, once they were done with the job. Meanwhile, the diagnostic continued on the *Barataria*'s systems, and the data search was initiated by the *Enterprise* computer, comparing the download of the computer to the *Barataria*'s core memory.

"Computer, notify me if there are any deviations in the source path," Spock ordered.

"*Affirmative,*" the computer acknowledged.

From the shuttle bay, Spock went directly to his science lab station on deck 2. The skilled science teams were already working on determining the source of the shock-wave radiation. Several preliminary reports were awaiting his analysis.

Along with the disruptions in the gravity field, the

ship's internal sensors read abnormally high levels of gamma radiation in flux, indicating the shock wave involved some form of subspace incursion. The shields had not been effective in deflecting the multiflux radiation. Yet present levels of gamma particles were well within normal.

Malfunctions had occurred within the ship's electroplasma systems, causing strong power fluctuations and fusing conduit circuits. Spock could detect no coherent pattern in the location or severity of the malfunctions. He also had no theory for the cause of the multiflux radiation, other than its connection in some way to the destruction of the Romulan bird-of-prey. However, since he had ascertained the composition of the multiflux radiation, he had obtained what the captain had requested.

He hit the comm button. "Spock to Captain Kirk. I have a preliminary report."

Kirk was down on one knee next to Scotty, examining the dilithium crystals. The articulation frame was raised to expose the glowing crystals.

"Yes, Spock?" Kirk asked, raising his head.

"The shock wave consisted of multiflux gamma radiation, Captain. Source unknown." Spock paused. *"However, there is a great deal of wreckage from the Romulan bird-of-prey dispersed throughout the area. It might be possible to gather some debris for analysis."*

Kirk shook his head silently. Right now, with only thrusters functioning, he didn't want to move the *Enterprise* out of the sensor shadow cast by the Badlands. It wasn't every day a Romulan bird-of-prey blew up, and that shock wave must spread the word for light years. Surely some vessel was bound to come see what had happened. Stuck in unknown space with a Romulan smuggler ship in his shuttle bay and the debris of a bird-of-prey floating around. . . .

"Not now, Spock. I'll let you know when we can proceed with salvage. Kirk out."

Scotty was shaking his head as Spock signed off. "I dunna know of any kind of radiation that can make dilithium crystals expand. Even multiflux radiation."

Kirk bent closer to look at the sparkling interior. It took a great deal of precision control to harness the matter/antimater reactions that drove the *Enterprise* to warp speed. Yet each dilithium crystal was smaller than his fist. "You say they've expanded by as much as 4 percent?"

"Aye," Scotty confirmed. "I wouldna' bring the warp drive on-line now, sir. Not 'til we know whether the structural integrity of the crystals has been damaged."

Kirk rubbed his mouth, wondering when and if other Romulans would arrive, and whether they would be cloaked. "How long will the scanning take?"

"More than a day, maybe two," Scotty admitted. "It's not an easy job, Captain. We have to scan each crystal. And there's still the electroplasma taps to replace an' all those circuits."

"Do we have phasers?"

"No, sir. I can make it a priority . . ."

"What about impulse power?" Kirk asked.

"Any time now," Scotty assured him.

"I want impulse power first, Scotty," Kirk ordered. "Then you can deal with the phasers, then warp drive."

"Aye, Captain." Scotty braced himself as he got to his feet. "I'll get to work on it."

Kirk wasn't very pleased as he crossed engineering. There were too many people missing to get all the repairs done as quickly as he would like.

That was his next stop. Sickbay.

Chapter Four

DOCTOR MCCOY was curious about the Romulan smuggler, so at the first lull in the triage, he grabbed a medical scanner and went to see her.

The ears reminded him of Spock at first. But after she greeted him with a very un-Spock-like smile, he decided that her ears were nothing like the Vulcan's. She had dainty, shell-like ears, and the points only made her seem mischievous.

"Thank you for coming to see me, Doctor," she said gratefully. "I seem to be ill."

"There was a radiation burst when the Romulan bird-of-prey exploded." McCoy pulled out his medical scanner.

She stood up and held out her arms, as if that was expected. She was taller than the doctor, and very elegant, standing there as if ready to submit to an ordeal.

45

"Is that how the doctors scan you in the Romulan Star Empire?" McCoy asked.

"We get scanned all the time," Commander Teral told him seriously. "Entering and leaving buildings, random scans in the corridors, scans when we sleep . . ."

"*Who* does these scans?"

"Docking agents, Romulan militia, various officials, security for the royal family." She shrugged. "Whoever has an interest in finding contraband on you."

McCoy's mouth was open. "That sounds terribly invasive. What about your personal privacy?!"

One corner of her mouth curled up. "Why do you think I run the *Barataria?* I want to get away from all that. I dislike being scanned."

McCoy glanced down at his medical scanner. "Well, this is just for health reasons." He quickly passed it over her chest. "Exposure is only 100 rads. You got off lightly."

He adjusted the hypospray to provide a mixture of cysteamine and polymuons so her biosystem could absorb the medicine properly. "You'll be fine. Drink lots of fluids and rest. Sit down."

"Is that another scan?" she asked, warily glancing at the unit in his hand.

"Not at all. This regenerates your cellular structure."

She seated herself, crossing her legs. The doctor carefully passed the cellular regenerator over arms and chest, down to her legs. "You'll need to get one cellular regeneration treatment a day for the next few days."

"Thank you, Doctor," she said.

McCoy chatted with Commander Teral for a few more minutes, asking about her work. But Kelley was waiting patiently near the door, and he had patients waiting for him in sickbay, so he cut their conversation short.

As McCoy hurried through the corridor, heading back to sickbay, he ran into Captain Kirk.

"You look cheerful, Doctor," Kirk said abruptly. "I thought you had an emergency situation down here."

"Uh, we do. That is, I just came from seeing Commander Teral," McCoy explained lamely. "She's traveled the galaxy, you know. The stories she tells . . ."

"Oh, really?" Kirk responded. "She seemed rather severe to me. I take it you didn't find anything in the scan."

McCoy shook his head. "No, nothing unusual. She has a mild form of radiation sickness, rash, some nausea. It could be worse."

As they neared sickbay, the situation became apparent. Several patients were waiting in the halls, and only one was still standing, hunched over. The others were sitting or lying on the deck.

McCoy felt a pang of remorse for staying away so long. He had been talking with Commander Teral while all these people needed his help.

He helped Specialist Trey into the examining room, so he could sit on a mat along the wall. Trey immediately lay down, groaning.

Kirk was holding up Lieutenant Marley from the science lab. Her knees were buckling, but she was trying to walk. As he helped her sit down, Kirk told McCoy,

"Spock says the *Enterprise* was hit by multiflux gamma radiation."

"Multiflux *gamma* radiation?" McCoy repeated incredulously.

Kirk slowly straightened up, looking at the full room and listening to the sounds of people moaning in the next wardroom. He asked, "Isn't there anything you can do to help these people, Doctor?"

"I'm trying!" McCoy irritably took the padd Nurse Chapel was holding out to him, and checked the number of people who had arrived since he'd left. The medical staff was commandeering the nearby quarters to bed down all the casualties. Nurse Chapel was already directing a medical technician to take the overflow patients to the temporary wards.

"How many crew members are ill now?" Kirk asked.

"Forty-two. It comes on with hardly any warning."

McCoy rapidly accessed the medical database and ran through the recommended procedures for gamma radiation exposure. There was no mention of multiflux gamma radiation except as a theoretical phenomenon. "There's nothing I can do but give them cysteamine to reduce the biological effects of the irradiation. And perform regeneration and DNA resequencing."

"Spock has filed his preliminary analysis," Kirk said. "Perhaps that has additional information."

McCoy accessed the science report and compared the information to the patient data that had been gathered. "Exposure must have been at least 30 kilovolts to cause this amount of damage. The first casualties came from the ship's perimeter, but they weren't the worst cases. I've seen crew members from every section on the ship, including the bridge."

Kirk glanced up sharply. "Who?"

"Chekov." McCoy gestured with his head. "He's lying down inside."

Kirk paced over to the door, glancing into the darkened room. "Chekov . . ."

McCoy joined him, his voice low and urgent, "Jim, I don't think we're dealing with gamma radiation—at least, not just gamma radiation. The length of onset time, the severity of the symptoms, even the dispersal pattern doesn't fit typical gamma particle reaction. I need to know *more*. Gamma decay is usually the product of other types of radioactivity. So what was the source? And what put the radiation into a state of subspace flux?"

Kirk considered it, then hit his comm badge. "Scotty, do we have impulse power?"

"Aye, sir, just getting impulse engines back on-line now."

"Very good." Kirk relaxed, as if he was glad to finally have something go right.

McCoy stood nearby as the captain signaled Spock on the bridge to proceed with the salvage of Romulan wreckage. "Try to stay within the sensor shadow of the Badlands. And send anything you discover to Dr. McCoy," Kirk ordered.

"Aye, Captain," Spock acknowledged.

"Kirk out."

After overhearing their terse exchange, McCoy was

ready for Kirk's next question. "Bones, when will the injured crew members be back on duty?"

"With exposure to gamma radiation, up to 60 percent of the acute symptoms disappear within several hours. Some of these people may be up and around by evening shift." McCoy frowned at the data graph that the medical diagnostic had computed. "But from what I can tell, it could take as much as a day or two for them to fully recover. And the worst cases will need regular regeneration treatments for several weeks."

"Do whatever you can, Bones."

"I will, Jim." McCoy felt a familiar sinking feeling, the kind he got when he was faced with a seemingly insurmountable problem. "I'm not going to sit around and wait for Spock to pick through that wreckage. I'll start a reverse spectral analysis of these blood samples—that could tell us something. . . ."

Yeoman Harrison tightened her arm around her stomach. She stumbled the last few feet through the door. The effort of getting to sickbay without passing out had caused sweat to break out on the back of her neck.

She had started to feel ill in the communications lab, while preparing the logs for dispatch to Starfleet Command. There had been an urgency in her work— after seeing one colleague after another fall sick, she felt as if a strange plague had struck the *Enterprise*. She fought the first waves of nausea. She tried to ignore the prickly heat rising in the skin on her arms.

And when she finally fled to sickbay, walking had been excruciating. Every step jolted her head and stomach.

She braced herself against the desk. The examination room was filled with people, but no one noticed her at first. She tried to catch her breath to call to Nurse Chapel, a distant blurry figure in blue.

Then she saw Captain Kirk standing with Dr. McCoy in the door to the wardroom. Kirk's expression was strained, and he was saying, "Do the best you can, Bones. I need to repair the ship, and a third of my crew are flat on their backs!"

Harrison's first instinct was to flee. She couldn't let him see her like this. She couldn't bear to let him down. The nausea wasn't that bad, and she had ointment she could put on the rash that was reddening her chest and neck.

Swaying, she tried to get away before they saw her. But Nurse Chapel called out her name.

A wave of dizziness hit her, and Harrison couldn't see for a moment. She felt Chapel steadying her, reassuring her, "You'll be all right, dear."

Then she felt stronger arms take hold of her, holding her up. "Yeoman, you're sick," Captain Kirk said.

Adrenaline made her stand up straighter, and she forced herself to look him in the eye. "It's not too bad, sir. Just give me a hypospray and I can get back to work."

From somewhere behind her, Dr. McCoy said, "Put her here."

Kirk guided her to a medical bed. She wished her

legs didn't feel so wobbly. She also shook with frustration at appearing so weak in front of the captain. It had taken her many long months to gain his respect, and she intended to keep it.

She took slow, regular breaths, closing her eyes as she lay back and let Dr. McCoy perform his examination. Her pulse beat was fast, too fast, and she knew she had to get herself under control.

By the time she opened her eyes, the captain was standing next to the bed. She tried to offer him a reassuring smile. Maybe it was because she was lying down, but she was starting to feel better already. She tried to sit up.

"Stay still," McCoy ordered. He expertly filled and administered a hypospray. She felt it going in, but nothing noticeable after that.

"You'll have to get some rest," McCoy told her. His hand fumbled with the cellular regenerator as he ran it over her shoulder and down to her fingertips. The rash was maddening, itchy and burning at the same time. She couldn't bear to touch it, but the compulsion was almost too strong to withstand. Her fingers twitched next to her thigh.

Kirk watched as the doctor passed the regenerator up the outside of her leg, carefully following the contours of her calf and thigh all the way up to her short uniform skirt. She was watching his face, and for a moment his eyes met hers.

"Well, it looks like you're in good hands," Kirk said suddenly. "I'll leave you in the doctor's care."

"Uh . . . yes . . . ," Dr. McCoy replied vaguely.

The captain didn't see McCoy sway because he was already heading toward the door. The doctor braced himself for a moment against the bed, and the regenerator bumped into her.

"Doctor?" she asked.

He slumped forward, supporting himself with his arms. "Sa'right . . ."

She lifted up on her elbow, trying to brace him. "Doctor, what's wrong?" Her voice raised, "Captain! Something's wrong with Dr. McCoy."

Kirk rushed back in time to catch Dr. McCoy and keep him from falling. "Bones!"

Harrison slid off the bed, helping Kirk pull the doctor onto it in her place. Beads of sweat were forming on McCoy's forehead, and his head moved back and forth slightly. She recognized that utter preoccupation. He was feeling so dizzy he didn't know which way was up and which way was down.

Nurse Chapel ran over with a hypospray. Kirk bent over McCoy, showing far more overt concern than he had shown toward her. But then again, she had been feeling like McCoy was now, blinded with nausea and unable to see anything, when Kirk had helped her to bed.

The room reeled and she closed her eyes. Here it comes again, she thought. Her stomach clenched. She thought she was going to die.

"You'd better sit down," Kirk told her. He was supporting her elbow again, helping her to sit on the deck of sickbay. She knew her skirt had shifted absurdly high, but she almost didn't care.

Curling her legs underneath her, she bent far over, bracing herself with her hands, trying to keep from passing out. With every ounce of strength, she raised her head to blink up at the captain. "I'm sorry, sir."

"It's all right, Yeoman," Kirk said gently.

He couldn't blame her or McCoy. They both looked as if they had been dragged through a conduit during a coolant leak. The yeoman's grooming was usually impeccable, uniform neat and hair meticulously tended. Now she looked disheveled—and very, very ill.

Nurse Chapel began passing the regenerator over McCoy's face, which was turning bright red. "Look at his arms, too," she said, pushing up his sleeve.

Kirk noticed that her hand was shaking as she held the regenerator. He gave Chapel what he hoped passed for a reassuring smile. "We'll get through this."

McCoy was muttering something about "getting to work on that reverse spectral analysis."

"You're staying right there," Kirk told him. Not that it looked as if Dr. McCoy or Yeoman Harrison were in any shape to defy him. The doctor had said a few hours would see them over the worst of it. Kirk hoped he was right. Otherwise they would be left with no functional crew at all.

They had to complete their mission. If they just could find proof that Commander Teral carried the information on the plasma beam weapon—then they could leave the Badlands, even if only at impulse power. . . .

Suddenly the red alert klaxons went off with a penetrating sound that cut through everything else.

"Captain Kirk, to the bridge please."

Kirk moved away from McCoy's bed. "This is Kirk. Report."

Spock's voice came on line. *"I have a vessel on long-range scanners, sir."*

"What kind of ship is it, Mister Spock?"

"Sir, according to the remote sensor relay, it is a Klingon battlecruiser."

Chapter Five

KIRK STEPPED onto the bridge and went straight to the captain's chair. Spock slipped out of the seat to stand next to him. Kirk noted that Lieutenant Meghann was at the helm, Mister Chekov's usual station.

"Status report," Kirk ordered.

Spock faced the viewscreen. "A Klingon D7-type battlecruiser is advancing toward the Badlands at warp 7, Captain."

"Have they seen us?" Kirk asked.

"Negative, sir. The *Enterprise* has remained within the sensor shadow of the Badlands."

Kirk leaned closer to Spock. "Did you find anything in Commander Teral's ship?"

"No additional storage spaces have been detected," Spock said. "However, the diagnostic is not yet complete."

Kirk dismissed Spock to his station. "Put the Klingon battlecruiser on screen."

"Switching to visual," Sulu confirmed.

The starfield shifted, but there was no sign of the ship.

"Go to full magnification," Kirk ordered.

"Full magnification," Sulu confirmed.

"There she is," muttered Meghann at the helm.

The bulbous nose of the green battlecruiser swept through space. Kirk felt a tingling in the back of his neck. The Klingon vessel was moving with stealthy speed, straight towards them.

Scotty was staring up at the screen, distracted from his analysis of the dilithium crystals. Unable to restrain himself any longer, he exclaimed, "But Captain, it can't be the Klingons! Not in this part of space."

Kirk silently agreed. Klingon territory was on the other side of the Federation, curving to meet the opposite end of Romulan space. Yet Kirk hoped it *was* Klingons, however unlikely that might be, because the alternative would be worse. Romulans had recently acquired Klingon-design battlecruisers, incorporating their own cloaking technology into the deflector shields.

If that was a Romulan ship on an intercept course, it would be very difficult for him to explain why the sector was full of pieces of an exploded Romulan bird-of-prey. Or why a Romulan cruiser was in their shuttlebay.

"Ready phasers," Kirk ordered.

"Aye, Captain, all banks ready," Scotty acknowledged.

Shields had automatically been raised when they went to red alert. But without warp drive, they couldn't escape.

They waited as the battlecruiser rapidly closed with the plasma storms. It slowed to warp 3 as it approached the sensor shadow. Like the *Enterprise,* it finally had to drop out of warp because of the ion interference from the plasma.

"The battlecruiser is changing course," Spock announced.

"They've seen us," Kirk said grimly.

"Affirmative," Spock agreed. "They have entered the sensor shadow."

"Captain, we're being hailed," Uhura said.

Kirk stood up, his feet spread wide as if bracing himself for a physical confrontation. "On screen."

The starfield slowly dissolved to reveal the proud head and shoulders of a Klingon commander. His mustache started at the outer edges of his lip, creating thick tails that hung on either side of his mouth, mingling with the hair of his beard. Much like the Romulans and Vulcans, his Klingon brows curved up expressively.

"Dorak, son of Ronh," the Klingon barked. "In command of the *Tr'loth.*"

Altogether a fierce sight, but Kirk breathed a sigh of relief. At least it wasn't the Romulans. He knew how to handle Klingons. Every time he encountered Klingons, they were trying to take advantage of somebody. That made them predictable.

"Captain Kirk of the Starship *Enterprise,*" he said

flatly. "You're a long way from home, Commander Dorak."

"As are you." Dorak's eyes didn't blink. "What ship was destroyed here?"

"A Romulan bird-of-prey."

"*You* destroyed a Romulan bird-of-prey?" Dorak laughed, throwing back his head to show his pointed teeth. "I've heard of Captain *Kirk* and the Starship *Enterprise!* I would sooner believe a babe would fight Kahless the Unforgettable!"

Kirk stayed calm. There was no need to rise to meaningless insults. "The Enterprise was damaged at the same time the bird-of-prey was destroyed."

"*Who* destroyed the bird-of-prey?" Dorak demanded.

"We don't know what happened." Kirk said with all the patience he could muster. "We were some distance away from it."

"Why are you here, so far from the Federation?"

Blandly, Kirk gestured in the direction of the Badlands. "We're engaged in deep-space exploration. Our science labs are analyzing this region of plasma storms." Dorak's expression remained dubious. "What about you, Commander? It's a long way to Klingon territory. And I somehow doubt you're on a scientific mission. . . ."

Dorak's eyes narrowed, and he glared from Kirk to the other members of the bridge crew. Then the screen when blank. When the starfield resumed, the Klingon battlecruiser was growing larger. The malevolent green glow made Kirk's lip draw up in disgust.

"The *Tr'loth* is closing," Mister Sulu reported.

"They'll soon be within phaser range," Scotty assured him.

Spock looked up from his scanner. "Sir, their shields are at maximum and disruptors are on line. They also have maneuverability on their side."

"Spock, can they scan us?" Kirk demanded urgently. "Can they tell there's a Romulan ship on board—or a Romulan, for that matter?"

"Negative, sir, not through our shields."

"Very good," Kirk replied, relaxing somewhat.

Kirk could have sworn the Klingon commander was surprised to find the *Enterprise* here. Almost as surprised as Kirk was to find Klingons arriving in the area.

"Busy little spot, wouldn't you say, Mister Spock?" he asked.

"Aye, Captain. There seems to be an unusual amount of traffic for this area of unclaimed space."

Kirk narrowed his eyes. "What's the current status of the Klingon-Romulan alliance?"

Spock consulted with his computer for the latest Federation intelligence data. "The Klingon-Romulan alliance is unchanged. Active exchange of trade and military information."

"Perhaps it's not as active as the Klingons would like," Kirk murmured.

Scotty turned. "Sir? You think the Klingons were the ones the smuggler was to meet here?"

"A plasma beam weapon would be very useful to the Klingon Empire," Kirk commented. "Especially if the Romulans—their allies—have been holding back on them."

"We have no record of Klingons using plasma beam weapons," Spock agreed. "If the technology fell into their hands, it could upset the balance of power."

Kirk settled back to wait. If the Klingons were expecting to meet the smuggler, Dorak would not know if the ship had arrived yet. The bird-of-prey could have picked up the smuggler before it exploded, or both vessels could have been destroyed during a battle.

"The *Tr'loth* is slowing, sir. Eighty thousand kilometers away," Sulu announced.

The Klingon ship eased into place off their bow, positioned as if it were hanging over the *Enterprise.* The Klingon commander was deliberately assuming a threatening posture.

"Captain," Uhura said, "we're being hailed by the *Tr'loth* again."

Kirk stayed seated this time, casually leaning back on one elbow. "On screen."

Dorak was standing up, his hand braced on a bulkhead, looking down at the screen. Kirk could see other Klingons in the background, because of the wider angle. They were hunched over their instruments, with only the backs of their heads visible; but the low grumble of their voices was audible.

"We have scanned the area. It appears that you speak the truth. A Romulan bird-of-prey was destroyed." Commander Dorak leaned forward. "We still have not determined the cause."

"Neither have we," Kirk said patiently.

"You may be on your way," Commander Dorak said

with a magnanimous wave. "According to Klingon-Romulan agreements, we have salvage rights."

"I didn't know Klingons made jokes, Commander." Kirk didn't move. "I'm sorry to say, that wasn't a very good one."

"Many would be grateful not to have to *fight* to get away," said Durak.

"Commander, the *Enterprise* is not going anywhere." Kirk knew it wouldn't matter if he told them what their own sensors could detect: there were no matter/antimatter emissions from the nacelles of the *Enterprise*. "Our warp drive is off-line until we finish some repairs. It looks like we're stuck here for a few days."

"How unfortunate. Considering that we just signaled the Romulans and informed them of the destruction of one of their birds-of-prey." Dorak gave him a toothy grin. "They should be here within a few days."

"Calling for reinforcements already, Dorak?" Kirk prodded.

Dorak pursed his lips. "Stay away from the wreckage, Captain Kirk! It is ours."

"We will proceed with our investigation," Kirk countered.

"Then we will destroy your ship and salvage *your* wreckage!"

Kirk knew the *Enterprise* couldn't risk dropping shields to pick up debris while the Klingons were in the area, or they would discover the Romulan ship in the shuttle bay. They might even be able to detect the Romulan captain on board.

But Kirk wasn't going to let any Klingon dictate terms to him. "You'd better not make that threat unless you're willing to act on it." He stared at the screen, right into Dorak's eyes. "Kirk out."

Kirk terminated the connection himself.

Everyone on the bridge waited, expecting some sort of reaction from the Klingons. Kirk had practically slapped Dorak in the face with the back of his hand.

"The *Tr'loth* is scanning us, Captain," Spock announced.

"Shields?" he asked.

"Shields are holding, sir," Scotty assured him. "They'll not get anythin' on us!"

"They're moving off, Captain," Sulu reported. "Bearing zero-two-eight mark ten. One-half impulse power."

Kirk took a deep breath. So Dorak had chosen not to fight now. That must mean his mission was more important than putting an upstart Starfleet captain in his place.

Kirk quickly accessed Scott's engineering report on the dilithium crystals. They had just begun scanning the complex crystals in the science lab. It would take at least another two duty shifts before they were done, and another two days, at least, to replace the damaged EPS taps and bring warp drive on-line. *If* the dilithium crystals hadn't been structurally damaged.

"Get that warp drive back on line, Scotty," Kirk ordered, knowing he wouldn't have to tell his chief engineer how important it was.

"Aye, sir," Scott said fervently. "I'll go help with the scanning."

Kirk went over to Spock's station. "Our priority now is to find the specs on the plasma-beam weapons. Commander Teral must have the data. There's no other reason for the Klingons to be here."

"That would seem to be a logical explanation for their arrival," Spock agreed.

"Get down there, Spock, and turn that ship inside out if you have to. We've got to find that information."

"Aye, captain," Spock acknowledged. Kirk trusted that if the data was there, Spock would find it. Others seemed to find Spock's supernatural calm unnerving, but to Kirk it had always been reassuring.

Kirk settled in to see what the Klingons would do next, while waiting for Spock's report. He knew it would be no use confronting the Romulan captain again until they had proof of her guilt.

Not that he was fooled by the Klingons. They could act like they were just nosing around out there, innocently scooping up wreckage, but Kirk knew they were here to get the data on the plasma-beam weapon. And he couldn't allow that to happen. Even with one third of his crew incapacitated and so many vital systems off-line, Kirk knew he would have to beat the Klingons at their own game.

Chapter Six

LEAVING THE BRIDGE, Spock first went to the science lab to review the analysis of the scans of the *Barataria*. The interior scan correlated with the exterior scan to within .0003 microns. The downloaded computer memory banks were identical to the core in source patterns, and there were no overlaid sequences.

Then Spock proceeded to the shuttle bay to complete a scan of the *Barataria*'s systems. He nodded at the two security guards on duty in the shuttle bay.

Spock checked the examination of the *Barataria's* systems, but it was not yet completed. He returned to the exterior of the shuttle with his tricorder to scan the blackened scoring. He compared the dispersal pattern with logs of the *Enterprise* from over two years ago, when their hull had been damaged by the Romulan plasma-beam weapon.

Once the variations in structural materials were taken into account, the scoring pattern on the *Barataria* correlated with the damage done to the *Enterprise*. Spock concluded that Commander Teral's assessment had been correct: the *Barataria* had been at the extreme range of the plasma beam. Otherwise, her ship would have been destroyed.

Spock returned to the interior of the *Barataria*. The hatch opened into a general storage area, with a short corridor leading to the command center. The portable diagnostic unit was humming on the floor next to the captain's chair.

It was clearly a one-person ship. Spock was impressed with the meticulous order of the supplies and computer logs. Even Commander Teral's personal belongings, such as clothing and discs, were organized and immaculately maintained.

In addition, the subtle tones in the gratings and bulkheads were aesthetically pleasing. The command center was a model of efficiency, and there was an inherent symmetry in the structure of the ship.

Spock braced his hands on the back of the chair and leaned forward to read the power levels. Minimal, with engines powered down.

His hands lingered on the texture of the chair. Soft, pliant, yet strong. His fingers flexed, sinking in deeper.

Then he saw her face, the face he had been trying not to think of since Commander Teral had emerged from her ship. The Romulan Commander—he would not think her name, for that was too intimate, an intimacy he had betrayed for Starfleet.

Only a few months had passed since he had encountered the Romulan Commander. He could not forget how he had touched her hand and her face, even her lips. Captain Kirk had ordered Spock to distract the commander so he could steal a Romulan cloaking device for the Federation. But in the end, Spock could not say he regretted the time he had spent with her. She was an exceptional woman. . . .

The scanner beeped, indicating that it was finished, but for a moment Spock didn't notice.

When he realized the examination had been completed, Spock got to work. He noted that the only anomaly in the scan was in a subroutine linked to Teral's communications grid. This subroutine wasn't in the data; instead, it was an autosystem curled within the other subroutines. The only thing that would have detected it was a level-one diagnostic, which would have taken several hours to complete.

Spock attempted to access the subroutine, but it was coded shut. Carefully examining the physical structure, he noted a power linkage, which meant it was probably designed to self-destruct if opened without the proper access codes.

Spock notified Captain Kirk. "Sir, I have discovered a subroutine that is encoded. We will need the access codes to open it without damaging the data."

Kirk immediately replied, *"She must have them—Commander Teral."*

"Agreed, sir."

"Get them from her, Spock. And if you can't, I'll come down there and do it myself."

"Understood, Captain." Spock signed off.

On his way to deck 6, Spock reviewed his options. Commander Teral had no other logical choice but to relinquish the access codes. He would be ruthlessly honest, and she would realize the truth and accept it, as logical beings tended to do.

At the door to Commander Teral's temporary quarters, Spock told the security guards, "I must see Commander Teral."

Kelley opened the panel to the controls and operated the door. The chief of security gestured for another guard to stand by the controls as she followed Spock inside. "Captain's orders," she informed him, when he glanced back.

"Of course," Spock said.

Apparently, Commander Teral was startled when the door opened without warning. She stood up next to the couch.

"I am Commander Spock," he told her. "First Officer of the *Enterprise*."

"Good, I would like to leave now, Commander Spock," Teral told him. "I have been delayed here long enough."

"I regret that I cannot comply at this moment," Spock said.

She lifted her chin, her perfectly composed expression revealing strength of character. "What are the charges against me?"

"There are none, yet," Spock said. "However, fifty-five bottles of Romulan ale were discovered in a bulkhead inside the *Barataria*."

Commander Teral sighed and turned to the viewscreen. It showed the Klingon battlecruiser moving in the distance. A white beam shot out from its deflector grid and anchored a spinning piece of debris. The beam shortened, drawing the debris towards the cruiser.

"What are the Klingons doing here?" Commander Teral asked, following his gaze.

"How do you know that is a Klingon vessel?" Spock politely asked. "Romulans also employ the D7-type battlecruiser."

"The markings indicate it is Klingon." Teral had a slight edge of scorn in her tone. "What are they doing here?"

"Perhaps the Klingons are here to obtain the information on plasma-beam weapon that has been smuggled out of Romulan territory."

Teral lifted one brow and looked at him as if she hadn't thought of that. "Interesting idea. But it has nothing to do with me."

"The Klingons would undoubtedly detain your ship if you left the *Enterprise* now," Spock pointed out.

"That is my concern, not yours."

Spock was not convinced. "I have located the information," he informed her.

"Oh?" she asked, surprised. "What information?"

"The data is located in a subroutine concealed within your communications processor."

Her expression eased. "Oh, that. That's not the information you want."

Spock held up one hand to stop her from turning way again. "May I ask what it is?"

"Those are my . . . contact files, my black files. I keep them in the subroutine in case I'm searched. But most officials don't put this much effort into it." She glanced away in exasperation. "Starfleet! Have you got nothing better to do?"

"I must request the access codes so I can examine the data," Spock told her.

"No. That is my information."

Spock stepped closer. "Nevertheless, I must examine it. The data we seek are vital."

"Not to me," she said defiantly. The black kohl encircling her eyes made her stare seem piercing.

Spock was reminded again of how fierce yet composed Romulan women could be. "I do not believe you have any choice, Commander Teral. If you do not give me the codes, I will attempt to open the subroutine without them. Whether I succeed in obtaining the data or not, Captain Kirk will then be forced to deliver you to a Starbase for further questioning."

"So now the Federation believes people are guilty until proven innocent?"

"The subroutine would seem to be evidence of your guilt," Spock pointed out.

"That's Romulan thinking, Commander Spock. I thought Vulcans were different." She looked toward Kelley guarding the door. The security chief's strong-boned face was expressionless, but the phaser hanging on her belt was clearly visible. Teral was a prisoner.

She sighed. "The contact information is extremely sensitive. I would not like it falling into the wrong hands."

"If the subroutine does not contain the data on the

plasma weapon, I assure you it will be returned to you intact and uncopied."

Teral tilted her head as if judging him. "A lifetime of contacts within Romulan territory are in that subroutine. Starfleet would love to get their hands on it. You could be lying to me."

Spock ignored his sense of déjà vu. The other Romulan commander had also wondered aloud if he was lying to her. That time, Spock had assured the commander he was telling the truth.

This time, he said, "You do not have to believe me, Commander Teral. Your actions will prove your innocence or guilt."

After a moment, Teral turned and picked up a padd. "Here are the access codes. As you so logically pointed out, I have no choice."

She keyed in the codes and the proper sequence for opening the data seal. Before handing it over, she said, "Mister Spock, I hold you personally responsible for my files."

Spock inclined his head, retreating to the door. Security Chief Kelley stood down from parade rest, ready to follow him out.

"And Mister Spock," Commander Teral called out behind him, "when you conclude that I *don't* have the information you seek, please tell your captain that I want to speak to him."

Much later, Spock turned off the diagnostic display of the data in Commander Teral's subroutine. He sat in the captain's chair on the *Barataria,* his fingers steepled thoughtfully as he considered his findings.

The information was exactly what Teral had claimed it would be: contact information, names, places, computer codes, drop points, and verification passwords. It was detailed, organized, cross-referenced, and did indeed contain a lifetime of smuggling experience. Spock wondered what this exceptional woman could have made of herself if she had put her effort into a legitimate pursuit.

Teral had contacts within the Romulan Senate and even with those who surrounded the Praetor's administration on Romulus. Spock speculated on the possibility that Teral had blood ties with the Romulan elite. That would explain her regal bearing.

According to the numerous other contacts detailed in the database, the captain had traveled widely. Spock had not heard of some of the places she frequented, such as "Ferenginar" and "Bajor."

The information served to build a convincing picture of a captain with a fast ship serving high-level clients with peculiar tastes. One of the entries under "preferences" was for a mature Orion animal woman with blue-green skin rather than the traditional olive green. Another entry was for a biannual delivery of half a kopec of Delavian chocolates. Another standing request was for an inverse-flux spectrometer. Apparently Commander Teral specialized in hard-to-find items. Some were legal in the Federation and in the Romulan Star Empire, but more than half would be considered contraband.

Spock had run cross-checks on the subroutine as well as on the routines it was nestled among, searching for buried layers of information or subsubroutines. But there was nothing.

Spock downloaded the summary of his report. Mainly it contained negative findings on the searches that had been conducted on the *Barataria*. The Romulan ale was the only concrete evidence they had found. As he had promised Commander Teral, Spock did not include the data contained within the subroutine, since it was not pertinent to their primary mission.

Spock proceeded directly to the bridge, where he knew Captain Kirk would be waiting for his report.

Spock was aware that every officer on the bridge was watching him as he approached the captain. On screen was the Klingon battlecruiser, maneuvering closer to a piece of nacelle debris from the destroyed bird-of-prey.

"Did you find anything, Spock?" Kirk asked.

He didn't bother to lower his voice. "Sir, I was unable to locate the information on the plasma beam weapons."

"No?" Kirk's brow furrowed in concern. "Are you sure, Mister Spock?"

"Yes, sir." Spock clasped both hands behind his back, standing at attention near Kirk. "Commander Teral operates a small smuggling operation specializing in rare or illegal luxury items. Fifty-five bottles of Romulan ale were located inside a concealed compartment. The manifest and navigational logs are consistent—the destination was an Earth Outpost in sector 7449, on the border of Federation territory."

"What about that subroutine?" Kirk asked. "Didn't you find anything in it?"

"The subroutine merely contained Commander Teral's contact information."

"She *must* have the weapons information . . . ," Kirk murmured, "that's why the Klingons are here."

Spock cleared his throat slightly. "Sir, Commander Teral has requested permission to speak with you."

Kirk acknowledged, knowing he would have to wring the information out of the Romulan himself. Kirk thought that Spock was acting strangely. Maybe it was because he hadn't found the data they were looking for . . . Spock was a perfectionist, so he was probably irritated by his failure, though he would never admit it.

"You have the bridge," Kirk told Spock. But as he got out of the chair, he hesitated. "Tell me, Spock, what do you think of Commander Teral?"

Spock stiffened slightly, as if returning to attention. "Commander Teral is a highly efficient individual."

"I understand," Kirk said, even though that was not the descriptive term that immediately leaped to his mind when he thought about Commander Teral. Kirk noticed the others were listening in curiously. "Carry on."

In the turbolift, Captain Kirk ordered, "Deck 6."

After a moment, he told the computer, "Captain's log, supplemental." He knew he couldn't wait any longer to file his log. The next dispatch would be sent to the relay soon, and he must keep Starfleet Command notified. "In spite of the fact that the Klingon battle-cruiser is in the area, we've continued our salvage operation of debris from the Romulan bird-of-prey. We are conducting scans on each piece of debris, trying to locate primary components. Thus far, we've only found one important piece of debris, about the size of a communicator, that came from the plasma-flow integrator. We dropped shields to beam it on board. There was no reaction from the Klingon vessel, so we believe they did not notice the microsecond interruption, due to scanner disruptions within the sensor shadow of the Badlands. We continue with repairs and to search for the specs on the plasma-beam weapon."

Kirk signed off on his supplemental log, sending it to communications to be posted along with the others. He had postponed his log in hopes that Spock would discover the plasma-beam specs.

Their situation had not improved much in the past few hours, though the flow of sick crew members had finally stopped at forty-seven. According to reports from sickbay, the injured crew members were stabilized but still incapacitated. Nurse Chapel had confided that Dr. McCoy was finally asleep and resting comfortably.

At deck 6, Kirk nodded to the trio of security guards. Perhaps there didn't need to be so many.

"I'm here to see Commander Teral," he told the chief of security.

"Aye, sir," Kelley said.

Kirk stopped Kelley before she could manipulate the door control. "Did you scan Commander Teral for weapons?"

"Aye, sir, and Dr. McCoy gave her a bioscan."

Kirk nodded. "You can wait out here."

"Acknowledged, sir."

When the door opened, Commander Teral was sitting on the sofa under the viewscreen. One leg was tucked underneath her, and she was sitting back, her arm lying on the back of the couch. Her metal-mesh jumpsuit was open at the collar.

She slowly stood up, bringing her face out of the shadows. He hadn't taken a good look at her in the shuttle bay—he had been too busy watching her gun hand and wondering whether there were other Romulans hiding in the *Barataria*.

Now he could see her full lips, and the way her dark brows were so finely curved. She was different from the last Romulan woman he had encountered—the other Romulan commander. He hadn't meant to capture that commander after he had stolen the cloaking device from her ship. But she had been in their custody until they transferred her to Starbase 12, where she was probably still waiting to be returned to her own people.

Kirk wondered if *that* was Spock's problem. He had apparently become quite . . . intimate with the Romulan commander. But Kirk knew that Spock hadn't spoken to her while she was in custody on board the *Enterprise*.

Teral was even more imposing than the Romulan military commander had been, quite tall and commanding, with an arrogant expression.

"Yes, Captain?" She crossed her arms. "Did you come just to have a good look at me?"

He ignored her fighting stance and grinned. "You asked to see me."

"I am waiting for an apology." Her expression was distant, as if she really didn't care whether he apologized or not.

"I'm still not convinced you're telling the truth." Kirk continued smiling, because Teral was not.

Teral glared at him for a moment longer. Then she sighed, lifting one hand as if in defeat. "I should have expected you would not admit you were in error." Suddenly she smiled back at him, as if she had been caught doing something she knew she wasn't supposed to do. "I've been trying to figure out what's going on."

"There are many things I would like to know, too," Kirk agreed. "Such as, why was that Romulan bird-of-prey chasing you?"

"Sit down, Captain," she said, gesturing to the sofa. She sat down, too, absently tucking her leg underneath her again. Only one pointed ear and the side of her face caught the light.

"Captain, I believe the Romulans were under the same impression that you are, that I was carrying the plasma-beam data."

"Explain," he demanded, leaning forward to see her eyes better in the shadows.

"I believe I was hired to be a decoy."

"Then you admit being involved in something more than smuggling Romulan ale?"

"Yes, but I didn't know it involved *this*."

Kirk sat back, considering this new twist. Could

there possibly be another ship, and the *Barataria* just a decoy? "If that's true, then where is the other ship?"

"It must have been behind me, watching to see who followed me. It could be anywhere by now." Her hand turned palm up. "All I know is that I was ordered to go straight through this system while I was making a run to drop the ale. And I was paid well for it, through an anonymous contact."

"But the Klingons are here waiting for the smuggler," Kirk said.

"If you hadn't been here, I would have passed through this system with the bird-of-prey behind me. The other ship could have easily met the Klingons."

"You have a point," Kirk admitted.

"Now they will have to set up a new contact meeting. It will take more time, but the most difficult part is over. *I* served as decoy for the other ship to get out of Romulan territory. *I* am the one who almost got pulverized by a plasma beam. *I* am the one who was captured by *you*. They certainly got their money's worth out of me."

The explanation seemed airtight, but a little too convenient. He studied her face—her watchful eyes, her calculated smile. In spite of it all, he wanted to believe her.

Then a sudden realization brought him up short. Why was he so eager to give her the benefit of the doubt? He heard sincerity in her voice, in the way she moved, in the way she *looked* . . . perhaps that was it: she looked like Spock, whom he trusted implicitly. His belief in Spock's honor and integrity was so deep that it was affecting the way he felt about this woman. Many of her mannerisms, her subtle expressions, and especially her facial characteristics were similar to Spock's.

"Let me go," she told him, leaning forward to press her point. "The Klingons will give chase, and you can stay here and pick up the wreckage."

"If I let you go, the Klingons would stop you exactly as we did."

"The *Barataria* is a fast ship, captain. You only caught me because you ambushed me." Her voice grew harder. "It is my choice. I have already stated I will pay the fines for smuggling Romulan ale. If you do not bring further charges against me, then you must let me go."

Kirk was beginning to wonder about that himself. He was bending the law quite far already, nearly to the point of unlawful detention.

But he shook his head. She had already admitted some involvement in smuggling the plasma-beam data. He couldn't let her go. Besides, if she had managed to somehow conceal the plasma-beam data, she would hand it over to the Klingons once they captured her. "I can't let you go until I have proof one way or the other. You have to give me *something*."

"What can I give you?" she asked, her eyes pleading. "I have only the truth to give."

They couldn't leave until their warp drive was back on line, and he couldn't let her go to get caught by the Klingons. If she didn't have the information they sought, the Klingons wouldn't content themselves with simply scanning her.

She saw his grim expression, and realized she wasn't going to be released. She looked down at her hands in her lap as Kirk got to his feet. He couldn't see her expression.

"I'm sorry about the inconvenience," Kirk told her.

She looked up, a light glinting off her eye. "You could lessen the inconvenience by not charging me for smuggling Romulan ale," she told him. "And give me back those bottles. Then it will not be necessary for me to complain about this."

Kirk's mouth opened slightly. "That would be against Federation regulations."

"So is holding someone without informing them of the charges," she pointed out.

"That's an interesting proposition," he told her. "Can I think it over?"

"Take your time," she told him with a little wave of her hand. "If you would like, you can give me your answer this evening."

"This evening?"

"Yes, if I do have to stay in this room alone, I would appreciate some company for my evening meal."

Again Kirk felt as if things were turning in a direction he had not anticipated. "I suppose it's the least I can do."

Commander Teral was smiling as Kirk left. He wasn't sure what he was going to do about the Romulan ale. It would be convenient to scrub the charges to make up for detaining her—*if* she wasn't the smuggler they were looking for. But that was a fairly large *if*.

Chapter Seven

SPOCK FOUND IT fascinating to watch the reactions of the crew as, hour by hour, day by day, they endeavored to get the *Enterprise* back in working order.

Because stellar distances were so great, it would take weeks to get help from Starfleet. If the dilithium crystals were now flawed due to the radiation burst, it could take years to get back to the Federation under impulse power alone. They were on the edge of nowhere, and clearly had to fend for themselves.

Meanwhile the Klingons circled around them, picking up debris and never letting them slip out of sensor range within the shadow of the Badlands. Spock had to admire Commander Darok's subtle intimidation ploy. His maneuvers continually pushed the *Enterprise* right to the edge of a fight.

Spock had been allowed to send additional probes

into the Badlands to obtain scientific data. Since the captain had informed the Klingons that the *Enterprise* was here to study the plasma storms, it made sense to continue with their scientific research.

They were well into their third day of yellow alert when Sulu announced, "I've got another one!"

Spock switched from his scans of the Badlands to access the sensor array. There was a piece of debris that scanned positively for theta-matrix compositing particles, an essential component of warp drive systems.

"Tracking," Mister Chekov reported.

Chekov had returned to his duty station two days ago. Most of the injured crew members were also now back on duty, including Dr. McCoy. He had already been on the bridge once this morning, complaining about something. Spock had been too involved in an analysis of the plasma gases to listen.

"Confirmed, Captain," Spock said, examining Sulu's findings. "It is part of the converter assembly, consisting of tritanium, approximately 1.2 kilograms in weight."

"The biggest we've found," Kirk said thoughtfully.

"Indeed, it is quite sizable," Spock agreed.

"Location of the Klingon battlecruiser," Kirk requested.

Chekov checked the helm. "Two hundred thousand kilometers off our stern, sir."

"Close . . . ," Kirk said, disappointed. "Too close."

"Perhaps we could create a diversion," Sulu suggested. "Vent some plasma from our nacelles."

"They know we're working on our warp drive,"

Chekov agreed. "It would make sense to vent the systems."

Spock detected an eagerness from the crew to do something—anything—to break the monotony and stress. "Captain, the risk may be too high," he cautioned. "None of the other debris beamed on board has revealed any information relevant to our current mission."

"It could tell us *something*," Chekov insisted, sounding frustrated. "Especially if they had an engine overload."

All eyes turned to Captain Kirk. Spock could tell by the way he shifted in his seat that Kirk, too, was eager to do something. But Kirk was too canny to fall into that trap.

"Hold position," he ordered. "Keep us between the Klingon battlecruiser and the debris. We'll wait until they move off."

Barely suppressed sighs greeted his order. But the crew obediently settled back to their duties.

"Engineer Scott to Captain Kirk."

Kirk shifted his hand to press the button to respond. "What is it, Scotty?"

The chief had been ensconced in engineering for the past day. The only time Spock had seen him was when he had assisted in calibrating the dilithium crystal scanner to ensure that the entire crystalline structure had been analyzed. Dilithium was a notoriously difficult substance to work with.

"Th' dilithium is sound, sir," Scott jubilantly reported. *"I've realigned the crystals in the articulation frame, and the new EPS taps are containin' the stream.*

We can power up the warp engines in the next hour or so."

There were quiet exclamations of relief among the officers, as Kirk said, "Good work, Scotty. Let me know as soon as warp drive is back on-line."

Spock returned to his work. Their situation would obviously change soon, so he needed to obtain as much data on the Badlands as he could within that time frame.

Kirk was tired of waiting, but he contained his impatience as warp drive was slowly powered up. It had been a game of nerves for the past few days. The Klingons had kept creeping closer than he was comfortable with, and the *Enterprise* had to keep constantly running away while trying to act like it wasn't.

Kirk had become more and more convinced that the Klingons were waiting for the smuggler to arrive. It was not like Klingons to lurk. They were in-your-face types, quick to attack and depart. If the situation was bothering *his* crew, the Klingons must be ready to explode.

Most revealing was when Commander Darok had hailed them yesterday, irritably demanding to know whether they had encountered any other vessels in the area. Kirk had blandly admitted to seeing several vessels in the area, but he couldn't get Darok to specify what type of ship he was looking for. Kirk didn't want to reveal anything else while they were still without warp drive. They were too vulnerable to get in an entanglement with the Klingons.

But now . . . Kirk knew he needed to resolve the situation. He had spent the past two evenings with Commander Teral, talking about a wide range of subjects, people and places, trying to figure her out. Yet Kirk was still not sure if she was telling the truth. She had certainly traveled extensively both inside Federation and Romulan territories as well as in the outlying regions. He found himself almost envying her freedom. She admitted she could have retired to a small planet somewhere by now, but she said she enjoyed roaming about.

One thing Kirk knew for certain—he couldn't trust his own judgment when it came to the Romulan commander. And Teral had also thoroughly captivated McCoy, who went to "check on her" soon after he was able to get out of bed. McCoy had been there when Kirk had arrived the night before—the doctor had almost invited himself to stay for dinner. Kirk had observed that Spock at least had not spoken to Teral since he had confronted her over the access codes.

Since Kirk couldn't get the proof from Teral, he decided it was time to try another route. He would provoke the Klingons, to find out if they were in the Badlands to meet the *Barataria*.

When Scotty confirmed that warp drive was on-line and that they could engage it, Kirk was ready. He checked their location and was pleased to see they were close to the edge of the sensor shadow, where they could go to warp.

"Does the battlecruiser have weapons systems on line?" Kirk asked Spock.

"Affirmative, sir. However, their targeting system is currently on standby."

"If we drop shields, how long before they could lock on and fire?"

"Approximately thirty seconds," Spock replied. "Assuming Commander Darok decides to attack the moment our shields are down."

"I don't think the Klingons are prepared to do that." Kirk stood up and moved forward to the helm. "Sulu, drop shields and leave them down until my order. Mister Spock, scan the battlecruiser and let me know when they lock on weapons."

Chekov seemed confused. "Shouldn't we dispel some plasma as a distraction, sir?"

"No," Kirk told him.

Sulu turned to look up at him. "But sir, at this range the Klingons will know we've dropped our shields. They'll be able to scan us."

"That's what I'm counting on." Kirk gazed speculatively at the battlecruiser on the viewscreen. "I want them to scan us. Let them see we've got a Romulan on board." He glanced around as the bridge crew realized what he intended to do. To bring the weapons systems on line, he now ordered, "Red alert."

"Red alert," Uhura announced to the ship as the red light began flashing. "All decks report status. Red alert." After a moment, she reported, "All decks report ready, sir."

"Chekov, move away so they can see that piece of wreckage we've been hiding.

"Acknowledged, sir."

"Mister Sulu, after you drop shields, beam the

wreckage over and take it to the science lab." It would serve as an excuse for their lowering the shields.

"We are clear of the debris, sir," Chekov reported.

"Drop shields," Kirk ordered.

"Dropping shields," Sulu reported. His hands moved across the console.

Kirk kept an eye on Spock, who was gazing into his scanner.

Spock didn't look up as he reported, "The *Tr'loth* is scanning us, Captain."

"Hold position," Kirk said calmly. "Beam aboard the debris."

"Aye, sir," Sulu acknowledged.

Most of the officers on the bridge shifted, instinctively uneasy with the idea that the Klingons were scanning the ship.

"Twenty-five seconds," Sulu reported.

Kirk knew the Klingons had been working with the Romulans for many years now. They probably had a good understanding of each other's physiology and lifesigns. It wouldn't take the Klingons long to find the Romulan in their midst.

"Thirty seconds," Sulu said.

"Their weapons are locking on, sir," Spock announced, after a few moments.

"Raise shields," Kirk ordered.

"Shields raised," Sulu replied, so fast that the sequence must have already been keyed in.

"Evasive maneuvers," Kirk said. "Heading four-five-zero mark forty."

The battlecruiser shifted out of view on the screen as

the *Enterprise* headed for the edge of the sensor shadow. Kirk checked the readout on his arm console. The Klingons weren't firing, but they were in pursuit.

"Sir, Commander Darok is hailing you," Uhura said.

Right on cue, Kirk thought. "On screen."

The Klingon glowered down at him, his face filling the screen. "Kirk! You have Romulans on board your ship!"

Kirk affected an innocent smile. "Actually, only one Romulan. Commander Teral of the *Barataria*."

"Release the commander immediately," Darok demanded.

"What is your interest in Commander Teral?" Kirk asked.

Darok narrowed his eyes. "I will speak with the commander *now*."

An interesting suggestion, and one Kirk was prepared for. Teral might take the opportunity to exchange recognition signals, or perhaps convey a message in code. It was a calculated risk, but he was willing to take it to resolve the situation. Darok was not a subtle person, so surely he would give away his intentions.

Kirk pressed the comm to the captain's quarters. "Commander Teral, the Klingon Commander Darok would like to speak with you."

After a moment, Teral replied, "I have nothing to say to any Klingon commander, Captain Kirk."

Very smart, Kirk thought, exactly what she would say if she was innocent of smuggling plasma-beam data from the Romulans to the Klingons. But maybe she *was* innocent. . . .

He signaled Uhura to put the Darok back on the

screen. "Commander Teral doesn't want to speak to you, Commander."

"You lie!" Darok blurted out. Spittle caught on his lower lip, making it shine. His brows stuck out wildly as he glared at Kirk.

Kirk was disgusted by the display. He leaned back, silently gazing at the commander.

"Release her now!" Darok insisted. "Or you will regret it. . . ."

Kirk went very still. "How did you know Commander Teral was a woman?"

Darok was momentarily caught off guard. "You said—"

"No, I didn't mention it."

Darok glanced away briefly. "The scans show a female Romulan."

Kirk suppressed his grin of victory. Darok had said—"You have Romulans on board." If they couldn't tell there was only one Romulan, then they certainly hadn't been able to pinpoint gender.

Now Kirk was certain that Teral was lying. She must have the specs on the plasma-beam weapon.

The Klingon commander was growing purple with rage, thinking Kirk had possession of the information. Darok slammed his fist against something off screen. "Release that ship now!"

"I have no intention of doing that," Kirk said steadily.

"You will suffer the consequences." Darok seemed pleased at the prospect as he cut transmission.

"Full impulse power," Kirk ordered. "Scotty, we're going to need warp power."

"Aye, Captain!" Scott called from the engine room.

The swirling plasma clouds shifted out of view as the *Enterprise* dived away from the Badlands.

"Standby," Kirk ordered. "Distance, Mister Chekov?"

"The battlecruiser is at 100,000 kilometers and closing fast, sir."

"The *Tr'loth* is firing phase disruptors," Spock announced.

"Shields, full power to the rear." Kirk braced himself, as did the others on the bridge.

The *Enterprise* rocked under the impact and explosion. Kirk caught the arm of the chair to keep himself from being flung out.

"Direct hit to our rear shields," Spock said. "Shields at 82 percent."

"Lock phasers," Kirk ordered. "Bring us about for attack."

"Changing course," Chekov replied eagerly.

"Phasers locked," Sulu confirmed.

As the *Enterprise* turned, the *Tr'loth* continued on for a few seconds before starting to veer away.

"Fire!" Kirk ordered.

The whine of the power couplings signaled phasers firing from all banks. The beams repeatedly struck the port side of the battlecruiser.

"Direct hit," Spock announced. "Their shields are holding."

Kirk didn't need Spock to tell him that the Klingons had fired their disruptors again. The energy streaks darted away from the battlecruiser.

The *Enterprise* was diving to evade the disruptor beams when they hit the top of the saucer section.

Steadying himself, Kirk could hear the strain on the hull, and a muffled explosion from the deck below. The crew was scrambling to stay at their stations.

"Shields down to 63 percent!" Spock announced.

Kirk checked his arm console. The Klingons were forcing them back towards the plasma storms. Chekov cursed under his breath as he tried various evasive maneuvers to bring them back on course.

Suddenly gravity generators seemed to shut off. Kirk raised his arms, startled, rising up from his chair. Uhura screamed, a piercing cry of disorientation. Kirk hung in the air, kicking out one leg as he slowly turned. The rest of the bridge crew were up-ended and floating.

Several heartbeats later, gravity abruptly returned.

Kirk landed heavily on the deck. His ears were ringing from the disruption in the environmental systems. He had to swallow hard to bring his balance centers back under control.

"Spock—what happened?" he asked, rolling to his feet.

"Sensors are off-line, sir," Spock promptly replied, sounding intent and preoccupied as usual with his data. "A gravity flux occurred for 6.4 seconds—"

"*Scott to Captain Kirk!*" Scotty interrupted though the intercom. "*The warp core is off-line.*"

Kirk gripped the arm of the chair. Not again! "Scotty, we need warp drive."

"I canna give it to you, Captain," Scott cried out. *"I don' understand it, but the dilithium alignment is off again. We had to shut down the antimatter stream."*

"What about impulse power?" Kirk asked.

"I'm trying, Captain," Scott assured him. *"But we have to reroute the electroplasma energy through the conduits. The new circuits have blown."*

"Do what you can, Scotty." Kirk fumbled for the button. "Spock, that was the same thing that happened when the Romulan bird-of-prey exploded."

"There is a correlation in the type and severity of malfunctions." Spock turned around, removing the receiver from his ear. "Sir, it appears that the *Tr'loth* is in trouble. Their shields are down and the ship is foundering."

"Sir!" Chekov exclaimed. "We're being drawn toward the Badlands. Thrusters aren't holding us. . . ."

Over the comm, Kirk ordered, *"We need impulse power now, Scotty."*

Scott acknowledged from engineering, even as another EPS circuit failed. He began to bypass the injection relays manually, keeping a graph of the circuit stress displayed on the panel so he could tell which one to shunt to next. The best he could give the captain at the moment was thrusters. Thrusters would not be enough to keep them from resisting the strong gravitational pull of the Badlands. If only they hadn't been heading toward the plasma storms at full impulse when they foundered!

"Check the flow valves," Scott ordered his best power man, Lieutenant Klancee. The slush deuterium used as fuel for the impulse engines was almost as volatile as antimatter. Scott hadn't even looked at the dilithium crystals yet—he was too busy trying to get the impulse engines on-line.

Scott tapped in a quick scan. Readings indicated that subprocessors were failing all over the ship, unable to link to the main computer as many of the protected circuits failed. Alternate linkages were failing, too, and at an alarming rate.

Virtually every control panel and terminal operated the ship's systems via a subprocessor link. With the data stream interrupted, there was no way for the crew to control the ship. Backup systems were engaging in all the major systems, from navigational control to life support.

Technicians were replacing circuits on the power conduits as fast as they could on all decks. But even with all the practice they had had over the past few days, it still took time to remove the old ones, sterilize the surfaces, and install a fresh circuit or tap. It was taking far too long to get impulse power going. Scott glanced at the display of their location, dismayed by how much closer to the storms they had been pulled.

"Kirk to engine room," came through the speakers. *"What's happening down there!"*

The impulse engines pulsed red and orange, coming to life with audible strain as the power stream fluctuated. Having to switch electroplasma circuits manually was causing flow disruptions. Scotty could tell the other technicians, then the junction nodes were also manually stabilizing the stream. They couldn't go on like this for very long.

"A few more seconds, Captain, and I can give you one-quarter impulse power!" he called, unable to go to the comm. He used the long plasteel power converter with the magnetic nodes to manipulate the manual routing controls.

"Flow valves holding," Klancee reported as he returned. He quickly slid open the panel under the main engineering console and began replacing the fused EPS taps.

"Plasma storms at 300,000 kilometers," Sulu announced through the comm.

The deck shifted beneath Scott as the artificial gravity control reacted to the stress of the nearby plasma storms. The entire ship began to vibrate as if they were rolling over rough planetary terrain. Scott had never felt the *Enterprise* react this way before.

Muttering under his breath, Scott checked the shields, noting they fluctuated between 23 and 42 percent. It would have to do, until impulse power was stabilized. If they lost impulse engines, shields would drop. Scott didn't want to think of what all that plasma would do to the hull of the *Enterprise.*

"We need impulse power now," Kirk prompted from the bridge.

"Captain, I'm working as fast as I can!" Scott exclaimed. "It's a miracle we're keeping her going at all!"

The jolting caught Lieutenant Klancee and caused him to bang his head on the console while he was shifting to the next panel. He cursed under his breath and hauled the large EPS tap into place without pausing.

Scotty didn't like the feel of the shuddering, as they were buffeted by the discharge around the plasma storms. The strain of holding the shields up was reflected in energy spikes in the impulse engines—but now, with some of the faulty circuits replaced, Scotty was finally starting to make progress.

"I can give you one-quarter impulse, Captain," Scott said into the comm. "But there are still some conflicts in the reaction control system."

"Understood," Kirk said curtly.

"Wallowin' around like a drunken whale," Scott muttered as he tended to the relays.

Under the console, Klancee gave a muffled snort that reflected a lack of humor about their situation. "Almost done here, sir. I'll do the command coordinator next—"

Klancee broke off as he sat up, a shocked expression on his face. "Sir! Behind you!"

Scotty whirled around, expecting to see at least two or three Klingons invading the engineering section. What he saw was less frightening, but even more odd.

The bulkhead was glowing.

Scott went closer to see. The light was coming from the metal itself, emanating from the bulkhead. The curved support from floor to nearly eye level sparkled with many different pinpoint colors.

Scott checked it with his tricorder while Klancee moved his hand closer. "It feels warm," Klancee said.

"Don't go near it," Scott ordered. "I'm reading gamma radiation."

The *Enterprise* lurched more roughly, and they both went back to work. But Scott kept glancing over at the bulkhead. He sent the data from his tricorder straight to the science lab, but was unable to take another second away from the systems until they had stabilized impulse power.

When the shuddering slowed and finally eased, Scott let out a long sigh. The were moving away from the plasma storms. He let himself slump forward for a moment. At least if the shields failed now, they wouldn't be fried.

Scott went to the portal to check on the battlecruiser visually. The Klingon ship was clearly having her own troubles. Though the *Enterprise* sensors were still down, he could tell from the lack of distortion fields around the hull that the *Tr'loth* had no shields. Without shields, the Klingons weren't going to be picking another fight any time soon. The chief breathed another sigh of relief.

Then he glanced over at the still glowing bulkhead as he hit the comm. "Scott to Mister Spock. There's somethin' strange down here I think you should see."

Chapter Eight

YEOMAN HARRISON had been assigned to a repair crew because of the emergency power failure. She had recovered from the radiation sickness, with only one lesion on her neck. Dr. McCoy had removed the dead tissue and healed the area with a skin grafter, and he told her that many of those who became ill had suffered from the same symptoms.

So Yeoman Harrison was able-bodied, unlike the crew members who had been hit first and hardest by the radiation. She figured that almost a dozen were still confined to bed rest in their quarters.

Harrison first helped replace electroplasma circuits in sickbay, and when those were completed, she continued up to the scanning grid on deck 6 along with the rest of her team. When they passed by the quarters of Commander Teral, Harrison realized she should probably look in on their guest. Captain Kirk had assigned Harrison to serve as liaison to Teral, so the yeoman was supposed to make sure the Romulan had everything she needed.

There was only one security guard outside Teral's door. Captain Kirk had reduced the number of guards the first night Teral was on board.

The guard nodded familiarly as Yeoman Harrison approached. "She's been asking what happened."

It was just as Harrison suspected. Commander Teral was not one to sit calmly on the sidelines while other people fought her battles. The guard opened the door and followed her inside.

"Are you injured?" Harrison asked Teral.

Teral ignored her inquiry. "What happened? No one has answered my calls. Why did the Klingons attack us?"

"Maybe it's because you wouldn't talk to them," Harrison said somewhat more tartly than she had intended. She had heard rumors of what had happened on the bridge. She kept trying to ignore the fact that Captain Kirk had spent the past two evenings in Teral's quarters. It was none of her business.

"I want to speak to Captain Kirk," Teral imperiously demanded.

"The captain is busy right now," Harrison said, remaining courteous. "But I can take a message to him if you would like."

"Yes, tell him to come here," Teral ordered.

The yeoman watched her pace back and forth in front of the viewscreen, focused on the image of the Klingon battlecruiser. Even from this distance, it was clear the ship was moving slowly, when it moved at all.

But Harrison was more interested in the Romulan woman than in the threat the Klingons posed. She couldn't understand why Captain Kirk and Dr. McCoy were so interested in her.

Teral could be very nice when she wanted something, very complimentary and friendly, like when she asked Harrison to get her some outfits more casual than the mesh jumpsuit. But there were other times, like now, when she was cold as ice and meaner than a mugato. Harrison wondered if the two men simply never saw this side of her.

"Don't just stand there," Teral told her. "I want to see Kirk now."

"I'm sure he's busy," Harrison retorted. "But I'll pass along your request."

Harrison was heading toward the door when it opened from outside.

Captain Kirk stood in the doorway. "What's going on here?" His expression eased when he saw the security guard inside.

"I came to make sure Commander Teral was all right," Harrison said.

"Oh, very good," Kirk told her, seeming preoccupied.

As well he should be, Harrison thought, with the *Enterprise* in such disarray. Though she felt a flush of pleasure that Kirk was pleased with her performance, she didn't like the self-satisfied expression on Teral's face. Who did Teral think she was, able to demand and immediately get the presence of the captain of the flag-ship of the Federation?

Kirk realized Yeoman Harrison was upset. That tiny wrinkle between her brows was deepening.

No wonder, he thought, when he caught a glimpse of Teral's smug look. The way Teral came up to him, smiling possessively, was enough to make anyone jealous. Somehow the Romulan shifted closer to him, making it clear that she and Kirk had formed a bond.

That seemed to infuriate the yeoman even more. Her glossy brown hair trembled as she lowered her chin, her hands fumbling with the large round circuits she carried.

"You're both dismissed." Kirk wondered if he should have someone else liaison with Commander Teral. But that was of little importance right now.

He waited until both Yeoman Harrison and the security guard had left and the door slid shut behind them.

"You can't lie to me anymore." Kirk turned abruptly on Teral. "I know Darok is here to meet with you, to get those specs on the plasma-beam weapon."

She blinked, caught. But she quickly said, "I think the Klingons are here for the same reason, because of what you were told."

"What do you mean?" Kirk asked.

"What if the Klingons were given the same information as you? That a smuggler carrying the specs on the plasma-beam weapon would arrive at this very spot? They would try to stop the Federation from obtaining the weapon—they want it for themselves."

"Are you trying to say this is all a hoax?" Kirk asked flatly. "Who would benefit from that?"

"The same people who hired me to lure a bird-of-prey to this place," she told him. "Spies and informants thrive on war. Why not bring the three superpowers together in a distant star system? Let them destroy each other over information that was never there. That would start a tidy little war and keep the credits flowing in their direction."

"Wild accusations," Kirk said.

"*I* think I know who did it," she said. "And if I have time, I can prove it. I will give that information to Starfleet in exchange for sanctuary in the Federation."

"You want to stay in the Federation?" Kirk asked in surprise. She had been so eloquent about the beauties of Romulus and the excitement of working in the Romulan territory compared to the staid Federation. "That's not what I expected from you."

"Do I have any choice?" she asked. "I was dragged into something much larger than I anticipated. Obviously I cannot return to the Romulan Star Empire, not if there are rumors that I have acquired plasma-beam technology."

Kirk shook his head, running his hand across the back of his neck. For a moment, he felt dizzy. Then it passed. "If what you say is true, I'm sure Starfleet would grant you asylum."

One brow lifted slightly in surprise. "That easily? How can you be so sure?"

"It is . . . who we are," Kirk told her. "I'll take you to

Starbase 33. You should have no trouble dealing with the Federation."

Kirk realized something was wrong when it felt as if he was speaking from a great distance. His voice seemed disconnected from his body. He shifted his shoulders, feeling cramped, as a bead of sweat ran down the side of his face.

He could tell that Commander Teral was not happy with his suggestion. Her eyes narrowed for a moment, and the confiding, entreating look disappeared in a flash of irritation.

"I don't have the data!" she snapped. "Why not call off that guard and end this charade?"

Kirk reached out to steady himself against the table. Why was the room spinning?

Teral exclaimed out loud, startled when he went down to his knees. She reached out to help him, then stopped. With her face swimming in and out of his sight, Kirk could tell she was rapidly considering the situation.

He tried to speak but couldn't.

"Guard!" she called out, going over to hammer on the door. "Guard, help me! Your captain is hurt!"

The door slid open and the guard took in what was happening. Teral gestured toward Kirk, frantically pulling on the guard's sleeve to bring him closer. The guard knelt by the captain.

As the guard's face came closer, Kirk could see Teral behind him. "No . . . ," he whispered.

Teral snatched the phaser from the guard's belt. He turned, shocked. But she stunned him before he could stop her. He fell forward, landing on Kirk.

Kirk fell back. When Teral aimed the phaser at him, he did the only thing he could do—he passed out. At least he pretended to, but for a moment, he didn't remember anything.

When he opened his eyes, his legs were pinned beneath the guard. He still felt dizzy, but it wasn't quite so bad now. For a moment he was tempted to close his eyes again.

But every instinct fought against oblivion. His mission was to stop the smuggler and get the plasma-beam data. He had no intention of failing.

Clenching his teeth, Kirk rolled onto one elbow. The guard was dead weight on top of him. The exertion made him pant harder. Desperately he looked up at the comm panel near the door. If only he could get there, then he could send out an alert that Teral had escaped. Groaning, he pulled his right leg out from under the guard.

With one leg free, it was easier to sit up and roll the guard off him.

Getting to his feet was more difficult. Every step was agonizing. He almost doubled over from the pain in his gut. For a moment, he swayed, in agony between his pounding head and his stomach. He wanted nothing more than to lie back down next to the guard.

But he couldn't.

With an iron will, he clenched his teeth against the nausea and the spinning of his head. Mind would conquer body.

Step by step, he went to the comm panel. He hit the wall harder than he anticipated, bracing himself against it with one shoulder. Pushing the comm button, he said, "Alert! All decks, alert! Commander Teral has escaped. All hands . . . be on the lookout for . . . a Romulan woman. She's armed."

He started to sink to the deck as Spock's voice returned, with an anxious edge. *"Acknowledged. Captain, are you all right?"*

"No. Send McCoy," Kirk said, his knees buckling. "Emergency. . . ."

Teral was in the turbolift when Kirk's alert went out. She *knew* she should have stunned him, too. But he had looked like he was about to die from radiation poisoning, and she didn't want to risk killing him with a stun. She had discovered early in her career that you could get away with almost anything except murdering a starship captain.

The turbolift slowed. She twisted the handle harder, hoping that would keep it from stopping. But it slowed its downward motion, then stopped. It was deck 15.

Several technicians were waiting for the lift. They were carrying packs, and were obviously one of the repair teams that were trying to fix the damaged circuitry of the ship.

Teral burst through the gathering just as they realized who she was.

"Stop!" two of them yelled, running after her. She knew the other one would report her location.

Even with the scanners malfunctioning, it was only a matter of time before she was caught. Before Kirk alerted the crew there had been a possibility she could gain access to her cruiser and disable the forcefield on the hanger deck. Now the likelihood of capture was so high, she proceeded to implement her backup plan.

She was on the environmental level of the secondary hull. It was an easy matter of slipping into a room to hide as the two technicians hurried past, calling advice to one another. One peered into the lab where she was hiding, but she slid under the console where he couldn't see her.

Once they had passed, Teral found the closest access tube leading down to the next deck—engineering. Medical stations were also on this floor, and there were quite a few crew members milling about in the corridors. She could hear someone groaning nearby.

Teral didn't have time to think about the strange radiation sickness that had struck Kirk down right in front of her eyes. She had never been in such a tough situation before; then again, she had never transported such high-credit information before. She had thought long and hard before deciding it was worth the risk to sell the specs of the plasma-beam weapon.

Getting the information had happened almost by chance, though one of her informants had subsequently died at the hands of the Tal Shiar, the Romulan intelligence service, because of his involvement. Because of his slipup, Teral would have to arrange a new identity and buy a new ship before going back to work. *If* she decided to continue working after this. With the credit she would receive at all Klingon supply depots, she would be set for the rest of her life.

She slipped into the narrow crawl space between the banks of reactor coils, knowing that would help mask her lifesigns. She figured the ship's internal sensors were a low priority for the repair crews. But she wouldn't put anything past that Vulcan first officer, Mr. Spock. He might be able to find her.

Her plans were always nestled within plans, to make for smooth transitions. She was used to switching in midstream, and it was her ability to refrain from panic that had enabled her to get so far in her chosen profession. She was generally acknowledged to be very good—perhaps even the best—at smuggling information and goods.

That was because she knew how to become whatever people wanted her to be. She had talked Dr. McCoy into giving her the lightest possible bioscan, and even Mr. Spock had apparently not turned over her informant contacts to Starfleet. But that Captain Kirk . . . he should have trusted her. She had given him every reason to believe in her, and all the evidence was on her side. Yet he had stubbornly continued to post a guard at her door.

She had waited patiently to get free of her prison. Accessing information about the ship's blueprints and schematics had been easy using the specially adapted tricorder she had obtained from a contact in the Tal Shiar. That was how she knew the location of every exterior port on the ship.

The engineering deck she was now on had several exterior ports for easy disposal of hazardous waste. She edged through the banks of coils to reach the one she had targeted.

It was a simple unit with an automated lock. She keyed in the proper engineering code, also gleaned from her covert computer searches. The round hatch, approximately an arm's length across, opened with a hiss.

Glancing around to be sure no one could see her, she reached up to her hair. The knot was formed around a silver sphere. She hefted it in her hand. It hadn't been easy distracting the doctor while he performed his bioscan. Yet even a bioscan would have trouble identifying the stasis sphere as anything but a hair accessory, and it was specially designed not to trigger a weapons scan.

But a Federation detention center would spot the stasis sphere instantly. They would open it up and discover the specs for the plasma-beam weapon inside.

She activated the subspace beacon, which would remain inert until signaled by the frequency she had coded in. Placing the sphere inside the exterior port, she closed the hatch. It cycled automatically. The stasis sphere was designed to act like a buoy, and it would float nearby forever, if necessary, waiting for her to come back and pick it up.

Now she had to get as far away from this spot as possible before she was captured. It was likely, with all the malfunctions occurring in the ship's systems, that the cycling of the exterior port would be overlooked.

She found the next access tube and slid down the ladder four decks. She picked up speed near deck 21, and had to jump off.

That should confuse Mister Spock for a few moments.

The recreation area was deserted, as all personnel had been called into repair teams and emergency duty assisting the injured. She ran through the large rooms filled with games and diversions, wondering how people who were so soft could have presented such a challenge to her skills. She had encountered Starfleet before, but she had never had such a problem dealing with them.

She took another access tube down when she heard voices. That brought her to the food prep facilities, where there were more people around. As soon as she could, she ducked through a storage room to another ladder. Back up on deck 20, she entered the shuttlecraft maintenance shops.

Now she was nearly under the hanger deck itself. There were several access ports and a hydraulic elevator leading up to the hanger. Undoubtedly there were security guards alerted and waiting up there for her.

She was torn between trying to get to the *Barataria* or giving up right now. If she could get to her cruiser, she could hide inside the plasma storms until both the *Enterprise* and the *Tr'loth* left. Then she could come back and pick up the sphere with the plasma beam data. She was sure she could make new arrangements with the Klingons to exchange the data.

Teral decided to try to get to the *Barataria*. Being stunned was an unpleasant experience, but if she didn't do everything in her power to get away, they might think it was suspicious and start interrogating her for real.

Just inside the maintenance shops were rows of helmets worn by the workers when they were welding with plasma torches. She grabbed the first one and jammed it on her head. It was small, but she was able to flip down the protective visor. Now, no one would be able to recognize her immediately as Romulan.

There weren't many crew members on the hanger deck. She slipped past a dismantled shuttle, noting that the entire impulse engine came out as one unit. That would be a handy way to transport an impulse engine, she thought, always on the lookout for a good product. She had a Ferengi contact who would pay quite a bit of latinum for an impulse engine.

At the rear of the maintenance shops, she found the hydraulic elevator shaft. Just as she suspected, there were hand-and footholds going up one side: a maintenance ladder.

She carefully crawled up the ladder, hoping the hydraulic elevator wouldn't start up or down. Moving faster, she strained her eyes to see to the top. It was too dark to tell what she would have to deal with.

When she got to the top, she realized there was no access hatch on this level. The elevator was all the way up and locked into position. She could see a thin line of light from the shuttle hanger slanting down into the well of blackness. She could also hear voices, orders to prepare, and running feet.

She started to climb back down, knowing it had been a mistake going up the blind ladder.

Suddenly light shone up at her from below. "There she is!" someone called.

Teral climbed down faster, hoping they wouldn't try something stupid like moving the elevator.

A security guard grabbed her leg as she neared the maintenance doorway, almost making her fall down the rest of the elevator shaft. "Let go!" she hissed. "I will come out."

The hand tightened. "Drop your phaser!"

All she could see was an arm and a hand grabbing her ankle. She was tempted to stun the guard just on principle, but they would surely stun her if she tried to fight.

"Here it is," she said, leaning over to toss it through the maintenance doorway. There was a shout and a scramble as the others went after it.

Once the hand let go, she was able to climb back through the maintenance door. Resolutely, she shut her mind off. She hated authority enforcers—whether they were Federation security guards or Romulan peace-keepers. She didn't respond to their questions or react when they pulled off the welding helmet, knowing the enforcers would be particularly unpleasant because she had stunned the guard in her quarters.

As they marched her through the maintenance shops, she ignored their little indignities, like their binding her wrists together in stasis cuffs. Instead, she occupied her mind with what she would do with the credit after she turned the plasma-beam specs over to the Klingons. There was a gorgeous planet in outer Hyperia she had stumbled on, and she had long wanted to return.

Her pleasant daydreams were interrupted by the appearance of Captain Kirk coming out of the turbolift. He looked quite ill, breathing heavily and sweating a great deal.

"You should lie down, Captain," Teral told him. "You look unwell."

Kirk stared at her, licking his dry lips. "I knew you couldn't be trusted."

Teral narrowed her eyes at him. "If you were in my position, Captain, you would have run, too. Klingons and Starfleet fighting, with me caught in the middle . . . not a good situation. Besides, you should thank me for not stunning you. In your condition, it could have killed you."

"I want her thoroughly scanned," Kirk ordered, turning away. "And put her in the brig."

Chapter Nine

THE SECURITY GUARDS rushed Captain Kirk to sickbay, alerting Dr. McCoy that they were on their way. McCoy was angry at Kirk for ignoring his order to report immediately to sickbay. Instead, the captain had insisted on receiving a hypospray that would alleviate some of the symptoms of nausea and dizziness so he could go down to the shuttle bay to confront Commander Teral.

McCoy had protested and argued until Kirk ordered him to administer the hypospray. Knowing that the captain wouldn't be able to rest until he knew that Commander Teral was recaptured, McCoy had reluctantly complied.

When he saw Kirk being helped into sickbay by Security Chief Kelley, McCoy regretted having given in.

"Jim!" he exclaimed. "You look terrible. Put him there."

Kelley gingerly helped Kirk to the medical bed, trying not to offer too much support. Kirk motioned her away so he could sit down on the edge of the bed. McCoy ignored his protests and assisted in lifting his feet onto the bed.

The heart monitor immediately activated, indicating his heart rate was faster than normal. Kirk also had a fever, and his gastrointestinal tract was inflamed. Much of the skin on the upper half of his body was irritated, and many of the minor blood vessels showed injury.

McCoy grumbled as he worked, watching the damage manifest in front of his eyes. That's the way it was with radiation. Once the bone and tissues of a body were exposed, there was nothing that could be done to prevent the decay. Molecules had already been ionized, and now all the doctor could do was fight the symptoms as they manifested.

Kirk groaned, his arms clutching at his stomach. But he still tried to look around the sickbay, even as McCoy was stabilizing him.

"What happened, Bones?"

"Same thing as before," McCoy said sharply. "Gamma radiation coming out of nowhere, Spock tells me."

"Spock . . . ," Kirk whispered.

"He's on the bridge, watching the Klingons. I wonder how they're doing? According to rumors I've heard, they just let their sick *die*."

Kirk managed a weak smile. "Glad we don't follow that philosophy."

McCoy silently agreed, having gone through the

same pain of radiation exposure. He would hate to endure it without medication and cellular regeneration. Without the treatment, many of the injured on board the *Enterprise* would have been approaching death in the next few weeks.

The graph on the medical bed revealed the level of Kirk's exposure. It was at least 400 rads, which was the equivalent to the absorption of 40,000 ergs of energy per gram of tissue. A serious level of exposure, particularly for the bone marrow and lymphatic tissues. Without immediate treatment, such a dose would be lethal for some people.

"Doctor?" Nurse Chapel spoke quietly so as to not disturb the other patients who were flowing into sickbay. "Lieutenant Uhura has just arrived."

"That's two from the bridge," McCoy said. "Better convert the temporary wards again, Nurse. It looks like we've been hit by the same radiation as before."

Nurse Chapel hesitated as a lab technician helped Uhura to a bed across the ward. "What's causing it, Doctor?"

"Ask Spock," McCoy snapped. "He's the one who's supposed to be doing sensor sweeps."

Chapel turned away without another word, and McCoy immediately wished he hadn't said anything. He knew how Chapel felt about Spock—why did he let it irritate him? She was a good nurse and a good assistant, and he knew she deserved better than to be the brunt of his bad temper.

McCoy turned away with a sigh and began examining an ensign from food prep. This was her second dose, much milder than the first moderate one she had suffered through. McCoy shivered at the thought of being affected again by the radiation. It had been tough when his health was good. Right now, with his immune and lymphatic systems depleted as they were, he wouldn't get out of bed for a week. But no use wondering—he would know soon enough.

Reminded of the danger of repeat exposures, McCoy asked Nurse Chapel to go check on the patients who were still confined to bed rest. She would need to scan them to see if anyone had received a second dose.

When Kirk's medical bed signaled the end of the bone-marrow infusion, McCoy returned to Kirk's side to check on him. The captain's eyes were open, and he was trying to speak.

"My crew . . ." Kirk rasped. "How bad is it, Bones?"

"Twenty-six injured so far," McCoy told him. "If things go according to the last radiation exposure, they should keep coming in for the next couple of hours or so. I think it's worse than last time, Jim."

Kirk weakly tried to grab his arm but missed. "Tell Spock . . . alert Starfleet command. . . ."

"I'm sure Spock can handle the situation," McCoy assured him. "You have to rest now."

"No . . . ," Kirk muttered. "Have to finish . . . my mission."

"Not right now, you don't," McCoy said bluntly. He picked up another hypospray, this one filled with valurian, a Maltese drug that soothed the senses and relaxed the muscles. He injected Kirk with it.

For a moment, despite the mayhem in the ward as

people cried out for relief, the doctor stared down at Kirk. He had done all he could—cellular regeneration, tissue strengthening, bone-marrow infusion, injections of antimicrobial drugs. Now it was up to Kirk's immune system to fight the damage done by the ionizing radiation.

Nurse Chapel turned over the ward to the most senior duty nurse and picked up her medkit. She had been making regular rounds of the ten patients who were still confined to bed rest, so she knew exactly where to go. She had checked in via the monitor with each of them shortly after they realized that the *Enterprise* had been exposed to gamma radiation again, but none of them had complained of any new symptoms.

Chapel saw the signs of disorder everywhere. Panels had been removed and circuitry exposed. Repair teams seemed to be in every corridor. The medical database had finally come back on-line, but it had been a frightening moment when she'd realized the diagnostic beds weren't linked to the medical computers. She had taken pulses and temperatures using handheld scanners.

Chapel made her rounds, noting the nervous tones and the way crewmembers huddled together in small groups to talk. It was as if a signal had flashed through the ship, and everyone knew that their captain was lying in sickbay, unable to take charge of the unstable situation. There was an ineffable feeling that things were breaking down. No one knew where the radiation came from or who would be the next to sicken and fall at their post.

Even Nurse Chapel, who trusted Mr. Spock implicitly, wished that Captain Kirk had not been struck down by the radiation. Who could guess what the Klingons would do? They could be aiming their weapons right now at the *Enterprise*'s weakened shields.

But she couldn't allow her own apprehension to upset her patients. As she paused in front of each door to request admittance, she shook herself, settling a pleasant smile on her lips. The sick crew members would be worried enough without her compounding the problem. Mental health was an extremely important component in recovery.

As Chapel checked each patient, it was usually a matter of passing the hand scanner over them while making reassuring conversation. Four crew members demanded to be released from confinement, and she agreed. They were not fully recovered, but then again, none of those irradiated the first time had fully recovered. The nature of radiation poisoning was such that it progressed over weeks. Medical technology ensured that most of the damage could be lessened if caught in the first few hours, but the full course of treatment lasted up to thirty days.

One patient had already returned to duty, and Nurse Chapel noted on her tricorder to place a medical reprimand on Ensign Leesan's record. She should know better than to return to duty before she was released, but Leesan was a top technician and the prospect of so much work to be done must have driven her from her quarters.

Of the remaining five patients, Chapel found that

two had been irradiated again. She stabilized them with hyposprays of cysteamine, then signaled the medical technicians to come fetch the sick crew members.

As they carried Lieutenant Matheson from his quarters, Nurse Chapel followed, nervously biting her lower lip. Matheson had gotten a dose of 200 rads the first time; now he'd taken another 400 rads. He wouldn't be returning to security duty for at least a week. But he wasn't as bad as Specialist Calloway, who had taken close to 600 rads both times. Chapel was very worried about Calloway, who was unconscious as they carried him from his room.

Now that she didn't have patients to reassure, Chapel felt all her own doubts and fears flooding back. They were going to have to start sending the less injured back to their quarters to make room on the diagnostic beds. That meant recruiting more orderlies from the repair crews to help.

She hurried toward sickbay, knowing there was so much work to be done that soon she wouldn't have time to think about anything else. It was always that way in sickbay during an emergency.

Spock was at the science station, even though he was in command of the bridge. Between the repair crews and the radiation sickness, there weren't enough able-bodied crew members to staff every station.

He continued to monitor the movements of the Klingon battlecruiser. The *Tr'loth* was still not fully operational, though they were no longer in danger of being pulled into the plasma storms. Spock was prepared to offer assistance before letting the *Tr'loth* drift into the plasma storms without any shields.

"Spock!" McCoy exclaimed, as he burst from the turbolift.

Spock calmly turned to see the doctor rush toward him, waving the remains of what appeared to be the blue tunic of a Starfleet uniform.

McCoy stopped and looked around. "Where is everybody?"

"Mister Sulu just left for sickbay. It is unfortunate you were not on the bridge several minutes earlier." Spock noted the bridge did look deserted with only an ensign at the conn and the lieutenant at the helm. Lieutenant DeGroodt was overseeing the repairs from the engineering station. Chief Engineer Scott was in engineering attempting to realign the dilithium crystals, which had expanded by another 3 percent. Bringing warp drive on-line again was Spock's top priority.

"Forty-nine so far!" McCoy exclaimed. "If this doesn't stop soon, the entire crew will be disabled."

"I am aware of that, Doctor."

"Well, what are you doing about it, Mister Spock?!" McCoy demanded. "Where's that radiation coming from? How can we stop it?"

"Unknown at this time," Spock said. "There is no evidence of unusual levels of gamma radiation in this region. No evidence of gravity fluctuations."

"Yes but there *was* a radiation burst," McCoy insisted. "There *was* a gravity fluctuation."

"Precisely, Doctor. However the readings do not correlate with any known phenomenon."

McCoy held up the shreds of plush blue material. "Look at this, Spock. It's Specialist Calloway's uniform." His fingers dug into the material, and it shattered, fragmenting into brittle flakes.

Spock took some of the material in his hand, noting the silicate feel. He placed it on a sample dish and aimed his tricorder at it.

"Unquestionably most unusual," Spock agreed. "The molecular structure has been altered. It is similar to the damage done to the dilithium crystals and EPS circuits. At first it appeared that the power fluctuations had fused the circuits, but pathways were fused even in inert circuitry."

"The radiation must have done it."

"Indeed, there have been reports of luminescence in certain metallic compounds of the ship." Spock gestured to the shreds of tunic. "And polymers appear to be vulnerable to the radiation, as well."

"We're all vulnerable!" McCoy said, raising his voice again. "Where's it coming from, Spock?"

"The first time we observed a radiation burst was when the Romulan bird-of-prey was destroyed," Spock pointed out logically. "I have a theory that the Romulans incorporate subspace proximity detonators in their vessels that are released in the event of their total destruction."

"A booby trap!" McCoy exclaimed. "Of course . . . so if their ship is destroyed, they can still destroy their opponents. Ruthless."

"It is typical of Romulan behavior. However, it is only a theory."

"Well, it gives us something to look for," McCoy agreed. "Do you think these proximity detonators are cloaked? Why haven't we found any of them?"

Spock swayed slightly, but recovered immediately. "I am endeavoring to determine that, Doctor."

"You look ill, Spock." McCoy peered uncomfortably close into his face. "Quite green, in fact. Could that fine Vulcan physique be as weak as a mere human's?"

"On the contrary, Doctor. When I need your assistance, I will notify you."

McCoy pulled out his hand scanner and passed it close to Spock. "Exposure at least 300 rads!"

"Three hundred twelve to be exact."

"Spock, are you mad?! You have to come to sickbay right now for treatment."

Spock raised one brow. "May I remind you that I am currently in command of the *Enterprise*."

"May I remind *you* that you're half human." McCoy was already preparing a hypospray. "It's the best I can do until I run a diagnostic on your tissues and begin cellular regeneration."

"That will have to wait, Doctor."

The doctor grumbled, but Spock continued to scan for subspace disturbances, increasing the range to two parsecs and cross-referencing the data obtained from each sensor bank. It did not take much of his mental capacity to overcome the physical effects of the radiation exposure.

"Nothing affects you, does it, Spock?" McCoy said. "You can just keep on working in spite of radiation poisoning and a ship that's coming apart at the seams. You're one cold fish."

Spock glanced back at him. "Why thank you, Doctor. I believe that was a compliment."

McCoy threw up his hands in exasperation. For Spock, that was a common enough occurrence, so he ignored it.

"My prescription for you is rest," McCoy said.

"So noted." Spock didn't glance up. "Dismissed, Doctor."

Chapter Ten

KIRK WASN'T SURE where he was for a moment, then he remembered. Sickbay, they had brought him to sickbay after he had almost passed out in front of Commander Teral down in the shuttle maintenance shops. Checking the chronometer, he could tell that had been several hours ago. His body ached as though he had been running for days.

"I'm losing him!" McCoy exclaimed, hunched over the diagnostic bed next to Kirk.

Kirk pushed himself up to see. Dr. McCoy and Nurse Chapel were working over Specialist Calloway. The heartbeat monitor was blinking too fast, and the indicator dials were either too high or nearly at base level.

"Give me 15 cc's of tricortizine," McCoy ordered.

Chapel came running over with a full hypospray, handing it over. "Fifteen cc's, Doctor."

"He's convulsing again!" McCoy exclaimed, trying to hold Calloway down.

Kirk swung his legs over the edge of the bed. With two steps, he reached the bed Calloway was lying on. Kirk had to brace himself to remain standing.

McCoy hardly acknowledged him. The doctor was frantically trying to save Calloway. But the beep of the heartbeat monitor turned into a steady drone.

Bones lifted his hands, staring down at Calloway. "He's dead, Jim."

Kirk also gazed down at Calloway, limp now. He had been a crew member for over three years. Kirk had promoted him to Specialist himself. He was a brilliant physicist.

Nurse Chapel shut off the diagnostic monitor, and the drone stopped.

McCoy was slowly shaking his head. "He received two high doses of radiation, Jim. There was nothing we could do. His circulatory system was irreparably damaged."

"I know you tried, Bones," Kirk whispered. "How many are sick?"

"Sixty-four, Jim. None so bad as Calloway, but if we get hit again . . . there's no telling how many people will die."

There is no dignity in this death, Kirk thought, as two medical technicians came forward to shift Calloway's body onto an antigrav pallet. They would take him to the morgue, and tomorrow or the next day Kirk would be standing next to a coffin at an exterior port. He would try to say a few words to make sense of the loss, while Calloway's friends gathered tearfully around to bid him farewell. And that was the positive scenario.

"You should lie down," McCoy told him. "You're stabilized now, so someone will help you to your quarters. We need the diagnostic bed for the injured who haven't received bone-marrow infusion."

"I should get to the bridge," Kirk said, still bracing himself against the bed.

"Spock has everything under control," McCoy said sharply. "The Klingons have just gotten impulse power, but their shields are still down. Besides, you couldn't sit up for ten minutes straight, Jim."

Kirk watched as the medical technician gently pushed away the antigrav pallet carrying Calloway. Kirk knew he couldn't lie in bed while his crew died one by one from this strange radiation poisoning.

"Ah, here's Yeoman Harrison," McCoy said with relief. "Make sure Captain Kirk gets to his quarters, Yeoman. Put some fluids by his bed so he won't have to go to the food slot."

"Aye, sir," Harrison replied seriously.

She took Kirk's arm, supporting him. Kirk smiled at her weakly. "You're not sick this time?"

"No, sir."

He could swear she reddened. "I guess this time it's my turn," he said.

Kirk let her help him out of sickbay, which was full of injured crew members. All of the rooms that lined the corridors near sickbay had open doors, revealing the injured lying in makeshift biobeds.

"I have to go to the brig," Kirk told Yeoman Harrison as they entered the turbolift.

"But, sir, Dr. McCoy said—"

"It doesn't matter what McCoy said." Kirk took hold of the turbolift control. His hand was shaking, and he had to lean against the railing. "Deck 19."

"Are you sure you'll be all right, Captain?" Harrison asked anxiously, caught between letting him stand on his own and trying to support some of his weight.

"I will be after I talk to Commander Teral."

Kirk got a report from Spock on the way down to the brig. The situation was much as McCoy had said—the Klingons were slowly but surely pulling their ship together. The *Enterprise* was also being repaired, and Scotty had nearly finished realigning the dilithium crystals. They hadn't bothered to do the lengthy scanning procedure this time. They were betting everything on the crystals' integrity.

Kirk left Yeoman Harrison waiting in the security section while he went into the brig.

"Commander Teral says she feels sick," Security Chief Kelley said. "Nurse Chapel came down and gave her some 'sprays. Said she got over 400 rads and needs cellular regeneration. But I wouldn't release Teral to sickbay without direct orders from you."

"Good work," Kirk said. He was sweating again, and feeling dizzy.

Kelley sat down behind the table again as Kirk entered the tiny cell of the brig. Commander Teral was curled up on the bench, rocking back and forth slightly.

"I hear you're ill," Kirk said flatly.

"What happened?" she groaned. "I feel like I'm dying."

Her hair was loose and flowing down her back, while her eyes were reddened and watery. She looked haggard, and Kirk suddenly realized she was older than he was. She had such a commanding presence that until now he had not considered her age.

"Spock thinks this might be a Romulan booby trap. Have you heard of the military using subspace proximity detonators?"

"I don't know . . . I don't think so . . . but it could be true. . . ." She blinked, her mouth open slightly as she tried to breathe without passing out.

Kirk knew exactly how bad she felt. Slowly, he eased down on a chair. The sick interrogating the sick. At least he was better than she was. She hadn't received any cellular regeneration or marrow infusions. Maybe she wouldn't realize that he barely had the upper hand.

"Soon the Klingons will regain shields," he told her, "and they're going to attack us because they know you're on board."

She tried to protest, "But I don't have the information on the plasma beam—"

"We don't have time for your lies!" he interrupted. "The Klingons want those specs, and they'll destroy the *Enterprise* now that they know *we* have *you*. If the Klingons don't attack first, another radiation burst could kill us all!" Kirk swallowed. "I just saw Specialist Calloway die. He got over 400 rads the first time, just like you. It took one more exposure to kill him."

She was clenching her arm around her stomach as she tried to sit up. "Leave! We must get away from here."

"I'll give the order as soon as you give me those specs."

Her face contorted. "You wouldn't kill your crew over blueprints for a weapon!"

"We're prepared to die to complete our mission." He wiped the sweat from his forehead, wondering how much longer he could sit upright. "If you hand over those specs now, I can guarantee the Federation will grant you asylum. All charges will be dropped."

She panted, looking up at him. "You guarantee it? Your word as a Starfleet captain?"

Kirk felt a leap of hope. "I have the jurisdiction to grant you amnesty and full immunity,"

Teral lay back down, one arm over her face. "My head is bursting . . . I cannot think."

"You don't have to think." Kirk stood up, stumbling forward to lean over her. "Tell me where those specs are and you'll be safe!"

She looked up at him, her large dark eyes finally meeting his. "Very well, I will tell you how to find the data."

Yeoman Harrison knew Captain Kirk had been successful as soon as he stepped out of the brig. He seemed energized, and he shrugged off her offer to support him as he walked.

"You can take her to sickbay for cellular regeneration," Kirk ordered Kelley. "I'm going to the bridge."

Kirk left the security section and headed down the corridor with hardly a wobble.

But Harrison wasn't about to leave him until she had carried out Dr. McCoy's orders. Kirk's face was flushed, and there was a moment when he paused next to the wall and she thought he might pass out. Then he got control of himself again, and kept on walking.

In the turbolift on their way to the bridge, Kirk signaled Spock. "Send out a tone on subspace frequency Omega-nine. It should activate a homing beacon on a stasis sphere that is floating in the area."

"Indeed," Mister Spock replied.

"Commander Teral put the specs inside the stasis sphere."

"I will endeavor to locate it immediately," Spock agreed.

Kirk signed off. His lips were compressed from the effort of standing up.

"Sir, if I may ask," Harrison ventured. "What did you say to Commander Teral to make her give you the information?"

Kirk just smiled. "I pointed out that she had no other reasonable choice."

Harrison was glad to see Kirk smile in spite of how sick he was. She figured she never would know what happened between him and Teral, but the result confirmed her faith in the captain's power of command.

Kirk was pleased that Yeoman Harrison stayed back as they entered the bridge. He didn't need her hovering over his command chair.

Aside from Spock, only three officers were on the bridge—DeGroodt at the engineering station, and two young officers at the helm. Yeoman Harrison hesitated, but when Kirk gestured, she took the communications station where Lieutenant Uhura usually sat.

"I have located the stasis sphere," Mr. Spock reported. "I am beaming it to the bridge."

Kirk turned just as the sphere materialized near Spock. It floated for a moment, then fell with a solid thunk to the deck.

Spock picked it up. "Ingenious. A self-contained stasis bubble that would appear invisible to any standard-level weapons scan."

Kirk's mouth felt dry, and he whispered, "Does it have the data, Spock?"

Spock scanned it with his tricorder. "The sphere contains data stored in an electromagnetic strip. It will take some time to extract the information."

Kirk swallowed, wondering how long he was going to be able to continue this. Waves of vertigo seemed to roll up and down from his head to his feet.

"Status," Kirk demanded.

"We have left the sensor shadow of the plasma storms," the helmsman reported. "The Klingon battle-cruiser is 300,000 kilometers away. They are on an intercept course."

"The *Tr'loth*'s shields and weapons systems are back on-line," Spock confirmed.

Kirk hit the control to engineering. "Scotty, do we have warp drive?"

"Aye, sir," he wearily replied. "The power-up se-

quence is well underway. Pressure is up to 72,000 kilo-
pascals. We're ironin' the timing discrepancies out now."

"Tr'loth is at 250,000 kilometers."

Kirk wished they had more time. "Spock, did you
find out what caused the radiation burst?"

"Negative, Captain."

Kirk glanced briefly at the screen, where the Klingon battlecruiser could be seen lumbering closer.

Kirk wanted to stay, to be sure the stasis sphere wasn't
another trick by Teral, and to find out where the radiation
bursts were coming from. But he couldn't afford to start
a battle with the Klingons with his crew in their present
condition . . . and he couldn't shake the memory of
McCoy's voice saying, "If we get hit again by that radiation, there's no telling how many people will die."

Kirk muttered to himself, "Sometimes you have to
be content with getting away with your hull and your
crew intact."

"Sir?" Harrison asked, turned to see what he wanted.

"Plot a course back to Starbase 33," he ordered.
"Helm, take us out of here. Warp 4."

Kirk sat back in the command chair, watching as the
Badlands slowly crossed the screen. They had not penetrated the mysteries of the ruddy plasma storms any
more than they had discovered where the radiation came
from. But he was certain Teral was not lying this time.
The sphere contained the specs on the plasma beam
weapon, and Starfleet headquarters would be pleased to
get the debris from a Romulan bird-of-prey to analyze.

"We've completed our mission," Kirk told everyone.
"We're going home."

PART 2

Stardate 45091.4
Year 2368

Immediately after "Ensign Ro"

Chapter One

CAPTAIN PICARD settled himself in the command chair. It had taken most of the duty shift to travel through the Badlands sector toward the plasma storms. Meanwhile the crew had prepared the shuttlecraft *Hawking* for its voyage into the storms.

The excitement on the bridge was building as the shuttlecraft launch approached. Though many other science vessels had investigated the infamous and dangerous Badlands, this was the first time that the *Enterprise* was exploring this unusual cluster of plasma storms.

Counselor Troi entered the bridge and walked down the ramp to the command center. She smiled at Captain Picard, no doubt able to sense his eager anticipation of what they might discover. Thus far, Starfleet vessels had barely penetrated the plasma storms, which remained a tantalizing mystery.

Deanna Troi seated herself next to Picard. "Did I make it in time?"

"We are preparing to launch." Picard thought she looked quite striking, wearing a royal blue dress and matching headband to hold back her thick black curls. She often wore clothes from her own wardrobe rather than her uniform, a choice that might bother Picard if another officer did the same. But Counselor Troi said it made it easier for the crewmembers to open up to her when they weren't constantly reminded that she was their superior officer, and Picard saw her point.

The image of the Badlands grew larger, bleeding off the edge of the viewscreen. The plasma formed swirling reddish clouds that spread through a vast region of space, an area that would normally be occupied by several solar systems.

Picard enjoyed scientific and research missions. They had been ordered to perform a thorough survey of sector 21305, commonly known as the Badlands sector. Picard was intrigued by the question of how this unique phenomenon had been created, and also what fueled the continuous energy in the plasma storms. It would take an incredible amount of power to sustain the ionization of all that matter.

"Are there any other vessels in the area?" Picard asked Worf.

"None, sir," replied Worf, his Klingon Chief of Security.

"Good. Take us into the sensor shadow of the Badlands," Picard ordered.

"Heading three-one-four mark two," Ensign Ro Laren confirmed.

They had already sent sensor probes into the plasma storms, with few results. The distortion and interference in telemetry caused by the plasma made it difficult to receive sensor data. Yet the *Enterprise* couldn't actually go into the Badlands because plasma tended to clog the plasma grid, the part of warp drive responsible for power conversion levels.

However, earlier surveys had confirmed that a much smaller vessel, such as a shuttlecraft, could safely venture into the plasma storms under impulse power. Picard had assigned his first officer, Will Riker, and Commander Data to take the *Hawking* into the Badlands.

"Picard to shuttlecraft *Hawking*. Are you prepared to depart?"

"Aye, sir," Commander Riker responded from the hanger deck. *"Shuttlecraft Hawking is ready to go."*

"On course for dropoff point, sir," Ensign Ro reported.

Picard acknowledged, leaning his chin on his hand. Ensign Ro Laren was a new addition to his crew. The Bajoran had assisted in their last mission, to seek out Bajoran terrorists who were attacking the Cardassian colonies along the border.

The seemingly simple mission had been complicated by a conspiracy at the top levels of Starfleet. Admiral Kennelly was now in custody, undergoing a hearing regarding his covert assistance to the Cardassians. Apparently, the admiral had tried to destroy a powerful group of Bajoran rebels.

Captain Picard had already submitted his testimony regarding the incident to Starfleet Command. He knew that Ro Laren had not yet submitted her report, and he would have to remind her at shift change to do so. She was a key witness, since Admiral Kennelly had covertly ordered Ro to offer weapons to the Bajoran terrorists. It was part of Kennelly's plan to lure the terrorists out where the Cardassians could attack them.

The Cardassians were bound to be displeased that Starfleet had backed Captain Picard's decision to protect the Bajoran terrorists. The Cardassians also wouldn't benefit from the public disciplinary hearings against Admiral Kennelly. The fragile truce with the Cardassian Empire was only two years old, and anything could turn them into adversaries again. The first Federation-Cardassian war had been long and bloody. Most Starfleet officers had tangled with the Cardassians in recent memory.

Picard thought it would be in their best interest to avoid Cardassian contact on this survey mission. But the Cardassian border was in the neighboring sector. Anything could happen, which was why Starfleet had sent the *Enterprise* rather than a smaller science ship to perform the survey.

First, the *Enterprise* had completed an initial survey of the Badlands sector. It had taken several days to circle the sector and perform an initial scan of the solar systems and celestial phenomena, including the corkscrew Kamiat Nebula.

They had picked up several small vessels on long-range sensors, but had never come within hailing range.

Ensign Ro suggested that they could be Bajoran terror-ists, who typically used the Badlands as a place to hide from Cardassian warships. The smaller vessels had avoided the *Enterprise,* disappearing soon after they were detected.

"Approaching dropoff point," Ensign Ro reported.

"Very well," Picard acknowledged. "Slow to one-quarter impulse power."

"Aye, Captain."

Picard stood up. The complications of galactic poli-tics could be intriguing at times, but he was glad this was primarily an exploration mission.

He smiled slightly. "Shuttlecraft *Hawking,* this is Captain Picard. You are cleared for departure."

Commander Riker waited until the flight-deck offi-cer confirmed clearance before responding, "Affirma-tive. Departure sequence initiated."

"Impulse engines on-line," Data confirmed.

"Engaging thrusters." Riker grinned at Data. He en-joyed piloting the shuttlecraft. The flight controller was a hands-on system, unlike the conn of the *Enter-prise.*

The shuttlecraft lifted smoothly, then turned. Two other shuttles were parked on the opposite side of the enormous bay. Riker aimed the nose of the *Hawking* at the wide mouth of the hanger.

"Tractor beam locking on," Data noted.

Riker usually arranged with the flight officer on duty to be allowed to pilot the shuttle out of the hanger with-out using the precision short-range tractor beam. His pilot rating was high enough for him to perform a manual launch.

But Lieutenant Aston was a stickler for procedure. Since he had been promoted to flight officer he'd refused every one of Riker's requests for a manual launch. It was one of those situations where the commander was sorely tempted to pull rank, but his sense of honor wouldn't allow it.

Still, Riker had been standing rather close to Aston this time when he made his request. To be fair, he had only realized what he was doing when Aston cleared his throat and looked up nervously before denying his request.

As the shuttle was passively conveyed through the shuttlebay hanger doors, Riker replayed the incident in his mind. He knew Deanna would scold him for using his tall stature to try to intimidate Aston, even if it *was* subconscious. So he figured he wouldn't tell her. He would just be more careful next time.

Riker took the controls, ready for the tractor to disengage. "I've got the helm," he told Data. Either of the two forward panels could control the shuttle, but Data was preparing to conduct the sensor scans inside the plasma storms.

Riker opened a channel to the *Enterprise.* "Shuttlecraft *Hawking* to the *Enterprise.* Proceeding toward the Badlands at full impulse."

"Acknowledged," Captain Picard replied.

The closer they drew to their targeted entry point, the rougher the ride became. The Badlands began to stretch overhead tens of thousands of kilometers away.

In front of them, the leading edge of the mass was glowing orange, red, and pink, with streamers of plasma continuously rippling into normal space. Discharges along the edge flickered like lightning inside a storm cloud, reflecting gold through the ionized plasma. Other parts of the storm were shadowed, as if denser than the rest of the mass.

"Steady as she goes," Riker said.

"Increased power to the structural-integrity field," Data reported.

As they moved closer, they could see that the plasma was constantly churning. Riker felt as if they were about to dive into rapidly boiling water. The shuttlecraft shuddered harder as the discharges affected the stability of subspace.

"Transferring auxiliary power to the forward shields," Data said calmly.

"Slowing to one-quarter impulse power. Five seconds to the plasma field," Riker reported back to the *Enterprise*. His voice shook from the vibration of the shuttlecraft.

He knew the captain and bridge crew would be watching the *Hawking* on the viewscreen, through the lines of static that appeared whenever they entered the shadow of the Badlands. Riker preferred the view from the shuttle over the one from the bridge.

The *Hawking* shook harder. He could feel the attitude adjusters slip under his hands.

"Entering the Badlands," Data announced.

Streamers of re-ionizing plasma gas obscured the viewscreen.

The white-and-gray gauzy streamers lessened as the shuttle went in further, clearing every now and again to show a vast layered field of pink and orange clouds. The layers were joined together by funnel-shaped flares, moving like a mirror image of a tornado, narrowing in the center and widening to a swirling vortex above and below.

"Sensor range is limited," Data reported. "The plasma is interfering with our imaging systems. I am increasing the bandwidth to compensate for the interference."

The shuttlecraft rocked violently for a moment, then settled down to a continuously bumpy ride. Riker told Data that he was trying to use thrusters to stabilize.

"Reading high levels of magnetic turbulence," Data reported, his voice slightly altered by the force of the vibrating ship. "Hull pressure reaching dangerous levels."

One plasma flare swerved quite close. *Where did that come from?* Riker wondered wildly. One minute it wasn't there, then the next it was sideswiping their hull.

"Increasing speed to one-half impulse," Riker said grimly. Under conditions like these, he needed more power.

As their speed picked up, the shuddering grew worse. Riker banked around the twisting plasma flare and headed toward the upper layer of clouds. There were more whirling flares off their port where the plasma was denser. Riker changed course again to get clear around them. The shuttle was still riding rough, as if there were timing delays in the Optical Data Network relays.

"Shields at 78 percent," Data announced. "Shuttlecraft *Hawking* to *Enterprise*. Come in, *Enterprise*."

Riker was too busy getting the rhythm of the plasma storms to pay much attention as Data went through the standard communications protocols for an away team that has lost contact with their ship. No one had really expected communications contact to be sustained inside the plasma storms anyway.

"Nothing within 100,000 kilometers," Data reported.

"We need more sensor range," Riker muttered. "If there is anything in here, we'll hit it before we see it."

"Understood," Data said, manipulating the sensor controls. "I will attempt to modulate the emitter pulse to increase sensor range."

They flew on, both concentrating on their work. The light was muted inside the shuttle compared to the glowing plasma field on the viewscreen. It was occasionally lit brighter by flashes of ion discharge.

"Sensors reading 250,000 kilometers," Data reported. He sounded almost regretful when he added, "At that aperture the beam is narrowed approximately to a 12-degree arc directly in front of the shuttlecraft."

"Great," Riker muttered. "We might as well shine a handlight out the portal to see if anything is coming."

Data blinked, his glowing yellow eyes turned to Riker. "Commander, I fail to see how the use of a handlight would improve our situation."

"That's a joke, Data."

Data shook his head, focusing back on the control panel. "I see. Once again, I have misjudged a situation in which a joke would be appropriate."

"It's not really appropriate now," Riker smiled briefly.

He enjoyed being able to baffle Data once in a while. It was impossible to do it when it came to facts and figures, but the simplest things could sometimes make Data seem like a child—rather than the most intelligent creature Riker had ever known.

Data had done a good job, as usual. The enhanced sensors were much better, even if they did narrow their field of view. Riker compensated by flying a zigzag pattern.

They were quite deep inside the plasma when they came upon a thick cluster of flares. Riker threaded the needle between two whirling funnel clouds. He had a better feel for their wide swinging movements now.

But then streamers of plasma drifted across the viewscreen, partially obstructing the view. "Data?"

"We appear to be approaching an area of relatively thin plasma," Data reported.

The heavy clouds thinned, and the layers pulled apart. There were no plasma flares for as far as the sensors could read.

"Sensor range increasing," Data noted, magnifying the view.

"What have we here?" Riker mused, opening up his search pattern. After a few moments, he said, "Is that what I think it is?"

"It is a gas giant with six iron-core moons in orbit," Data confirmed.

"A gas giant . . . ," Riker repeated, gazing at the aquamarine and green stripes that banded the planet. He gave it a wide berth, wanting to avoid intense gravity fluctuations, which would be amplified by the plasma fields.

"I am also reading one Class-O planet," Data reported, "and one Class-M planet. They are in orbit around an orange dwarf star."

"An entire solar system," Riker said in amazement. "Swallowed by the plasma storms. Could there be others?"

"It is probable, considering the size of the Badlands," Data agreed.

Riker shook his head as they flew through the system, gathering readings on the various planets. It was an odd scene; the planets appeared to be floating in the plasma, but the subtle ripples in color and light showed their massive movement as they orbited the dim, distant sun. Riker felt like he was in an ancient city that had been swallowed by water. The atmosphere was murky, yet currents flowed around the ruins, choking and isolating them.

He whistled low under his breath, and double-checked the imaging device. He wasn't sure he could describe this accurately in his report. But in this case, one view of the planet swimming past would be enough to send chills down anyone's spine. He couldn't imagine what conditions would be like on the surface of the class M planet. Even if there was an atmosphere, this much ionization would surely harm life-forms.

The shuttlecraft bucked as they reentered the denser plasma field. Riker was glad they had the extra warp power to use as auxiliary energy to boost structural integrity and shields. The shifting plasma fields were straining all of their systems.

The solar system was swallowed up behind them by the plasma. Riker circled out and around, but there were no other distinguishable features, other than the endless plasma flares.

"Time to get back," he told Data, knowing that the crew would be waiting impatiently for their report.

Soon afterward, when Riker tried to navigate back to the point where they had exited the solar system, he discovered that he couldn't locate it again. Navigational systems appeared to be working perfectly, but when he ran the previous sequence against the interior map, he realized their bearings were shifting according to the fluctuating gravitational fields.

"We've lost our bearings," he told Data.

Data immediately understood what was happening, and he set to work trying to compensate. "We have lost primary navigation systems."

"Where are we?" Riker asked evenly.

"I am attempting to plot our coordinates according to the adjustments you made to helm control," Data informed him, rapidly calling up the sequence Riker had used.

Riker used thrusters to slip into the thicker plasma gas in the layer above them, hoping to be able to drift and avoid the flares while Data completed his computations. If anyone could navigate without the stars as guidance, Riker bet on Data to do it.

Data attempted to reverse the commands Commander Riker had input to return to the solar system they had discovered. When that proved ineffective, Data concluded that the plasma fields within the storms were in constant internal motion, changing their position in relation to the rest of the field and the surrounding galaxy.

Without precise measurements of the plasma fields and their interlocking currents, it was impossible to determine exactly where the shuttlecraft was in relation to its entry point. So Data attempted to determine approximately where the shuttlecraft was in relation to the closest edge of the plasma storm by calibrating the sensors to read the resonate frequency of the galaxy.

It was a unique and intriguing problem. However, Commander Riker clearly did not appreciate Data's enthusiasm for the task. Data limited himself to ten-minute updates when he realized Riker was clenching his fists in frustration, unable to do anything about their situation. Riker continued the sensor scans as they floated in the dense plasma, while Data worked out the difficult computations, using both his positronic brain and the shuttle's on-board computer.

Data sat quite still as he completed the process. Then he calibrated the sensors and determined the location where the resonate frequency was most distinct. "Proceed at bearing eight-one-five mark four-five."

Commander Riker relaxed somewhat. "I was beginning to wonder if we'd ever get out of here."

"Of course, Commander. It was simply a matter of narrowing the sensor feed to one frequency, taking into account the distortion of the—"

"Sorry I doubted you," Riker interrupted. He input the navigational bearing Data had provided. "Now, let's go."

Data took over the sensor scans, extending the beam to its limit. Using a pulse system, he shifted the sensor beam in a random pattern, gathering additional data and taking care to note the direction and intensity of the cross-translational plasma currents. They would need a better understanding of the movements within the plasma storms in order to attempt another interior survey. He also kept one bank of sensors tuned to the galactic frequency to keep the shuttlecraft on course.

For a long time Riker was silent, as they flew around the clusters of flares, avoiding pockets of turbulence and the denser areas of plasma, where they had to slow to thrusters. Data noted that the commander breathed a sigh of relief when the plasma streamers thickened. The plasma began to part, revealing a star or two.

"Leaving the Badlands," Riker announced.

Data waited until the starfield filled the screen, then he opened the communications channel. "Data to *Enterprise*. This is the shuttlecraft *Hawking*."

The low hum of static was audible to his ears, though Riker probably only heard silence. "The interference within the sensor shadow is too great."

"Let's see where we are." Riker watched the navigational computer run through a sequence of star patterns, trying to determine their location. A map appeared on screen. "Look, Data. We've gone through the narrow part of the plasma storms and exited the 'upper' edge. That's probably why they can't hear us."

The *Hawking* could not go to warp until they were some distance away from the Badlands. The gravitational forces of the plasma storms made it impossible to maintain a warp bubble.

So Data recalibrated the sensors to obtain additional long-range data. Since Riker was proceeding directly away from the Badlands, gradually the interference lessened, even though they were still within the sensor shadow.

His program to cut through the sensor interference succeeded as they neared the edge of the shadow. "Long-range scanners detect a vessel at bearing two-six-eight mark five-zero," Data announced.

"The *Enterprise?*" Riker asked.

Data considered the location of the sensor blip. Even at warp 8, which was impossible this close to the Badlands, the *Enterprise* could not have reached the specified coordinates. "Negative. Identity unknown. Sensors cannot maintain a lock due to the plasma interference."

Riker shifted uneasily in his chair, and the *Hawking* went to full impulse power.

As they neared the edge of the sensor shadow, Data noted something unusual. Sensors indicated a localized subspace disturbance. Before Data could warn Commander Riker, he had lost control of the *Hawking*.

Data instantly focused his positronic brain on a microsecond level to assess what was occurring. A subspace incursion took place within the *Hawking* for a total of 2.34 seconds. Sensors overloaded, as did the electroplasma power relays, shutting down major systems. The matter-antimatter injectors, on-line in preparation for warp drive, went into emergency shutdown as the shuttle shifted onto auxiliary power.

The red alert signal began flashing, and the computer announced, *"Main power off-line. Auxiliary generators engaged."*

In the red flashing light, their panels blinking with demands for immediate attention, Riker turned to Data. "What was that?!"

Chapter Two

RO LAREN fidgeted with her uniform collar. It itched. She wasn't used to having something tight around her neck. The prison jumpsuits she had worn up until a couple of weeks ago had been V-necked, gray and ugly.

Ro still wasn't sure she'd made the right decision. Despite four years of training at Starfleet Academy and duty on board a starship, she had landed in prison for disobeying orders and killing eight people. She didn't trust herself—and in spite of one successful mission with the *Enterprise*, she wasn't sure why Captain Picard trusted her.

"Retreat out of the sensor shadow," Captain Picard ordered.

"Aye, sir," Ro said, remembering to add the required "sir" this time. She input a bearing just outside the area designated as the sensor shadow and engaged full impulse power. The rendezvous time had long come and gone and there was still no sign of the shuttlecraft *Hawking*.

"Scan the region for vessels," Picard ordered.

"Plasma interference is reducing the sensor range," Worf regretfully reported. "However, I am reading no vessels in the area."

Picard lowered his voice, but Ro had no trouble hearing his question to Counselor Deanna Troi. "Can you sense anything from them?"

Ro leaned back further, trying to hear. She was unnerved by the Betazoid empath. She was never sure how much the counselor knew.

"Nothing, sir," Troi replied. "Not since they entered the Badlands. Maybe the ionization of the plasma storms interferes with empathic powers."

Ro shivered, wondering if Troi could read her emotions right now. She didn't like being transparent, but that's the way Troi made her feel during their counseling sessions. The questions she asked! Ro wanted to advise her to give up—there was no way to heal her wounds. There was no way for a Bajoran refugee to be "normal" like other people.

Since Ro figured Counselor Troi would report everything, she just kept saying she was grateful that Captain Picard was offering her a second chance. At one point, Troi had asked if Ro really wanted to return to Starfleet. Ro had quickly answered, yes. She didn't bother to add that aside from prison on Jaros II, she had no other place to go. She would rather die than return to a Bajoran resettlement camp to repair broken equipment or grow tubers in the dust.

"Leaving the sensor shadow, sir," Ro announced, bringing the ship to a halt.

"Worf, send out long-range sensor probes," Picard ordered. "Perhaps the *Hawking* left the Badlands at a different location."

Riker had to swallow several times to regain control. It had felt for a moment like he was being turned inside out.

"We have encountered a subspace field," Data said, sounding like nothing had happened.

"What kind?"

"Currently unknown, sir," Data replied.

Riker was having trouble controlling the *Hawking*. Intense subspace fields were known to disrupt the plasma flow. He sent the engine sequence into automatic shutdown. Other systems were shutting down, responding to the abrupt reduction in power. With only auxiliary generators, shields were at 30 percent.

"Was that a weapon of some kind?" Riker brought the *Hawking* to a stop, preferring to remain on the edge of the sensor shadow until they knew more. At least they were far enough away from the plasma storms to avoid being pulled in. "Where's that other vessel?"

"Sensors are still off-line, Commander."

"Okay, let's get to work," Riker said.

With both of them working, it didn't take long to replace the damaged circuits. They gave priority to the sensors, rerouting the power from the EPS system to the banks from the auxiliary fusion generators.

When Data could finally run a full scan, he immediately announced, "The vessel is on an intercept course. It is a Cardassian *Galor*-class warship."

Great, Riker thought to himself. They shouldn't have gotten so close to the edge of the sensor shadow. "Send a coded message to the *Enterprise*. If you have to, relay it to the Gamma 7 outpost. Let them know what our status and location is."

"Aye, sir." Data added, "The Cardassian warship is dropping out of warp."

Now Riker had to make a choice. They could dive back into the Badlands—where they would be at the mercy of the plasma storms with barely any shields and no impulse power. Or they could face down the Cardassians.

The thought of having to make an emergency landing on one of those planets inside the Badlands was enough to make up his mind.

"Open a channel to the warship," Riker said.

Data nodded. "Frequency open."

"This is William Riker in command of the shuttlecraft *Hawking*. Identify yourself."

Riker figured he would start off strong, since they didn't have a hope of winning a fair fight.

"I am receiving a visual response," Data reported.

"On screen."

The rapidly growing Cardassian warship was replaced by the image of a Cardassian—a female Cardassian. She was seated in a commander's chair that looked like a throne. On her head was a readout unit on which she could monitor the ship's systems.

"I am Gul Ocett, commander of the patrol in this region. Explain your presence here."

The ridges around her eyes and down the bridge of her nose were less pronounced than those of the male Cardassian who was standing behind the commander's chair. Riker also noticed that Gul Ocett had a blue tint in the depression in her forehead, and blue dots accented the outer ridges of her eyes.

"Explain your presence here," Gul Ocett repeated slowly. Anger glinted in her eyes.

"The *Enterprise* is on a mission to survey this sector," Riker explained. "As part of our survey, we took this shuttle into the interior of the plasma storms. The translational forces pulled us off course."

Gul Ocett turned her head briefly, her eyes narrowing at the small screen that was suspended from her headset. The male Cardassian continued to stare at Riker. His lips curved up slightly.

"We do not read the presence of the *Enterprise* in this sector," Gul Ocett told Riker.

"They're on the other side of the Badlands," Riker said reasonably. "Unless you've perfected a way to penetrate the plasma storms with your sensors. . . ."

Since this was clearly not possible, Gul Ocett ignored his comment. "A transport carrying Bajoran terrorists was sighted in this region. Have you encountered any vessels?"

"No, you are the first," Riker told her.

Gul Ocett again focused on the display in her headset. "How was your shuttlecraft damaged?"

"By the subspace field." At her blank look, Riker added, "Didn't you detect it?"

"No." Gul Ocett paused, turning her head as the

male Cardassian behind her whispered in her ear. Her expression was one of profound distaste.

Riker exchanged a quick glance with Data, raising a questioning brow. Since Data wasn't in the line of transmission, the android said quietly, "The warship was at extreme sensor range when the phenomenon occurred. It is possible they did not detect the subspace wave."

Gul Ocett nodded shortly, and turned back to the screen. "We will take your shuttle on board and transport you to the *Enterprise*."

Riker felt a chill of foreboding. Gul Ocett's stark expression and bloodshot eyes showed the strain she was under, making her proposal seem more like a threat than an offer.

"We will soon have impulse power." Riker smiled in a way he hoped looked unconcerned. "And we've already sent a message to the *Enterprise*. We should be able to rendezvous with them shortly."

Her irritation broke through. "Don't be foolish. It would take you days to get around the plasma storms on impulse power. Prepare for tractor beam."

The visual transmission ended, and the image of the warship reappeared on the viewscreen. After receiving Riker's nod of agreement, Data prepared the shuttlecraft for tractoring. They both knew that weapons were not an option. A *Galor*-class warship could give the *Enterprise* herself a challenge. And in the *Hawking*'s current condition, the warship could pulverize the shuttle with one well-aimed blow.

Riker had no choice but to allow the *Hawking* to be

seized by the tractor beam. But he didn't trust Cardassians. Maybe it was because of his years at Starfleet Academy, when the war was going strong and many of their battle simulations had focused on Cardassian tactics. The Cardassian Empire was a military-based society, yet unlike the Klingons, they were not known for their honor. If something could be done quietly and brutally, that seemed to be their preference. Riker found it hard to believe the Cardassians had finally agreed to peace with the Federation. Some of Starfleet's best tactical simulations indicated that the Cardassians had an ulterior motive for declaring a truce.

"Warship closing to 100 kilometers," Data reported.

Riker narrowed his eyes as the golden hull of the warship grew larger. Every instinct warned him not to allow the Cardassians to take possession of the *Hawking*. But he knew these were the wages of peace. If he and Data had to prove good faith in the name of Starfleet, then they would do it.

"Tractor locked on," Data announced. "We are being drawn toward the warship."

Riker put aside his doubts. The only way out was to go forward.

Chapter Three

DATA NOTED that Commander Riker looked disturbed. At first the android was busy locking down the systems, storing the information they had gathered in the Badlands. But with no sensitive data or systems on board the *Hawking,* he was able to finish his tasks quickly.

As they were drawn into the hanger of the Cardassian warship, they passed numerous energy-exhaust ventilators and weapons ports aimed at the *Hawking.* Observation windows lined only a few decks, with the vast majority of the hull consisting of layers of gold iridium plating. According to the latest Starfleet intelligence, the Cardassians achieved a 54 percent increase in structural integrity and shielding with their design, a fact that was stimulating debate on the design of future vessels at Starfleet Headquarters.

Data wondered if it exhibited a socialized prejudice to prefer the appearance of the *Enterprise* to this *Galor*-class warship. Then again, it could be his creativity program expressing aesthetic preferences. The *Enterprise* had graceful curves and sparkled like the starfield, while the Cardassian ship was angular and dark despite the golden gleam of iridium.

The green forcefield over the hanger flicked off just as the nose of the *Hawking* hit the threshold. Riker let out a hissing breath at the close call. Data reasoned this was typical Cardassian procedure; their military posture would dictate that shields be dropped for a minimum amount of time.

"Follow my lead," Riker told Data, as he went to the door. Data obediently fell in behind the commander. On the way, Riker glanced at the security bin, which held fully charged hand phasers, but he did not open it.

Riker opened the door to the *Hawking* and stepped outside. The lighting levels were lower than those in the shuttle, and Data's autonomic systems instantly adjusted the irises of his eyes to enhance the focus.

Several Cardassian guards in gray uniforms were stationed in front of the *Hawking*. One stepped forward, almost at Data's shoulder as he left the *Hawking*. The officer immediately entered the shuttlecraft and began scanning the interior.

"Is that necessary?" Commander Riker demanded.

"They are following my orders." Gul Ocett stepped from the shadows, coming closer. Her uniform consisted of black plated armor edged with darkly reflective strips to form a dramatic V-shape from her shoulders to her waist. She waited at some distance while the tallest gray-clad Cardassian held out a huge hand scanner. He passed it up and down in front of Riker.

"No weapons, Commander. No implants. This," he added, gesturing toward the comm badge, "is a communications device."

"If you had asked, I could have told you that," Riker said to Gul Ocett. He ignored the one performing the scan. "We aren't carrying any weapons."

Gul Ocett crossed her arms, waiting as the officer scanned Data.

"Commander! This one is not a biological life-form. Twenty-four kilograms of tripolymer composites, 12.8 kilograms of molybdenum-cobalt alloys, and 1.3 kilograms of bioplast sheeting."

"To be accurate," Data corrected, "my body consists of 24.6 kilograms of tripolymer composites."

"Some kind of machine?" Gul Ocett walked closer.

"I am an android," Data informed her.

Data was accustomed to the reaction of humanoids when they discovered he was an artificial life-form. But Gul Ocett was less tactful than most. She had no compunction about examining him closely, circling him, then peering into his eyes. She was slightly taller than Data, nearly as tall as Commander Riker. Data wondered what he would be feeling right now—*if* he had feelings.

"What is its function?" she asked Riker.

Riker raised one brow, nodding to Data to answer.

Data replied, "I am Commander Data, currently assigned to the Starship *Enterprise* as Second Officer and Operations Manager."

"A senior officer . . . ," she said doubtfully, drawing away finally.

"Commander!" announced the officer who emerged from the interior of the *Hawking*. "I have confiscated four hand phasers and disabled the vessel's weapons systems."

"Anything else you'd like to confiscate while you're assisting us?" Riker asked pointedly.

Gul Ocett didn't blink. She went closer to Riker, leaning into his face when she spoke. "A Cardassian outpost was attacked by Bajoran terrorists yesterday." Riker actually pulled back from her. "The terrorists destroyed two scout ships undergoing repairs. They fled into the plasma storms. Now we find you here. It seems like a remarkable . . . coincidence."

"I told you," Riker said, rigid with resentment. "We're on a survey mission."

"Yes, so you informed me."

"If you don't believe us, go find the *Enterprise* and ask them."

"I intend to," Gul Ocett said sharply. "I will also examine your logs. Give me your access codes now."

For a moment, Data was unsure of Commander Riker's response.

Then Riker started to smile. "Be my guest," he said, stepping back slightly to make a sweeping gesture toward the ship. "Data."

Data recited the access codes while Riker smiled at Gul Ocett. She was not amused.

"Perhaps you would be willing to exchange data with us," Riker suggested. "Share with us what you know about the Badlands. I'm sure you've had plenty of experience navigating through the plasma storms while you were chasing down Bajoran terrorists."

Data was not adept with nuances, but Riker's emphasis on "plenty of experience" seemed to cast aspersions on the Cardassians' ability to stamp out the rebellion by Bajoran nationalists.

Data did not believe it was wise to provoke Gul Ocett.

But Ocett simply told them both, "Come this way."

Data once again fell in behind Riker, noting that two of the Cardassian officers were bringing up the rear.

The narrow corridors were as starkly lit as the shuttle bay, with hard-edged lights and dark shadows. Data noted that Riker appeared uneasy, starting and looking more closely whenever someone appeared in the corridor. Data surmised that Riker was having difficulty seeing in the dim light.

The floor was hard and made a dull metallic ring with each footstep. Data amplified his hearing to detect the sound of hydraulic machinery operating the environmental systems and the hiss and whir of other mechanical equipment. He could hear few voices, yet Starfleet estimated that a crew of two hundred operated the Cardassian *Galor*-class warships.

Gul Ocett led them into a large room. Operational panels lined one alcove, partially concealed by blue grids with small round holes. A long curving desk filled the opposite end. Data recognized the male Cardassian who had been standing behind Gul Ocett during their first contact. He was seated behind the desk in a chair with the towering back that Cardassians seemed to prefer.

"Come forward," he said, beckoning them. The Cardassian stayed seated, leaning back and crossing one leg over the other. "I am Jos Mengred."

Data noted he was not in the Cardassian fleet uniform. His garments were of a finer material than Gul Ocett's—a mesh of black platinum chain mail. On his breast were insignia slightly different from the commander's. The flared top was identical, but the right lower tine was broken off, leaving only one sharp downward spike. The colors were muted and blurred, from purple to green.

Data quickly ran a comparison check. It was the insignia for the Obsidian Order, the ruthless and efficient Cardassian internal security police. The Obsidian Order maintained surveillance on virtually every Cardassian citizen in the Empire.

Mengred smiled as if he had been waiting for this. His eye-ridges were slightly gnarled and his face was creased into deep wrinkles on either side of his mouth, indicating that he was an older male. "Welcome aboard, Starfleet Officers."

Riker stood in front of the desk. "I am Commander Riker, and this is Commander Data."

Gul Ocett stood back, near the door. "The other one is a machine, Mengred."

His deep-set eyes fastened on Data. "The android?"

Mengred looked him up and down, slowly nodding his head. "I have heard about this one . . . Data, created by Dr. Noonien Soong."

Data detected a faint inhale from Gul Ocett, then, stiffly, she backed away two steps. She had not expected Mengred to know about his existence. It revealed a discrepancy in the distribution of information within the Cardassian government.

Riker interrupted Mengred's delighted appraisal of Data. "We would like to contact the *Enterprise*."

"Yes, I'm sure you would," Mengred said soothingly. "However, we are currently engaged in scanning the area for some Bajoran terrorists."

"Gul Ocett informed us that a Cardassian outpost has been attacked."

"Oh, she did? Gul Ocett is *generous* with her information," Mengred said thoughtfully, glancing at the commander. She didn't move a muscle. "I'm afraid you'll have to wait while we complete our primary mission."

"I have another suggestion," Riker said. "We'll take the *Hawking* and go look for a communications window to the *Enterprise*."

"Your shuttle has been damaged by the plasma storms," Mengred said regretfully. "It would be irresponsible of us to let you leave."

Data glanced at Gul Ocett. She did not look concerned about their well-being. "I can assure you, the *Hawking* is space-worthy."

"Ah, but we can't be sure of that without a thorough diagnostic of your systems. And that will take several hours to complete." Mengred smiled blandly.

"You're detaining us against our will," Riker pointed out. "There will be serious consequences."

"Not so serious as the possibility of your shuttle not returning to the *Enterprise* at all," Mengred assured him. "As long as you get back safely, I'm quite sure Starfleet won't complain about a little delay."

Data believed Mengred was correct. Federation dealings with the Cardassian Empire were strained enough at this juncture to excuse a few improprieties, such as a database search of their shuttlecraft and the detention of Starfleet officers.

"We will proceed to the communications point as soon as we can," Mengred told them.

Riker deliberately turned to Gul Ocett. "Set course for bearing seven-one-five mark ninety. That should take us within range of the *Enterprise*."

"Of course," Mengred replied for the commander. "Meanwhile, I'll have my aide, Pakat, show you to your quarters." He waved his hand and turned, letting the tall back of the chair conceal him.

Mengred's aide turned out to be a rather short Cardassian male with wide shoulders and stocky legs. Pakat looked powerful enough to roll a starship, and Commander Riker didn't doubt that the aide would do so if Mengred ordered him to.

Pakat didn't say a word as he showed Data and Riker to a narrow set of quarters with bunk beds along one wall. As the aide left, Riker said, "At least it's not the brig."

The door closed with a final hiss. Riker went over to it, but it stayed shut. "Or maybe this is the brig."

Riker began to look around, but he glanced at Data, covertly tapping his ear to indicate that Cardassians were likely monitoring the room.

Data nodded slightly, indicating he would reveal no tactical information. "Sir, Mengred and his aide wear the insignia for the Obsidian Order, the Cardassian internal security police."

"I knew there was something different about him," Riker said, as he circled half-way around the small room. "He didn't stand when Gul Ocett entered the room. Captain Picard would never put up with having an 'internal security agent' hanging over his shoulder on the bridge."

"It is an intriguing distribution of power," Data agreed.

Riker determined that there were no obvious ports allowing observation, but he was under no illusions. They were being watched. The panels were all welded shut, including the one under the wash basin. There was nothing loose in the room, and nothing that could be used as a blunt weapon. Even the drinking cup was attached by a cable to the wall. He filled it from the tap and drank.

"Metallic," he said with distaste, pouring the rest out.

"Orders, sir?" Data asked.

Riker tested the padding on the lower bunk, then lay down. "Now we wait," he said, putting his hands behind his head. "While Mengred calls his superiors and gets *his* orders. He isn't going to do anything without checking with his superiors."

* * *

Mengred leaned closer to the three-dimensional holo-image of the cell displayed on the black mirrored surface of his desk. Riker was no taller than his hand, and Data's slightly stiff movements made him look remarkably like a child's toy come to life.

Data took up a post near the door with his back to the wall, his hands clasped in front of him, and his eyes focused on the crack of the door. Then he went perfectly still, watching for the slightest movement while Commander Riker calmly lay in the bunk with his eyes closed.

Mengred had to admit that it was an impressive display of nonchalance. But then again, if he had a machine like Data to serve as his aide, he could rest easy too.

Mengred discounted Riker's ploys to gain supremacy, both his comments and his posturing. The Starfleet officer had managed to briefly discomfit Gul Ocett in the shuttle hanger, but she wasn't difficult to intimidate. She was a typical lumbering military officer. Riker's statement about his own captain refusing to put up with an "internal security agent" had even been useful in prompting an idea of how he could proceed in this matter. So he discounted Riker as not worth the effort of careful analysis.

On the other hand, there was Data . . . Mengred had read the reports about the Starfleet android as curiously as any other agent in the Obsidian Order. But he had never imagined coming face-to-face with the android. There was a standing order for all operatives to obtain any data they could on it's positronic brain, for future reproduction.

Mengred kept the holo-image activated, even while his call to Enabran Tain, the head of the Obsidian Order, was answered. Tain looked haggard, his down-turned mouth firmly set in displeasure. Mengred knew that things had not been going well for Tain lately.

"This had better be important," Tain barked.

"Sir, I have the android Data and Commander Riker of the Starship *Enterprise*," Mengred informed him. "We have their damaged shuttlecraft, and scans and data downloads are underway. They claim the *Enterprise* is in the area doing surveys and request to be returned to their ship."

Tain's expression lightened somewhat. "That is news, indeed, Mengred. Good work."

Mengred licked his lips, pleased by the rare praise. "Sir, if I may be so bold as to suggest a plan for exploiting this situation. . . ."

Mengred explained to Tain what he had in mind. But the entire time, he could see the tiny form of Data standing at perfect attention watching the door. If only he had an aide like that . . . knowledge instantly at his fingertips, power enough to overcome any attack, never sleeping, never tiring, the perfect guard. . . .

The *Hawking* was six hours overdue for its rendezvous with the *Enterprise* when La Forge suggested sealing the warp coils of the *Enterprise* so they could enter the Badlands on impulse power. Though Picard was reluctant to do so, he knew their options were rapidly running out. If his people were in trouble in there, he would have to pull them out.

"Search pattern completed," Ensign Ro announced, having run through a pattern that spiraled out from the area of the Badlands the shuttle had entered and eventually circled around and back to where they had started. "Nothing on sensors, sir."

"Very well," Picard said. The expectant eyes of his crew were on him, waiting for him to give the order. They wanted nothing more than to plunge into the Badlands to find their fellow officers. Yet somehow, his instinct told him that was not the right thing to do. . . .

"Sir," Lieutenant Worf spoke behind him. "You have an incoming message on a secured channel from Admiral Henry at the Gamma 7 Outpost. Priority two."

The Gamma 7 Outpost was the meeting site during the ongoing negotiations between the Cardassian Empire and the Federation. "On screen," Picard said, rising from the command seat.

Admiral Thomas Henry appeared on the viewscreen. "Captain Picard, I've just received word from the Cardassians. They have your missing men, Commanders Riker and Data."

"Where are they?" Picard asked, ignoring the muffled exclamations from the bridge crew at the news.

"They're on a *Galor*-class warship near the Badlands. I'm sending the coordinates to you now," Admiral Henry informed him, glancing down to send the transmission. "Along with the official Cardassian request submitted to Starfleet Headquarters."

"Information received," Worf informed the captain.

"Cardassian request?" Picard asked.

"Yes, Captain. When you rendezvous with the warship, your orders are to take on two Cardassians. The Detapa Council of Cardassia have requested that members of the Obsidian Order, Jos Mengred and his aide, be allowed to participate in the survey of sector 21305."

"Cardassians?" Ensign Ro blurted out.

Admiral Henry focused on Ro Laren. "Yes, Ensign, Cardassians. Or have you forgotten the Federation is at peace with the Cardassian Empire?"

"With all due respect," Picard said to the admiral, resting a hand on Ro's shoulder to keep her from saying anything more. "I know we've hosted Cardassian observers before, but does Starfleet really think it's wise to allow members of the Obsidian Order on board a galaxy-class starship?"

"I don't like letting their intelligence operatives on one of our ships any more than you do, Jean-Luc. But my hands are tied on this one." Henry narrowed his eyes and shook his head. "If we agree to their terms, the Cardassians will agree to designate the Badlands as neutral territory. I don't have to tell you how important that would be strategically, or how important it is for us to cooperate with the Cardassians."

"Of course," Picard said, remembering the recent damage done by Admiral Kennelly. "I understand the need to maintain relations."

"They have your people, Jean Luc." Admiral Henry's expression was closed, as if that said it all. "Before picking up the Cardassians, seal off engineering and don't let them have access to the ship's computers. They are obviously going to gather as much information about us as possible. Be polite but not too accommodating with technical data."

"Understood, sir," Picard agreed.

"Good, you'll have them for over a week, so stay on your guard. Henry out."

The Badlands appeared on the screen, blurred red and orange. Now Picard almost wished he had ordered the *Enterprise* into the plasma storms to search for the *Hawking*. Then they wouldn't have received Starfleet's orders. But he knew that facing a problem was the best way to overcome it.

"Worf, send the coordinates to the helm. How long will it take to intercept the Cardassian warship?"

"The direct route would take us through the sensor shadow," Worf replied. "At full impulse power, it will take just under two hours."

"That should be enough time to batten down the hatches," Picard said thoughtfully. "Worf, arrange for a complete security lockdown."

"Aye, sir," Worf replied.

"But sir!" Ro protested, turning around in her seat. "Just last week the Cardassians subverted a Starfleet admiral and tried to destroy a ship full of Bajoran refugees. Now you're cooperating with them?"

"You have your orders, Ensign," Picard replied, perhaps too sharply. "I'll be in my ready room."

Picard strode off the bridge and into his ready room. As soon as the door slid closed, he was able to relax. He was glad, as always, to have the ready room, where he could monitor the bridge operations from his desk without letting the crew see his concern. Right now, he couldn't allow them to know that he felt the same way as Ro Laren. How could the Federation deal honorably with people who refused to take a clear and honorable stand themselves?

Chapter Four

RIKER GROANED, instantly alerting Data. While monitoring the conditions in their cell, a significant portion of his positronic brain had been engaged in computing new formulas for the impulse reaction chamber on board the *Enterprise*.

But Data halted that task and gave Riker his full attention. "Commander?"

Riker half-rolled over, revealing a sweaty face. "My guts are tied in knots."

Data instantly went to his side. He was no doctor, but he had a great deal of medical knowledge stored in his database.

"How long have you been experiencing pain?" Data asked.

"About an hour now, I guess. It's getting worse."

Riker's pulse rate was 91.7 per minute, and he was

running a temperature of 101.2 degrees. His mouth appeared dry.

"My face and neck itch," he rasped. "Like I want to peel the skin off."

"That would not be advisable," Data told him.

"Thanks for the expert medical advice!" Riker snapped.

"I am not a medical diagnostician," Data informed him. "However, it is clear that you are suffering from some form of illness."

Riker rolled his eyes, a familiar reaction that indicated Data had stated the obvious. "How long have we been in here?"

"Two hours, twenty-seven minutes, and fourteen seconds."

Riker's muscles contracted, and he curled into a ball. His grunt of agony turned into panting. Data correctly ascertained that Commander Riker was unfit for duty and that he must now take command.

Data tapped his comm badge, but a dull buzz indicated their communications devices were being jammed. His internal sensors indicated they were being continually bombarded with electromagnetic energy.

"Data to Gul Ocett, this is an emergency." Data glanced up at the ceiling. They were undoubtedly being monitored. "We require immediate medical assistance—"

"No!" Riker exclaimed, still writhing in pain. "I don't want those . . . Cardassian butchers . . . touching me."

"With all due respect, sir, in your condition, you are not competent to make that decision."

Riker glared up at Data. But before he could protest, he gulped wildly and pointed toward the waste reclamation unit.

During the next hour, Data assisted Commander Riker in whatever way he deemed necessary. He carried the commander back to the bunk and removed his uniform jacket. Then he washed Riker's face with a cloth ripped from his own sleeve cuff. He wrung out the rag and placed it on Riker's forehead, an old method of helping to cool the head and bring down fever. Data even snapped the cup cord from the wall so that he could transport water to Riker.

Every three minutes, Data repeated his request for immediate medical assistance.

"Commander Data to Jos Mengred, we require immediate medical assistance. Please respond."

Mengred leaned closer to the screen, thoroughly intrigued by the android's actions. He alternated between calling for Mengred and Gul Ocett. It was quite the tactical move, since Ocett was calling him every time to say she must respond to an official request as per the detailed agreement Starfleet and the Cardassian Empire had entered into.

Mengred simply overrode her command, informing her to prepare a science bay for medical work. He wanted more time to observe the android.

The android stayed by Riker's side until the human's fit seemed to ease somewhat, and the commander lay quietly, his eyes closed and his black shirt heaving with every breath.

Mengred wasn't too worried about Riker. Humans were always getting sick. They sometimes blamed it on direct exposure to Cardassians, which had only started when they began meeting face-to-face in treaty negotiations two years ago. But Cardassians weren't getting ill with human viruses, so the Obsidian Order had informed their operatives that humans were a relatively weak and sickly people.

The android remained unaffected by his commander's lack of strength. His voice betrayed no anxiety, despite the lack of a response. He was efficient in tending to Riker and actually seemed to ease the human's suffering somewhat.

Then the android went to the door panel. He meticulously felt around the crack of the door, trying to insert his nails in to get a leverage point. But the door was self-sealing, to ensure that any gases pumped into the cell could not escape into the general atmosphere of the ship.

The android placed his ear against the paneling next to the door. Slowly he moved up and down, listening to the machinery behind the wall.

Mengred was intrigued. By listening along the wall, the android pinpointed the spot he intended to focus on. It was in the corner, far from the door. Mengred quickly accessed the structural specs and discovered that the door controls were located directly behind that panel.

The android backed up and began methodically kicking the metal wall panel. His strength was prodigious! Mengred quickly routed sensors to determine the cubic pressure applied with each blow, and was amazed by the results. The duranium filament membrane was layered with reinforcing tritanium sheets. It was rated to contain a class-two explosion.

But the android had already dented the shiny surface, and was methodically continuing to kick the same stress spot.

"Kee-ta!" Mengred saluted him under his breath. Very impressive.

"Gul Ocett to Mengred. Respond!"

At the interruption of the audio message, Mengred regretfully tore his eyes from the figures on his desk.

"What is it, Gul Ocett?"

"That machine is damaging my ship," Gul Ocett said darkly. *"It could batter down the wall panel and open the door."*

Mengred smiled at her urgency, the strain she must be feeling to so clearly exhibit her frustration. This little test had accomplished far more than he had hoped for.

Ocett's voice was rising, *"You do not have authorization to endanger this ship—"*

"Excuse me, Commander," Mengred interrupted. "I don't have time to discuss my authorization. I have to escort our guests to the science lab."

He could hear the strangled silence on the other end, before the channel snapped closed.

Data could feel the electron bonding give a micromilimeter with every impact. He continued with blows of the same intensity, intending to break off a section fourteen centimeters in circumference. That would allow him to access the gyro servos that operated the door panel.

"Worf!" Riker called weakly. "Worf, stop that banging. . . ."

"I am attempting to attract attention," Data informed the commander, though he knew Riker was incoherent and talking in a dream-like state because of his soaring fever.

The door hissed open, catching Data in midkick.

Mengred strolled in. "You've done an excellent job of trying to destroy that wall panel, android."

Data lowered his foot. "I have repeatedly requested immediate assistance."

"Sorry, we've been very busy." Mengred went toward Riker. "What is wrong with him?"

"Unknown," Data said, placing himself in a position where he could intervene if the Cardassian made a threatening move.

"He will be taken to the medical lab," Mengred said, snapping his fingers and gesturing. His burly aide and a Cardassian in a security uniform picked Riker up.

Data noted that they did not use their transporter to send Riker immediately to the sickbay, as they would have done on the *Enterprise*. They simply hauled Riker off the bed by his arms and legs while another guard fetched an antigrav pallet.

Data prepared to accompany them.

"You will stay here, android," Mengred told him.

Data quickly stepped around the aide holding Riker,

blocking him from moving forward. "I must stay with Commander Riker."

"Why?" Mengred asked him.

Data perceived a thoughtful quality to Mengred's question. "Because I am now in command of this away mission, and I insist on accompanying this officer to sickbay. If you refuse, I will make an official complaint to Starfleet Headquarters and the Detapa Council on Cardassia Prime."

"All that just to go with him for a medical examination?" Mengred pressed.

"Yes," Data said simply, feeling no need to address him as "sir" since he held no military rank.

"Very well," Mengred agreed.

Data followed the men carrying Riker from the cell. They placed him on an antigrav pallet that was stained and dirty from cargo. Data helped guide the pallet, staying near Riker's head in case he spoke.

Several security guards brought up the rear, their phaser pistols drawn and aimed at him. Data analyzed this new development and concluded their caution resulted from his demonstration of strength. It was highly likely the Cardassians considered him a threat after the damage he had done to their duranium-tritanium wall.

Mengred accompanied them, staying well behind Data. When he turned, the Cardassian was watching him: every move, every step, every blink of his eyes.

Data continued forward. The next time he looked back, Mengred was still watching him. The Cardassian did not attempt to conceal his interest in Data. But he completely ignored Riker, who groaned at every jolt in the passage through the corridors.

Data gathered useful information during their transit through the warship. He flagged Mengred's interest in himself as information to be considered in his tactical evaluation of the current situation.

Riker was pushed into a laboratory and lifted onto an activated diagnostic table. Data stood next to the table, examining the remainder of the room. It appeared to be a biology laboratory, with counters around three walls. The central table was attached to the computer console.

"This is your medical facility?" Data asked.

"Cardassians don't get sick," Mengred told him. "Injuries are handled in the aid center, but this appears to be a more complex situation which calls for a combined biological and medical facility."

Data refrained from comment. The room was equipped for active and passive scans, and his sensitive neural network detected both in use. The diagnostic table was emitting high-frequency electromagnetic waves in complex patterns.

Only Mengred and the Cardassian biology officer, who never offered his name, stayed in the room, while guards were posted at the door. Data endured the continual scans, remaining next to Commander Riker. From Mengred's reaction, Data deduced that the scans were investigating his composition as well as Riker's biological condition.

Since none of Data's schematics were restricted, and many aspects of his construction had been debated in cybernetics symposiums across the Federation, Data did not protest. If the Cardassians wanted a full record of his physiognomy, they could have obtained it in easier ways. But then again, Cardassians were notoriously suspicious and would probably believe that important information was being withheld.

Data knew the reason he was unique was much simpler than that—only Soong had been able to reproduce a viable positronic network. Data's own attempts with his daughter Lal had been both exhilarating and tragic, when she lived only two weeks.

"What are you thinking right now, android?" Mengred suddenly asked him.

Data looked up at Mengred, who was sitting back in a padded chair, watching him. The biologist was stiffly performing scans and comparing them to human readings on the computer console.

"I must contact the *Enterprise*," Data informed him. "I request that you immediately proceed to the communications window."

"Oh, your ship has already been contacted." Mengred smiled. "Did I forget to tell you that? The *Enterprise* should be arriving soon."

From Riker's bedside, the biologist announced flatly, "His cellular structure is exhibiting spontaneous decay. I can stabilize his systems with klysteamine."

Data immediately rejoined the biologist. "I would like to see the molecular composition of the klysteamine, and your recommended dosage size."

The Cardassian scientist didn't want to move away from his console, but Mengred ordered him to comply.

Data ignored the biologist's scowl and examined the klysteamine structure, accessing his own databanks to run a comparison against Starfleet standards. The Cardassian klysteamine was refined at a cruder quality level, but it had no additional chemical structures. Data determined that even if the Cardassian had misdiagnosed the symptoms, this dosage of klysteamine would merely reduce inflammation of the tissues and bring down Commander Riker's fever—exactly what was needed right now.

Data filled the injector himself and administered it to Riker. His temperature was 104.5—dangerously high.

"If Commander Riker dies, it will be due to your negligence," Data informed Mengred.

"He's not going to die," Mengred said, dismissing that with a wave of his hand. "You also contain medical knowledge?"

"I have access to a wide range of information." Data checked Riker's temperature again with the bioscanner. It had already dropped one-half a degree.

"And you truly feel responsible for that officer?" Mengred asked curiously.

"Yes."

Data stood stiffly as Mengred stepped closer. "A machine that thinks and talks like a human. Amazing. . . ."

Mengred continued to ask questions, and Data answered. The latest Starfleet orders were to cooperate with the Cardassians within the limits of the current treaty. Under section 233.5, the treaty specified that information exchange would be encouraged. Therefore, Data replied courteously and did not protest the continued covert electromagnetic scans. But their negligence of Riker's condition seemed to be calculated, and that indicated the need for caution, so Data provided as little concrete information as possible.

Mengred seemed to be mostly interested in Data himself. He asked about things Data had done, what he thought, why he had joined Starfleet, and why he had become a commander.

Throughout, Mengred kept referring to him as "android" until Data finally corrected him. "My name is not android. It is Data. I am a sentient being like yourself."

"Remarkable," Mengred said as if to himself. "Truly remarkable."

Data turned away to check Commander Riker's temperature. Over the past hour, it had dropped two-and-a-half degrees, bringing him out of immediate danger.

"Gul Ocett to Mengred."

A flash of irritation passed over Mengred's face. "What is it?"

"We have the Enterprise on long-range sensors."

Mengred glanced at Data. "Very well."

Data politely said to Mengred, "I believe that ends our discussion."

Mengred smiled. "For now."

Ensign Ro seethed inside. Her anger had been building ever since Captain Picard had acceded, almost without protest, to Starfleet Command's order to take on two Cardassians.

Ro was remembering why she had gotten into so

much trouble in Starfleet even before her court-martial. But she had to say something, when they went around asking for trouble! After all, what good did it do to allow Cardassians on board the *Enterprise?* Starfleet had everything to lose. It was complete arrogance, the arrogance of a people who hadn't been defeated for a few centuries. The Bajorans knew better. They knew you could always be beaten.

If the Federation territories had ever been occupied and their people enslaved, they would hesitate to allow untrustworthy Cardassians on board the finest starship in their fleet.

"Captain," Worf said from the tactical station. "I am reading a Cardassian *Galor*-class warship on long range sensors."

"Set an intercept course."

"Aye, sir," Ro said reluctantly. Worf had reported that the security lockdown was in place, but Ro was willing to bet on the Cardassians finding a way around even the toughest security protocols.

"Their shields are at full power," Worf announced. "Weapons are on-line."

"Open a channel," Picard ordered.

When the image of a female Cardassian Commander appeared on the viewscreen, Ro restrained the urge to spit at it. She knew the Cardassians were playing Starfleet for fools, and for her the contempt went both ways.

"Captain Picard, I am Gul Ocett," the Cardassian said bluntly. "Your officer is sick."

"Commander Riker?" Picard asked, rising to his feet. "Why were we not informed?"

"Your android stabilized the commander," Ocett retorted. "Prepare to receive the shuttlecraft *Hawking*. As per Starfleet-Cardassian Agreement Stardate 45117.6, your officers are accompanied by Jos Mengred and his aide Pakat. They will remain on your ship until Stardate 45120.6 while you conduct the survey of this sector."

Ro stifled an exclamation. It appeared that the only reason Picard was allowing the Obsidian Order on board was in exchange for his officers. That revealed a glaring weakness that would surely be exploited by the Cardassians.

Picard alerted sickbay. "Dr. Crusher, report to the main shuttlebay. Commander Riker is injured."

"*On my way*," was Dr. Crusher's immediate response.

Ro brought the *Enterprise* to a halt a bare 100 kilometers from the warship. The two starships would be fairly matched in a fight. The *Enterprise* had the edge, as it was much bigger, but the warship was powerful. How powerful, no one but the Cardassians knew for certain.

The *Hawking* emerged from the shuttle hanger, and everyone on the bridge breathed a sigh of relief.

"Picard to shuttlecraft *Hawking*," the captain hailed.

The viewscreen shifted from the exterior of the *Hawking* to the interior. "Data here, sir."

Data was clearly focused on flying the shuttle, but the view also included the entire width of the shuttle. The huddled form in back was probably Riker lying down on the bench. A Cardassian stood in the shadows to his side, while another Cardassian sat in the navigator's seat, his chair momentarily turned to face the back.

"Commander Riker is quite ill; however, he has been stabilized," Data reported. "Engaging docking sequence."

"*Hawking* is cleared for docking," Worf acknowledged as he dropped shields.

The other Cardassian turned to face the viewscreen. He didn't say anything. He simply looked from one bridge officer to another, assessing them. Ro shivered when she saw the insignia on his chest. The Obsidian Order . . . they were capable of anything, and had license to do everything.

She realized he was looking at her, smirking at the sight of her Bajoran nose and earrings. She fought to keep her hands from clenching and pounding the console.

Then he ignored her, exchanging greetings with Captain Picard.

As the *Hawking* docked, Ro concentrated on the control panel of the helm and didn't look up anymore. She didn't want to give the Cardassian the satisfaction of unnerving her like that again.

When Picard asked Worf to accompany him to go and meet their "guests," Ro shook her head. Her earrings made faint tinkling noises, but she didn't get any comfort from their weight. She didn't like this one bit.

Chapter Five

AFTER THE *Hawking* was seized by the docking tractor beam and set down, Data went to the rear to assist Riker. Data had urged him to remain as he was, but Riker had insisted that Data help him sit up. His legs were too weak to allow him to stand.

As soon as the door opened, Dr. Crusher entered the *Hawking*. "What happened to you?" she exclaimed, when she saw his condition.

"I don't know," Riker said, adjusting stiffly to see further into the shuttle bay. He had a ringside seat at Jos Mengred's introduction to Captain Picard. Worf was standing at attention behind the captain, an immovable hulking presence.

"Hold still," the doctor ordered, scanning Riker. "Inflammation of the intestinal tract and dermal tissue. Cellular degradation in the muscles and connective tissues. Moderate radiation exposure—but there aren't many free radicals left in your system. . . ."

Riker was too busy listening in on the Cardassian's conversation with Picard to pay attention to the doctor.

"I'm sure this will be an interesting experience for us all, Captain," Mengred was saying. Pakat stood stoically behind Mengred.

"Starfleet is pleased to cooperate with our Cardassian neighbors," Picard said.

"I recognize your name, Captain Picard," Mengred said conversationally. "When that rogue Starfleet captain destroyed a Cardassian facility in the K'alar system, you assisted the Cardassian Empire."

"Yes, that was almost a year ago," Picard said evenly.

Riker knew that was not the best incident to remind Captain Picard about. Picard had lost respect for Gul Macet, the lying Cardassian captain who had been in charge of the trio of military "observers" hosted by the *Enterprise.* Macet had known all along that the Cardassian "science station" that had been destroyed was really a weapons-supply depot.

Riker distrusted these two Cardassians as much, if not more than the military officers. Without their armor-plated uniforms, the Obsidian Order agents did not appear as formidable. But Riker knew better than to underestimate them.

"I was pleased when the Detapa Council said we would be allowed to accompany you during your survey of this neutral sector," Mengred said smoothly.

"Yes, of course." Picard seemed stymied by the Cardassian's enthusiasm. "Lieutenant Worf, Chief Tactical

Officer, will show you to your quarters. If you would like, he has prepared a tour of the *Enterprise* for both of you."

"Thank you very much, Captain. That will be delightful." Pakat didn't say a word as Mengred inclined his head in respectful greeting to Worf. "Lieutenant Worf. I have heard much about the ferocity and prowess of Klingons in battle. Is it true?"

Worf clearly had not expected a personal question at this moment. He glanced uneasily at Picard, who nodded for him to reply.

"Klingon tradition honors those who fight well in battle," Worf said bluntly.

"Then our people have much in common," Mengred said eagerly. "I look forward to comparing cultures."

From the look on Worf's face, Riker knew there was no cause to worry that the Klingon would be fooled by Mengred's charm.

Picard informed Mengred that there would be a reception for them later that evening in Ten-Forward, and asked to be excused from the tour of the *Enterprise*. "I must speak with my first officer," Picard added.

Mengred waved one hand in the direction of the *Hawking*. "I'm sure he'll be fine. Curious how quickly he took ill. He *seemed* to be a robust-enough individual." Mengred trailed off, shaking his head, as if to say one could never tell from appearances.

Riker shook with rage at the insult. He tried to stand up and nearly made it to his feet.

"Calm down!" Dr. Crusher hissed, pushing him

firmly back to the bench. "You're not exactly in fighting condition."

The guards he could see in the shuttle bay seemed to shift in embarrassment. Riker felt as if he had betrayed Starfleet by showing weakness in front of these Cardassians.

The tramp of feet echoed through the bay, and Riker slowly relaxed, knowing they were leaving. The hiss of the double doors on the hanger were unmistakable as they opened and closed.

Picard's voice came closer as he said, "Well, Data, I believe you have quite a lot to report."

"Aye, sir," Data replied.

Picard stepped into the *Hawking.* Riker again made a motion forward as if to stand, but Dr. Crusher put a hand on his shoulder. "What did I say?" she warned.

Riker leaned back as Picard joined them. "How are you doing, Will?"

"Better." Riker wished his voice was not so raspy and strained. "Data gave me something that lowered the fever. I was lucky he was there. Their medical facility looked like a torture chamber."

Picard placed a reassuring hand on his shoulder. "What's wrong with him, Doctor?" the captain asked.

She shook her head, closing her tricorder. "I'm not sure. He was left untreated for several hours. But that wouldn't account for the accelerated breakdown of tissue I'm reading. He needs cellular regeneration immediately."

"Were you exposed to something inside the Badlands?" Picard asked Riker.

Riker winced, unable to answer because of a sudden stabbing pain in his stomach.

Data offered, "Negative. However, when we left the plasma storms, a subspace shockwave disabled the major systems in the *Hawking*. We were taken on board the warship and exposed to continuous invasive scans. Long after the symptoms were exhibited, Commander Riker was placed on a biological diagnostic device."

"What frequencies were they using?" Crusher asked.

"High-spectrum frequencies in rotating complex patterns within a wide range of electromagnetic waves."

"Well, that *could* cause spontaneous decay in certain tissues. But not like this," Dr. Crusher said. She stood up and approached Data. "May I?"

Data nodded agreement to the medical scan.

"Minimal EM exposure in his biotissues," the doctor told him. "Not enough to cause damage."

When Riker was finally able to speak again, he weakly insisted, "The Cardassians must be responsible. They disabled the *Hawking* with the subspace field as an excuse to bring us on board the warship. The pain started not long after that."

"There was no medical alert from the computer on board the *Hawking*," Data said. "However, I can analyze the environmental logs to determine if the subspace field could have caused a biological reaction."

Dr. Crusher nodded. "Meanwhile, I'll do a thorough bioscan of Commander Riker. And begin the regeneration treatments."

"Proceed," Picard told Crusher. Then he turned to

Data. "I want a full report of everything that occurred since you left the *Enterprise*."

Riker leaned back as Dr. Crusher tapped her comm badge. "Two to beam to the infirmary."

Waves of dizziness washed over Riker, making it hard for him to think. He hated being shuffled off to sickbay to be worked over, while everyone else was dealing with the Cardassians. He felt as if he had brought a plague down on the ship and was now unable to do anything to help. He bowed his head to rest his forehead on his arms, unable to sit up any longer. It was the worst feeling he could imagine.

Worf nodded to his security guards to bring up the rear. It was an honor guard, he had insisted to the captain. But even without phasers, there was no mistaking the true nature of their orders.

Worf kept a close eye on the two Cardassians. Jos Mengred was the one in command; a tall, slender Cardassian who was older than the military guls and glinns whom Worf had dealt with before. His aide, Pakat, was much shorter, but had a well-developed musculature. He moved with the power and grace of a warrior yet he didn't have the arrogant swagger of the Cardassian military officers. These two agents for the Obsidian Order saw everything. Pakat never reacted to anything, and Mengred never lost his bland smile of approval.

"These are your quarters for the duration of the survey mission," Worf informed the two Cardassians.

The guards stayed outside as Worf entered the guest quarters on deck 5. Jos Mengred walked towards the huge slanted windows, where the *Galor*-class warship could be seen in the distance, motionless. Worf had no doubt they were scanning the *Enterprise* with every sensor grid they had.

"Another set of quarters are beyond that door," Worf informed them.

Mengred paced through the spacious 110 square meters. "We are each allocated quarters this size?" He seemed genuinely surprised.

"These are standard quarters," Worf said.

"You mean your crew quarters are like this, too?" Mengred asked.

"Yes." Worf was proud that the *Enterprise* was the biggest and best ship in the fleet. Yet he was uncomfortable with Mengred's surprise at the luxurious quarters. Much as he hated to agree with the Cardassian, Worf's Spartan tastes also ran toward less opulent surroundings. "I will return for your tour later," he said.

Worf started for the door, but Mengred interrupted, "I was not aware we are prisoners . . . do you intend to have guards watching us at all times?"

"Yes," Worf said flatly. "We were forced to confine one member of the last Cardassian *observation* team to his quarters after he attempted to access the defense codes from the ship's computer."

Worf pointedly glanced at the vacant desk. He had supervised the removal of the computer terminals from both rooms, sealing off the cables before they entered this section. But the ODN node was left tantalizingly exposed. Worf had tapped the ODN lines just before the seal, to alert him if the Cardassians tried to access the ship's computer. He hadn't yet had time to inform the captain about this precaution.

"You don't trust us." Mengred thoughtfully leaned against the desk. "I hope Captain Picard doesn't blame us because one of his men is suffering from space fever."

Worf grimaced. Space fever was a psychological disorder that resulted from confinement in a small spacecraft. "Your personal effects will be brought to you shortly. If you do not require anything else, I will return at 0400 hours."

"No, that will be all," Mengred said dismissively.

Worf left the room and ordered the two security guards to alert him if the Cardassians left their quarters. They were to accompany them at all times. The guards acknowledged, having already been briefed on where the Cardassians were allowed to go.

Worf trusted their abilities, and he felt confident in returning to the shuttle bay to examine the *Hawking* thoroughly. A security team was already performing scans on the personal effects of the Cardassians, which would be sent up to their quarters. They were also running a diagnostic on the *Hawking*'s systems and computer to determine if the Cardassians had tampered with the shuttlecraft.

After spending only a short time with Mengred and Pakat, Worf firmly believed they would find evidence of tampering. He was not surprised when his security team informed him that the memory core of the *Hawking* had been accessed and downloaded.

Worf oversaw the continuing scans and systems checks. If the Cardassians had performed any sabotage on the shuttle, he intended to find it and reveal that they had acted dishonorably. That would surely provide Captain Picard with a reason to send the Cardassians back where they belonged.

Mengred nodded to Pakat, who began scanning the room. The aide went over every particle of the place, checking under the cushions and dipping his tiny hand scanner into ornamental vases.

Mengred was particularly struck by the munificence of the quarters. The lighting was muted, much more suited to his taste than the glaring flat light in the shuttle bay and corridors. There was something soft spread on the floor, and subtle scents in the air. The cushions of the long, low couch were inviting.

It was just like those idiot military "observers," Gul Macet and his men, not to mention something as intriguing as quarters several times the size of the commander's on board a *Galor*-class warship. It was the little details that told so much about a people.

"Sir," Pakat reported, "I am reading no sign of scans or electromagnetic recording ports. There are several computer access nodes, but they read inactive. I believe it is a voice-operated system."

"Very good," Mengred told Pakat. "You can wait in the other room."

"Yes, sir." Pakat dropped his chin, turning away.

Mengred tapped the bone beneath his ear, activating his subdural cranial implant. Top-level operatives had enough implants to achieve their objectives without having to worry about carrying exterior equipment.

He began to subvocalize, speaking in the clipped dialect of his youth, which he had modified into his own private code. There were always watchers watching the watchers, so it had served him well throughout his career. He would go over his reports later, translating them into Cardassian before submitting them to Enabran Tain.

"Gul Macet is clearly a bumbling idiot," Mengred noted in his code. *"These Starfleet people know he was lying about the weapons facility destroyed by Captain Maxwell. Contrary to Macet's report, Captain Picard does not appear to be a gullible pacifist. He and his crew are highly suspicious of our mission and have taken precautions to monitor us at all times."*

Mengred knew that Tain was pleased that he had gained the opportunity for the Obsidian Order to place their own operatives onboard the Starfleet flagship. The military had released a highly edited version of Gul Macet's observations, and the inequity had lasted for nearly a year.

Mengred wondered what the Obsidian Order could have accomplished in the past year if the original observers had been their agents instead. He had downloaded Macet's report into his cranial implant to serve as a basis for comparison. Macet had said nothing about the android or the Klingon on board the *Enterprise*, yet these beings could be of vital importance to the success of the Cardassian Empire.

But Mengred was not so blunt an instrument as Gul

Macet. And he had time to gather the information he needed—he would lull their suspicions, show them that all Cardassians were not military men. To "break" a subject, one befriends him, then stabs swiftly and deeply. It was the only way to survive.

Ensign Ro went straight to Ten-Forward after her shift was over. She needed to talk to someone, and Guinan always seemed willing to listen.

Guinan was still listening even after Ro downed her first synthale and exhaled a litany of complaints.

"And here's the worst part," Ro exclaimed. "Captain Picard is actually letting Worf take them around the ship. They'll see everything!"

"Hardly 'everything,' I would imagine," Guinan said evenly.

"But Worf says the one in command talks all the time into a subdural implant. He's taking notes!"

"Well, they haven't been in here yet," Guinan pointed out, serving Ro another synthale. "Even though the reception is about to start."

"The other place they didn't go was to engineering," Ro said darkly. "I would have filed an official protest if they had. But I would have had to get in line after Worf. He's the only one who's taking this threat seriously."

"Laren, we're at peace with these people."

Ro rolled her eyes. "Well, *my* people are at war with them. I thought you would understand, Guinan. I bet *you'd* have a hard time making friends with the Borg."

Guinan shrugged one shoulder. "You might be right

about that. But the Borg haven't signed a truce with the Federation. The Cardassians have."

Guinan excused herself to complete the last-minute preparations for the reception.

Ro decided to hang around and see what happened. She didn't bother returning to her quarters to change, although she noticed that Counselor Troi had showed up in a fancy dress with her hair piled on top of her head. Ro wasn't sure why Troi made the effort. However, Ro approved of Worf's precautions. The big Klingon was already waiting near the door, having secured the large room.

She sat down at a small table where she could see the entire room. Sipping the Bajoran synthale, she savored the blue liquid. In prison, they had not been allowed luxuries like this. Funny how her current privleges reminded her of her past mistake. Commander Riker would certainly never let her forget it. She was glad that Riker wasn't going to be here tonight, though she wondered how he was doing. Stabilized but bedridden, were the rumors she had heard. Apparently it wasn't contagious, or the crew would have been alerted. It was probably just some noxious Cardassian bug.

"Speaking of noxious Cardassian bugs," Ro muttered under her breath as the two "guests" entered 10-Forward.

Captain Picard was right behind them. Apparently, he had come straight from the bridge. The Cardassian warship was still in the sector, though it had moved on around the Badlands, continuing its search for the Bajoran terrorists. Ro only hoped the trail had grown cold.

She sullenly watched the exchange of pleasantries, noting how easily Counselor Troi conversed with Jos Mengred. The other senior officers were introduced, except for Commander Data and Dr. Crusher. She overheard Troi explaining that their senior medical officer was still engaged in researching Riker's illness.

Ro tightened her fingers around the glass, draining it. They shouldn't show such weakness in front of the Cardassians!

Troi took both Cardassians to the bar, where Guinan greeted them with a placid smile. *Traitor,* Ro thought.

Both Cardassians ordered kanar, and Guinan fetched the tiny glasses full of the Cardassian beverage. They took sips and complimented Troi and Guinan on its authentic taste. Then the tall one smiled blandly around Ten-Forward, knowing he was the center of attention. The short one stayed in his shadow.

Ro stared at them with a sneer on her face. She didn't care when Counselor Troi stepped into her line of sight, making a clear signal for Ro to stop. Ro was more covert after that, but she made sure that every time the Cardassians glanced in her direction, they knew they weren't wanted by at least one crew member.

As the Cardassians made their way around the room, meeting the officers, Ro drained her glass and prepared to stalk out in protest. But to her horror, the short, stocky Cardassian drifted in her direction. She scowled at him, outraged that he would even think about approaching her.

Pakat paused right next to her table. His voice was

low and gravelly, as if something had permanently constricted his throat. "We didn't know that any Bajorans were on the *Enterprise*."

"I guess you don't know much, do you?" Ro said tightly.

His eyes wandered over her earrings and down her neck, to the rank insignia. "You are a Starfleet officer? Or is that uniform a courtesy?"

"Courtesy! I went through four years of Starfleet Academy."

Pakat looked at her and shook his head, as if he couldn't believe it.

"Look, *you*," Ro said bluntly. "Don't talk to me. Don't come near me. I don't want anything to do with your kind."

A spark seemed to light Pakat's eyes, and he actually moved closer. "Is that how it is? It has been a long voyage for me, too."

She pulled back. "Back off, lackwit."

He licked his lips, looking at her mouth. "I have not been with a Bajoran for quite some time."

She would have tossed her synthale in his face, but unfortunately her glass was empty.

Instead Ro shouted, "Get away from me!"

Everyone in Ten-Forward turned to look. She flung aside her chair and marched across the lounge. Somehow, the other Cardassian managed to stop her before she could reach the door.

"Get out of my way," she ordered.

"I must apologize for the misunderstanding," the tall Cardassian said, keeping his distance and holding his hands wide. He was clearly speaking for the benefit of the aghast onlookers in the lounge. "Among my people, irritation between a strange man and woman is taken as an indication of . . . mutual attraction."

Ro went nearly blind with rage. She had heard about Cardassians becoming more excited when women fought them. "Well, I'm *not* interested," she said through her clenched teeth. "Both of you, *stay away from me!*"

As Ro left, she could hear Counselor Troi apologizing to Mengred for her outburst. Ro wanted to turn back and make another scene, but she restrained herself. That would play right into their hands, making her look bad while the Cardassians acted like the injured party. They were tricky that way.

She hurried back to her own quarters, determined to stay right there as much as possible while they were on board. She would not open herself again to baseless Cardassian insults. She only hoped the *Enterprise* would survive this experience.

Chapter Six

DATA WAS AT the computer panel in his quarters long after the reception had begun in Ten-Forward. But he was completing the assignment the captain had given him earlier, to find out more about the subspace wave that had disabled the *Hawking*.

He discovered that thirty-three years prior to their survey mission, the Federation science vessel *Yosemite* had investigated the Badlands. The *Yosemite* was the first ship to explore the interior of the plasma storms, yet it was too large to penetrate more than 100,000 kilometers inside. So the *Yosemite* had explored the border regions and the vast sensor shadow surrounding the plasma storms.

When the *Yosemite* emerged from the Badlands she stalled, and it took several days for them to clean the clogged plasma from their warp nacelles. They remained inside the sensor shadow of the Badlands so they could continue to monitor the plasma discharge rate through special probes they had planted along the border.

They had almost completed the job when a subspace incursion, lasting nearly two seconds, had disrupted their power systems. After repairing their vessel, the crew of the *Yosemite* had completed their science mission without any additional incidents.

Since their probes had recorded many high-level discharges within the sensor shadow, the science team of the *Yosemite* theorized that the energized plasma created subspace incursions. It was similar to the way warp engines used plasma—created from matter and anti-matter—to generate the intense asymmetrical spatial distortion that imparted velocities through subspace.

Captain Indul, of the newly commissioned *Yosemite*, stated in her log that it was possible the ship had attracted the subspace discharge. She compared it to a lightning rod that formed the arcing point in a terrestrial electrical discharge.

Data created a simulation from the *Yosemite's* data and ran the same scenario for a vessel the size of the *Hawking*. When he compared the results to the logs during the power disruption of the *Hawking*, the data were identical.

Data believed that explained what had occurred to disrupt the systems of the *Hawking*. Captain Indul had theorized that direct hull exposure to the plasma fields increased the likelihood that a discharge would occur. Data intended to investigate that possibility further.

However, when he consulted the *Yosemite's* medical logs, there were no reported incidents of illness among the twenty-four crew members. Data soon determined that a subspace plasma discharge would not be a biological hazard.

Which indicated that Commander Riker's illness sprang from another cause.

Data downloaded his findings and completed his report, then sent it priority to both Captain Picard and Dr. Crusher.

Then he prepared himself for the reception. He was not worried about Commander Riker in the way a human would be. But he was concerned.

Before leaving his quarters, Data paused to tap his comm badge. "Data to Commander Riker."

"Riker here."

"Do you require any assistance, Commander?"

Riker chuckled weakly. *"Data, I'm flat on my back in sickbay. I wish there was something you could do about it."*

"Perhaps I can be of some use," Data said evenly. "I will come to see you after the reception."

There was a pause, then Riker said, *"Thanks, Data. I'd appreciate that."*

Data closed the channel. Before leaving, he made sure that Spot had plenty of water and that the nibbles she preferred this week were piled in her bowl. He wasn't human, with all the love and sorrow that implied, but at least he could be a responsible sentient being.

* * *

Dr. Crusher entered the latest diagnostic into the medical console. "Compare to diagnostic of Riker, William T. taken at 0430."

Crusher leaned back against the padding of her chair and closed her eyes. She had been working on the problem since the shuttlecraft had returned, and she still didn't have a solution that she could live with. Data's report, with the explanation of what had happened to the *Hawking*, only made things worse—

"Doctor?" Crusher opened her eyes to see Captain Picard standing at the door. "If this isn't a good time . . ."

"No," she said, sitting forward and straightening her coat. "Just taking a breather."

Picard entered and sat down opposite her desk. He looked tired, too.

"Did you just come from the reception?" she asked.

"Yes, such as it was." Picard tried to smile but couldn't. "It started out beautifully. Then there was a scene between Ensign Ro and the Cardassian named Pakat."

"Oh, my . . ."

"Pakat thought she was making . . . romantic advances, and he responded in kind."

"Oh, my!"

"Apparently Cardassians interperate irritation as some form of . . . flirtation."

Crusher was trying to absorb the image of a Cardassian flirting with Ensign Ro, and found she couldn't. "I'll try to keep that in mind."

"Do," Picard dryly advised.

Crusher was sorry she had missed it, but she was much too worried about Riker to think about anything else. "Jean-Luc, I don't know what to do about Will."

"Yes, I read your last report. You still don't know the cause of the cellular degradation? What about the radiation exposure you recorded?"

"The radicals disappeared extremely quickly," Dr. Crusher explained. "Likely it came from the invasive scans the Cardassians use. But there's something more serious going on here." The computer signaled that the diagnostic comparison was over. She examined the results for a moment, then turned the monitor so the captain could see.

"This indicates the rate of cellular degradation," she explained, pointing to a rapidly rising spike. "That's exponentially faster than any known EM exposure could cause. And there're other symptoms . . . ringing in the ears, itching and swelling of his toes and fingers. These symptoms fit nearly seven hundred thousand known ailments in the Starfleet medical database."

Picard shook his head. "I had hoped the runabout logs would shed some light on what happened."

"According to the *Hawking's* internal sensors, they encountered no unusual levels of electromagnetic energy. No anomalous readings at all, except for the odd subspace incursion that disabled the shuttlecraft."

Picard nodded. "And Data found an explanation for that in the *Yosemite* logs."

Crusher leaned forward. "So I ran a comparison of Riker's symptoms with case studies associated with Cardassians. Unfortunately, I came up with Myers disease."

"Myers?"

"Ambassador Myers spent a month on Cardassia Prime during the early negotiations of the peace treaty. He became sick with many of the same symptoms: vestibular disturbances in his neurons creating periods of disorientation and overstimulation of the nerves of the skin. The balance centers of the inner ear that contain otoliths were also affected, causing bouts of nausea and dizziness."

"Is this disease infectious?"

"No, according to every indication I can find, you have to ingest the microorganism."

"Ingest?" Picard asked.

"Riker says he drank some water while he was on the Cardassian warship. Data reports giving him additional water while the symptoms grew worse."

"They don't cleanse their supplies?" Picard asked in surprise.

"Well, Cardassians who get into space have already been exposed and are immune to the disease." She tightened her lips briefly. "Most of their medical literature boils down to 'survival of the fittest.' "

"Cardassians are notorious for valuing only the healthy members of their society." Picard considered the situation. "Do you believe the delay in treatment may have adversely affected Riker's condition?"

"Undoubtedly. He should have been treated immediately. That could have retarded the cellular degradation, though it couldn't have stopped the infectious agent from taking hold. But you should see him. He has terrible sores on his upper body, and I had to shave his beard off."

Picard glanced toward the sickbay. "What do the Cardassians say about this so-called Myers disease?"

"Apparently, they can carry the microorganism in their bloodstream without knowing it. Most Cardassians find out when they go into space, since it's triggered by pressure or gravity changes."

Picard stood up and walked over to the wall to avoid looking at her for a moment. Crusher understood, and she braced herself for the worst to come.

"So what is the treatment for Myers disease?" Picard finally asked.

"I can treat the symptoms, ease the pain somewhat. But Jean-Luc, there is no cure. It's an episodic, progressive disease that returns in short cycles. Ambassador Myers can no longer travel in space because of his sensitivity to pressure changes and gravity fluctuations."

Picard grew visibly alarmed, obviously thinking about Will Riker, the ultimate adventurer, confined to one planet for the rest of his life. "Have you told him?"

"I don't want to alarm him until I have no other possible explanation. If it is Myers, we won't know for sure for a few weeks, when it recurs. But I may have a preliminary diagnosis soon. I have a few more leads to run down. By morning I'll know."

"Keep me informed," Picard said.

"In the meantime, I think I should talk to him," she said, getting up to join Picard. "He's going a little stir crazy. He needs reminders to just take it easy until I have some real information for him."

Picard hesitated, and she understood why. She

would have a hard time speaking to Riker, knowing that he might never recover. If that happened, he would have to leave the *Enterprise*.

"No Beverly, let me," Picard objected.

That was Jean-Luc for you. He always accepted the responsibilities that landed in his path, no matter what they were.

"All right, but I've got to run another scan on him anyway," she said. "So I'll come with you."

Riker kept rubbing his chin and jaw. After several years of wearing a beard, it felt strange to be clean-shaven. At least rubbing his chin kept him from scratching the itchy spots that had appeared on his arms and chest. Dr. Crusher had sealed up the sores but the nerves were overstimulated and had not yet completely healed.

Dr. Crusher appeared from her office, along with Captain Picard.

Riker tried to sit up, but the doctor immediately ordered, "Lie back down. How many times have I told you to relax?"

"I've lost track, doctor. I keep hoping you'll give up." Riker tried to smile as usual as he lay back. But he could tell from Captain Picard's shocked expression that he wasn't fooling anyone.

Dr. Crusher busied herself with the medical scan, which Riker tried to ignore. They had prodded, poked, injected, and sucked tissue and blood from him until he thought he would run dry.

"The doctor says I can get out of here tomorrow," Riker told the captain.

"You *may* be able to return to your own quarters," Crusher corrected him.

"That's good," Riker said. "Nothing personal, Doctor, but I don't like being around sick people."

Dr. Crusher and Picard exchanged a glance, but neither said anything.

"So do you have any ideas what's causing this?" Riker asked, looking from one to the other.

"My diagnostic should be done by morning," Dr. Crusher assured him again. "So I'd better get on with it."

Dr. Crusher pocketed the scanner and returned to her office. Captain Picard remained standing next to the biobed.

"What's the situation with the Cardassians, Captain?" Riker had been thinking of little else since the last of the nausea and fever had eased under Dr. Crusher's ministrations. He was starting to chafe at being confined to sickbay. It was frustrating to be too weak to walk without help.

"The Cardassians are observing us," Picard admitted wryly.

"I hope that's all they're doing," Riker said darkly. He winced as he eased into a more comfortable position.

Picard lowered his voice. "I intend to lodge a formal complaint over their negligence towards you, Commander. Data said you were in pain for quite some time before they responded."

"I think it was part of their plan." Riker tried to push himself up straighter. "Sir, the Cardassians are known to use subspace carrier waves to deploy their weapons." Picard was looking down. "I think that's what caused my injury."

"Perhaps," Picard said. "Yet Commander Data has examined the sensor logs of the *Hawking*, and he has located another instance of a brief subspace disruption when the science vessel, *Yosemite*, was investigating the plasma storms. Their theory is that close proximity to the leading edge of the plasma storms, where the discharge is erratic and powerful, can affect subspace. These incursions can overload conventional power circuits."

"Yes, but the Cardassians were right there," Riker insisted. "And what about the way they treated us? Data says they were scanning us the entire time."

"You can relax, Will," the captain assured him. "We're all working to find a solution to this. Meanwhile, you look like you feel better than you did this afternoon."

Riker knew what the captain was saying. He may feel better, but he looked even worse. "I just hope I'm out of here tomorrow, even if I'm in my quarters—I can work there." He lowered his voice, glancing around to be sure no one could hear. "The latest intelligence says that the Cardassians have been experimenting with genetic weapons. Is it possible to deliver a genetic weapon through a subspace carrier wave? This problem I've got involves cellular degradation down to the DNA level. . . ."

"I'm sure Dr. Crusher is investigating all the possibilities," Picard assured him.

Riker kept trying to talk to Picard about the Cardassians, but the captain was strangely reluctant to discuss them. Crusher must have instructed Picard not to get him excited.

"Thank you for stopping by, Captain," Riker finally said, extending a hand.

Picard gingerly squeezed it. "I'll see you tomorrow, Will."

Then Riker was left alone, waiting for Data to stop by after the reception, as he had promised. Riker planned to ask Data to calibrate a Class II probe with enhanced long-range particle and field detectors. They could send it to the coordinates where the *Hawking* had been when it was hit by the subspace disruption. Perhaps the probe could track the particle residue back to the source.

He had intended to clear it with Picard, but the captain had more important things on his mind. Riker decided to speak to Data first, to set up the probe; then he would ask the captain.

Riker rubbed the edge of his chin. Waiting patiently was difficult for him, but he had learned at Starfleet Academy how to deal with inactivity. As long as it didn't last *too* long.

Chapter Seven

DEANNA TROI was sipping the last of her Gavaline tea, a favorite of her mother's. She smiled, thinking about their Cardassian guests waking up to a glass of fresh fish juice. She had learned a great deal about Cardassians last night, and had stayed in Ten-Forward until Jos Mengred and his aide, Pakat, finally retired.

"Dr. Crusher to Counselor Troi."

"Troi here," she said, setting down the cup of tea.

"Could you come to sickbay, Deanna?"

"Now?"

"Yes, please. It's urgent."

"On my way," she confirmed.

Quickly, Troi hopped a turbolift down to sickbay, absently nodding to crew members she passed on the way. She knew all of them. Many had shared some of their most private thoughts and feelings with her, so they viewed her as a close friend. Sometimes that made it difficult for her to walk through the corridors when her mind was on other things.

Right now, Troi was thinking about Will Riker. She had a bad feeling about this. Troi had consulted with Dr. Crusher yesterday, and the doctor had been very worried. She had promised to offer a diagnosis by this morning.

When Deanna saw Beverly, she became even more concerned. Dr. Crusher was visibly shaken, and Troi didn't need empathic powers to see that something very upsetting had occurred.

But when Dr. Crusher explained that Riker might have Myers disease, Troi's heart almost stood still. She had heard about Ambassador Myers' misfortune through diplomatic circles. She was as concerned as Starfleet about the wave of terrible diseases that had been unleashed on Federation humanoids once they began coming in physical contact with Cardassians.

"There is no cure, is there?" Troi asked, though she already knew the answer.

"Not yet, but I'm working on a treatment protocol." Crusher said grimly. "He's feeling better this morning. That makes it even harder. I had to tell him that Myers is known to be deceptive in its episodic attacks."

"Where is he?" Deanna asked, glancing into the sickbay. Riker was not in the main wardroom.

"He left. The computer says he's in his room, but he claimed he was going back on duty. I ordered the computer to override his commands." Dr. Crusher rubbed her eyes, which were reddened from staying up all night. "He went off swearing that he would find out what the Cardassians had done to him. I couldn't stop him. I hope he's all right."

"It must be a shock for him," Troi said, feeling stunned herself.

"I had intended to have you here when I told him," the doctor worried, "but he practically ambushed me as soon as I arrived. I didn't have time to call you—or security."

Troi made the appropriate soothing remarks. Beverly had obviously been working hard trying to find another explanation for Riker's illness.

"I'll go talk to him now," Troi added. "How sure are you about this diagnosis?"

"It's my chief suspect, but I'm not entirely convinced yet. He tested negative for the infectious agent, but the virus is notoriously difficult to detect." She shrugged in resignation. "However, the symptoms fit perfectly with Myers disease. If there is a reoccurrence, then we'll know for certain."

On the way to Riker's quarters, Troi kept hearing the dire tone in Crusher's voice, and the feeling of dread she sensed inside of her. Dr. Crusher didn't think there was much hope for Riker.

Troi steeled herself before signaling his door.

It took a few moments, but then Riker defiantly called out, "Come in!"

She carefully stepped over the threshold, unsure of what to expect. "Hi, Will."

Riker took one look at her and laughed shortly. "I should have known the doctor would sic you on me."

Troi was startled to see him without a beard, and

suddenly she realized she liked him much better without it. He looked younger this way, more vulnerable, like the Riker she once knew.

Then on closer examination, she realized that otherwise he looked awful. There was a reddened blotch on one cheekbone, and his neck seemed mottled, too. His general appearance was disheveled. He was wearing his favorite blue shirt, but it looked wrinkled.

"I'm not going back to sickbay," he told her flatly, pacing back and forth through the living room.

Troi seated herself on the couch. "That's not the issue."

"Oh?" Riker raised one brow. "Then you're just here to analyze me."

"I thought you would want to talk about this, Will."

"Well, you can save your concern. I don't have Myers disease."

Troi tried to breathe regularly. It was difficult to block his turbulent emotions when she was this close to him. With others, it was easier to resist the emotional pain. But she had been intimate with Riker, and even though it was a long time ago, it left her somewhat more open to him.

"Why don't you think it's Myers disease?" she asked.

"The Cardassians did something to me," Riker insisted. "They disabled the shuttlecraft, and there's no telling what else they did while I was on that warship."

"Then why wasn't Data affected?" she asked.

Riker looked away. "That agent, Jos Mengred, he

was interested in Data. He may have given orders not to harm him."

Troi considered the problem. Riker was having a typical denial reaction. He didn't want to accept the possibility that he faced a life battling an incapacitating illness. And she didn't need to rush the process of acceptance.

"Well, at least you got a shave out of this," she said lightly.

"That's not all she threatened me with. Look at this!" His fingers ran through his hair, pulling out thick clumps. Hair shifted down to the carpet.

"Oh no," Troi whispered.

"Started last night. You should have seen my pillow this morning." He shook his head. "Dr. Crusher lasered off my beard while I was still half-delirious. She wanted to do my head this morning, but I left before she could get hold of the laser-cutter."

Troi went closer to see. His hair was falling out in clumps, leaving bare spots. That was partly why he looked so wild and unkempt.

"You know, if you cut it short, it won't be as likely to fall out," Deanna said evenly.

He started to run his hand through his hair, then reconsidered the damage that would cause. "I don't care if I go bald. I just want to find out what's going on."

"Well, you can't go around the ship looking like that," she said. "If you saw one of your officers in that condition, you would give them a demerit on the weekly crew report."

Riker relaxed slightly. "Yeah, I suppose that's true."

"Let me get you into ship-shape condition," Troi told him. "Where's your laser cutter?"

"I could go to the barber," Riker said warily.

Troi pushed him back down. "I'll have you know, I'm a talented hair stylist. I should have opened a little shop on Betazed." She rummaged through the top drawer. "Ah, here it is."

Troi made Riker sit down on the chair under the light. He seemed tense, but she keep talking about her cousin who had taught her how to cut hair. His shoulders seemed to ease after a while, as she expertly flashed the laser cutter along the ends of his hair. Riker had been wearing it longer lately, so she cut off quite a bit, leaving it only a centimeter along the sides, and a few centimeters on top.

"There, that looks wonderful on you," she told him, stepping back slightly. She didn't want to mention that the back of his head was quite bald in patches. From the front it looked good. "You look very tough. I'd say you could go completely smooth, but we don't want to threaten the captain."

Riker gave her a grateful smile. But she still sensed that edge in him that always wanted to maintain control. As he examined his much shorter hair in the mirror, he nodded in approval.

Then he glanced down at his wrinkled shirt. "I have to change into my uniform."

"Don't you think you should rest first?" Troi suggested. "You're still very ill. You would probably feel better if you lay down on the couch and relaxed."

"I have to find Data. He started work last night on

recalibrating a probe to look for subspace carrier wave particles." He went to his closet to get a uniform. "I have to find out what the Cardassians did to me."

"You've been ordered to stay off duty."

"I know. I'm not going to the bridge." Riker pulled out a red-and-black uniform and went into the other room to change.

Troi hesitated, wondering if she should call Dr. Crusher. But unless Crusher sedated him again, Riker wouldn't stand for bed rest right now. He needed something to occupy his mind.

"As long as you alert sickbay if you start to feel worse," she called.

He emerged, looking pale but competent. "I'm fine."

She stopped him at the door. "I mean it, Will."

Impatiently he nodded. "I understand. I'll check on Data, then come back here to work. Does that make you feel better?"

"Yes." But she didn't feel better. She paused in the corridor watching him walk to the turbolift. He stood very tall, and her heart ached for him at the sight of the bald patches on the back of his head. He was trying so hard to not think about the worst because the worst was unthinkable. She wasn't sure what else she could do to help him.

She sighed as he disappeared into the turbolift. Captain Picard should be immediately informed about Riker's reaction to the bad news, she thought, even if it did make her late for her appointment with Ensign Ro. After the reception last night, the captain had asked her to have a talk with Ro.

Troi wasn't sure what she could do to help the ensign, either. When a humanoid went through the terrible things that Ro had experienced under the Cardassian occupation a full recovery was problematic. Ro had worked out some form of socialization, and she had made it through the Academy, but Troi had serious doubts about Ro's long term stability. In Troi's opinion, Ro was a time bomb that could go off at any moment.

Jos Mengred decided to visit Counselor Troi first thing in the morning. The Betazoid had been very accommodating last night, much more cosmopolitan than the other crewmembers, including Captain Picard. And she was the ship's counselor, with intimate knowledge of every person on board the *Enterprise.*

In many ways, Counselor Troi performed a similar function to his on board Commander Ocett's warship. Like Troi, he kept an eye on everyone and knew exactly what they wanted, what they felt, and what their weaknesses were.

Mengred dispatched Pakat to the bridge to oversee the survey operations. He didn't believe for a moment that it was a conicidence that the *Enterprise,* had been assigned an ordinary survey mission of the sector that just happened to border Cardassian space. But he was also quite sure that on the bridge, it would appear that a survey mission was underway.

Accompanied by one guard, Mengred proceeded to Counselor Troi's office. He was following instinct, as he usually did in his work. Over the years, as an agent for the Obsidian Order, he had realized that people subtly advertised the information that they held. The hard part was getting it out of them.

Even that wasn't so difficult once you knew what you were doing.

The office was open, so the guard escorted him inside. It took them a moment or two to ascertain that Counselor Troi was not yet in.

What trusting people, to leave their doors unlocked, Mengred thought. He would make the most of this opportunity.

The security guard, who had introduced herself as Lieutenant Rev, took up a station near the door. Mengred had tried talking to her, but she knew better than to do more than exchange a few pleasantries. Mengred understood security personnel—they were trained to be suspicious of friendly behavior. So after that, he maintained a wary silence with her, knowing that would soon lull her into complacency.

Mengred wandered around the spacious room. There were several sets of couches and chairs arranged for conversational purposes. At a sharp look from the guard, Mengred gave the counselor's desk with its computer monitor a wide berth.

A painting next to the security guard caught his attention. It was an image of Deanna Troi as seen from a distance. As he drew closer, the colors fragmented until they resolved into tiny dots of pure color.

"Very unusual," Mengred commented. Then he noticed the signature in the corner—Data. "The android did this?"

Rev glanced at Mengred, then the painting. "Yes, Commander Data is an artist."

Mengred waited until Rev's eyes slipped back to the painting. Then his thumb pressed the tip of his little finger. High frequency EM waves were emitted.

Rev hesitated, her gaze fixed on the painting. Mengred cleared his throat, but she didn't move. The EM waves caused a vibration in the occipital bone at the base of the cranium through which the medulla oblongata passed, linking the spinal column with the brain. This vibration extended to the adjoining bones of the skull, interfering with the firing of neurons and sensory transmissions from the spinal column. The result was a fugue-like state that could last up to several minutes.

Mengred moved quickly around the desk. He knew he was risking discovery if the counselor returned or if Rev snapped out of the trance too soon. But it was worth the risk. He wasn't worried about the internal sensors—the range of the cone of EM stunning waves was very short, and it wasn't likely they had reached the sensors in the ceiling.

Mengred found a locked drawer and inserted the nail of his middle finger. He counted five heartbeats before the locking mechanism was triggered. On a Cardassian lock, it would have taken at least a dozen heartbeats.

The drawer slid open, revealing a padd. Mengred accessed the short term memory systems. People rarely cleared out their short term files, and hand-held units were known to save up to several weeks worth of data automatically. Accessing the short-term memory wouldn't activate the computer uplink which could alert the counselor or security that someone was using her system.

He had to insert a virus that would open the data files when the proper code was supplied. He keyed in the code on the padd. A string of file-names of the latest data inputs appeared on the screen.

Mengred inserted the tip of his forefinger into the download port and copied the entire memory file into his fingertip database. He wiped the transaction from the memory file and shut down the unit.

He returned the padd to exactly the same position and closed the drawer. It locked automatically. How convenient. Now he wouldn't have to take the time to relock it.

Mengred hurried back to the security guard's side, and took up exactly the same position. So Rev wouldn't notice anything unusual, Mengred was turning away when Rev shook her head, coming out of the fugue state.

"Machines can do incredible things," Mengred said, gesturing back to the painting. "It's mesmerizing. . . ."

"Yes . . . ," Rev said, glancing from him to the painting again.

Mengred continued his tour of the room as if nothing had happened. Rev shook her head before resettling into her guard position. He was certain she was not aware of the lapse of time.

He sat down on the couch and pulled out his own hand unit. With his back turned to the guard, he inserted his finger-port. The information from the padd downloaded into his hand unit.

In no time, the latest entries were on his screen. Several were about Ensign Ro. Last week the Bajoran had been permanently assigned to the *Enterprise*. She had been present when Captain Picard had betrayed Admiral Kennelly's pact with the Obsidian Order. Kennelly had agreed that Starfleet would locate the terrorists and lure them out so Cardassian warships could destroy them.

As Mengred scanned the data on Ro, noting her discipline problems, he considered how unlikely it was that such a woman had destroyed Enabran Tain's carefully laid plans. Attacking the Federation outpost and making it look like Bajorans had done it had been easy compared to locating an admiral in Starfleet who could be swayed by Cardassian persuasion.

Mengred glanced up at the security guard and smiled. Rev had no idea he had just made off with a treasure trove of information.

He would have plenty of time later to assess the files he had obtained, but he enjoyed examining it right under Rev's eyes. He ran through the rest of the data files, picking up knowledge of crew weaknesses in several key leadership areas. He noted Troi's opinion of each officer or technician, but her rating system was soft, with carefully weighed pros and cons in each report.

Mengred paused when he crossed a name he knew— Lieutenant Worf. Troi was analyzing Worf's behavior during the recent conclusion of the Klingon civil war. Avidly, he read about the murder of K'Ehleyr, the mother of Worf's child. Troi mentioned that Worf was relieved that his family name was finally cleared when the Duras family challenge failed to gain the leadership of the Klingon High Council.

Tain will be pleased, Mengred thought. Cardassian knowledge of the details of the recent Klingon civil war was insufficient at best.

The last entry concerned Captain Jean-Luc Picard.

The entry was cryptic, but revealing. Troi had theorized that Picard's abduction by the Borg had revived his old fears of being drawn into his family's winemaking business and leading a life that was not his own. The Borg finally forced him to conform and subjugate his own will to that of the overpowering 'family,' the report noted.

So, a year after the Borg defeat at Wolf 359, Picard was still haunted by the memory of his assimilation. Tain would be pleased with that bit of information, too.

Mengred closed his hand unit, feeling quite invigorated. This assignment should offer no trouble at all.

He was further delighted when the door opened and Ensign Ro walked in. She stopped in midswagger, her mouth opening at the sight of Mengred.

Then she noticed the guard. "What are you doing here?" she demanded.

Counselor Troi's notations on the Bajoran were fresh in his mind. Mengred couldn't resist sowing some dissension among the crew. "I suppose I'm here for the same reason *you* are. Apparently Starfleet can't make up its mind between the Cardassians and the Bajorans."

Ro glared at him. "Starfleet knows better than to trust Cardassians."

Mengred stood up to go closer to her, knowing she would hate that. *"I'm* here, aren't I?"

"So is the guard," Ro shot back. "You notice there's no guard with me. I'm one of the crew."

The guard looked slightly uncomfortable, but she didn't interfere. Nearly professional quality, that one.

Mengred lowered his voice, moving closer to Ro. "I wonder at Starfleet's judgment. Reinstating you after you killed eight fellow officers. To me, that would seem to be the act of an enemy."

She was shaking, her hands clenched. "You would know. Cardassians know all about *killing.*"

"Really, my dear, you should control yourself." He laughed. "No wonder my aide was entranced by you. You have the most lovely flush when you're angry. . . ."

Ro raised her hand to strike him.

"Ensign!" The guard moved forward. "I think you should reconsider what you're doing."

Ro dropped her hand, and Mengred allowed himself to smile at her.

Ro stalked out of the counselor's office. In the corridor, Mengred could still hear someone calling for Ensign Ro to stop. Deanna Troi appeared in the open doorway. She took one look at Mengred, who raised his palms up innocently, then at the guard who was obviously on alert.

"What happened?" Troi asked.

Ro was standing in the corridor behind Troi, her arms folded and her head averted.

"I don't think Ensign Ro likes Cardassians." Mengred took the opportunity to make an exit. "I can see you are busy. Perhaps we can speak later."

Troi obligingly let him go. Mengred was pleased. He had everything he needed from her for the moment, and he liked leaving the situation in such discord.

The guard followed him out of the counselor's office like a silent shadow. It was almost like having his aide with him.

Further down the corridor, Mengred paused by a comm panel to ask, "Where is Commander Data?"

A female computerized voice answered, *"Commander Data is off-duty and is presently in the science lab."*

"Where is Lieutenant Worf?" he asked, unconcerned about the guard overhearing. Any second-rate intelligence agent would be able to predict the key people he would be interested in.

"Lieutenant Worf is on duty on the bridge."

Mengred knew that Data was the one he most wanted to investigate, but that would reveal too much, too soon. So he waved a hand at the guard without looking at her. "Show me to the bridge."

"This way," Rev replied evenly.

The guard led him down the corridor. Mengred felt his lip curl at the softness of Starfleet, from the pastel-colored walls and the springy flooring underfoot to the children running through the halls. Children! He heard laughter, and singing, even music. So many soft, murmuring voices. Where was the ring of boots, the brisk pace, and the crisp efficiency of military command?

He had been less than one day on board and already he felt nothing but contempt for these people. They may be more numerous, their territory far-flung and incorporating many different beings, but their foundation was *weak.*

Worf had determined that adequate security could only be maintained by enabling a continuous computer surveillance of the whereabouts of each Cardassian. The program was instructed to alert security if one of the Cardassians went into a restricted area, such as engineering or the weapons locker. The program was also instructed to alert security if the Cardassians attempted to access the computer.

The program displays included a moving blueprint of each deck as the Cardassians proceeded through the ship. There was also the on-board profile of the *Enterprise,* with tiny red flashing lights to indicate the location of each Cardassian. Each one was accompanied by a yellow light denoting security personnel.

One red light was on the bridge. Worf glanced covertly at Pakat in the command well below the tactical station. He was seated to the left of Captain Picard. Security Guard Zee was appointed to Pakat for this half-shift, and he stood poised at the end of the tactical station, watching the Cardassian's every move.

Worf knew Zee was prepared to jump the railing at the first wrong move Pakat made. Both Zee and Worf had tensed when Picard invited the Cardassian to sit within arm's range. But command had its privileges, even if it made it harder for everyone else to do their duty.

The other red light was moving up through the

decks. Jos Mengred had been in the counselor's office for twenty minutes, and was now on his way to the bridge. From the life-signs readout on the bottom of his monitor, Worf could tell that a Bajoran had entered and left, then a Betazoid and a Bajoran had entered as Mengred had departed. Worf knew that Lieutenant Rev would submit a report on what had occurred when she was relieved of security duty at half-shift.

"Proceed at full impulse power," Picard ordered.

"Aye, sir," helm replied.

The *Enterprise* was entering the Phylaris system, a G-type star. Their preliminary scan from outside the system indicated the star could have a class M planet in orbit. Worf was running the usual security protocols when entering an unexplored system. He was actively scanning for wave and particle emissions within the solar system, attempting to detect artificial sources of energy.

But at least half his control/display panel was occupied with tracking the Cardassians on board. He also kept several long-range sensors focused on the *Galor*-class warship whenever it emerged from the sensor shadow of the distant Badlands.

As the red indicator light representing Mengred reached the bridge level, Worf reduced the tracking program to a small cryptic readout on his panel. The turbolift opened and Mengred stepped onto the bridge. The agent for the Obsidian Order got a good look around.

"Captain Picard, Jos Mengred is on the bridge," Worf reported.

"So this is the bridge . . . ," Mengred said speculatively.

Picard looked back over his shoulder at Mengred. "You are welcome to join us."

Worf was proud of his foresight when Mengred approached a few steps closer to the tactical station. "May I stand here?" he asked courteously.

Worf said, "As you wish."

Security Guard Zee moved over, keeping his eyes on Pakat. When Zee didn't as much as glance at Mengred, Worf decided to commend him in his next report. Zee obviously trusted his fellow security officer, Lieutenant Rev, who was assigned to guard Mengred. Rev was already positioned at the back wall of the bridge; her eyes narrowed as she watched Mengred. She was clearly on the alert.

Worf quickly disengaged some operations, unwilling to let Mengred see their full detection capabilities. Meanwhile Mengred sauntered over to where he could casually examine the tactical readouts.

"Ah, the Phylaris system," Mengred said thoughtfully.

"You are familiar with this system?" Captain Picard asked.

"I know it offers nothing of any value," Mengred said. "No convenient moons to place a starbase. No planets worth colonizing."

At ops, Ensign Lita said, "I'm reading a Class-M planet, sir. Atmosphere ten percent oxygen, twenty percent nitrogen dioxide, fifty-seven percent CO_2. Almost five percent water molecules."

"Take us in closer," Picard ordered.

Mengred's voice cut through the bridge. "Don't waste your time. The land and plants are acid-based."

"I see," Picard said lightly. "Well, that is why we are here. To examine this planet."

Worf noted that everyone performed their duties with an efficiency tinged with tension. The Cardassians had transformed a relaxing survey mission into a diplomatic nightmare.

"Entering orbit, Captain," helm reported.

Worf was already programming a Class-III sensor probe. "Sensor prepared, sir."

Worf thought Mengred looked amused as the probe was deployed into the upper atmosphere. The data were meticulously gathered, with regular reports to the captain along the way. The planetary science lab would be thrilled with data from a new planet. Worf was not quite as excited.

When the probe was deployed into the lower atmosphere, there were increased readings of acid-based proteins. Shortly after the probe landed, the unit reported a highly acidic soil and atmosphere. Thereafter it began to malfunction, and soon ceased transmission altogether.

"This system has no tactical use, anyway," Mengred dismissed.

"That is true," Worf admitted reluctantly, having already reached that conclusion after examining the star chart. The system was strangely isolated, cut off from the closest star systems by the Badlands.

"Why don't you survey the plasma storms instead?"

Mengred asked Worf. "The systems inside have many strategic possibilities."

Captain Picard turned to answer him, "Commanders Riker and Data performed our preliminary survey of the plasma storms. While that data is being assessed, we are examining the rest of this sector."

Worf shifted uneasily as Mengred more or less rolled his eyes at Picard's answer. From that reaction and other things Mengred said over the next few hours, Worf got the distinct feeling that the agent thought the *Enterprise* was wasting valuable time.

He wouldn't dream of saying so aloud, but Worf was inclined to agree. It was clear that the system was uninhabited and uninhabitable. But there were survey protocols that had to be followed.

When they finished with the Phylaris system, Captain Picard ordered the Enterprise to set course for the Moriya system, on the far edge of the Badlands. Worf believed the Terikof Belt around the Moriya system would offer strategic possibilities, but the Cardassians already had mining claims in the area. The distant Kamiat Nebula would be surveyed after Moriya, and that too offered certain strategic possibilities.

While they were en route to Moriya, Captain Picard retired to his ready room, leaving the bridge to the crew. They wouldn't reach the Terikof belt until well into the next duty shift.

Mengred waited until Picard was gone to observe, "Starfleet certainly isn't a military organization."

Worf quoted from the book, "Starfleet Command is

the operating authority for the scientific, exploratory, and defensive activities of the Federation."

"Science, exploration, and defense," Mengred mused. "Not the sort of place I would expect to find a warrior."

Worf went rigid with resentment at the dig, and he refused to reply.

"I would think you'd take your rightful position in the Klingon Empire," Mengred told him. "Now that your people's difficulties are over. Surely a warrior such as yourself would be in command of his own ship."

Worf turned to face the Cardassian, noting Mengred's hungry eyes, looking for signs that he had struck a nerve. It reminded Worf of Klingon testing behavior, leading up to a physical confrontation. He could not allow things to escalate to that point in this situation.

"I will not discuss Klingon matters with you," Worf said quietly. Then he turned back to his station.

"Perhaps you aren't a warrior after all," Mengred said thoughtfully.

Worf whipped around so fast that the Cardassian was caught off guard. "Pahtk! You are without honor or you would not make a challenge you know I cannot accept."

Everyone on the bridge heard him. Worf was determined not to listen to the *pugh*, and though the Cardassian's lips moved, he did not hear him. Worf continued working, concentrating on his panel, coordinating with the science team to survey the approaching nebula.

When Mengred finally left the bridge, ordering Pakat to remain behind, Worf immediately enlarged the tracking monitor. The security chief was even more determined to know exactly where the Cardassians were at all times. He was certain that Mengred was not just here to observe. Mengred clearly had a goal to achieve, and it was Worf's duty to prevent him from harming the *Enterprise* in the process.

Chapter Eight

DATA WAS in command of the bridge during third shift. After several days spent surveying the rest of the Badlands sector, the plasma storms filled the viewscreen once again. For the past few days, science personnel had been busy at their monitors along the rear wall of the bridge, studying the plasma storms. Now they were gathering the last data they could obtain as they completed their circuit of the Badlands. Next, they would proceed to the rendezvous coordinates where the two Cardassians would be returned to their ship.

For Data, it had been a most intriguing week. He noted the varied reactions of the crew toward the Cardassians. Few people actively engaged them in conversation. Most avoided them, leaving Ten-Forward or the arboretum whenever one of the Cardassians appeared.

The exception was Counselor Troi. She had been unfailingly polite to them and generous with her time. The counselor had reported that Mengred's interests seemed general, but she noted a tendency for him to search out information about Data. Data suspected that even if he were human, he would not have been flattered by their attention.

"Prepared to launch probe number 22, Commander," the science officer announced.

"Execute," Data ordered. It was the twenty-second probe sent into the Badlands in the past few days. They were finally gaining an understanding of the complex plasma currents inside. There appeared to be hundreds of overlapping plasma storms, each with its own translational direction. Though the computer had created a navigational program, Captain Picard had vetoed another interior investigation.

At Commander Riker's insistence, Data had calibrated the long-range probes they deployed to include subroutines that searched for a wide range of residual particles from subspace carrier waves. Despite Data's report on the *Yosemite* and Crusher's opinion that he suffered from Myers disease, Riker remained convinced that the Cardassians had caused his injury.

As yet, none of the probes or modified sensor banks on the *Enterprise* had detected any form of subspace wave that could carry biological weapons. However, there was an increased level of tetryons in the region. Natural tetryon fields had been discovered in Federation territory, but tetryons were also indicators of subspace incursions. The findings were causing much excited speculation in the astrophysics lab. Studies continued to determine whether the plasma discharges were causing these increased levels.

"Probe launched," the science officer reported.

Data moved up to ops to monitor the telemetry himself. Maintaining a clear transmission from the probe continued to pose difficulties due to the interference. But Captain Picard had ordered the *Enterprise* to remain outside of the sensor shadow, to prevent a recurrence of the *Yosemite* and *Hawking* incidents.

Commander Riker was bitterly disappointed when the first probes returned no viable information. He had been very sick the first day after they returned from the Cardassian warship. He had only worked in the lab for a brief period of time before returning to his quarters. But Riker had monitored the telemetry, and Data had sent him regular reports as he analyzed the results.

Riker had finally returned to duty several days ago. He continued to call his illness an "injury." Data did not want to contradict the commander, but his recovery pattern conformed to the Cardassian syndrome that Starfleet called Myers disease. The symptoms usually went into remission for several weeks before returning as a chronic debilitating sickness.

"We've lost contact with probe 22, Commander," the science officer announced.

The flow of telemetry readings ceased. Data saved the information and sent it to the science lab.

"Acknowledged." Data ordered, "Helm, set a

course for the rendezvous coordinates. One-half impulse power."

The course he had plotted would allow the science team to continue to scan the Badlands for as long as possible. After dropping off the Cardassians, the *Enterprise* was scheduled to proceed to planet Melona IV to assist with preparations for a colonization project.

Data was monitoring the analysis of the data from the last probe, when the turbolift door opened, revealing Mengred. Mengred spent a great deal of Data's duty shift on the bridge. Data had duly reported to the captain the Cardassian's curiosity about cybernetics and his own operating systems. Picard had requested that Data submit daily transcripts of Mengred's questions.

"How are you functioning this evening?" Mengred asked.

"I am functioning normally," Data replied, as he always did.

Mengred made himself comfortable in the seat the counselor usually used. He didn't seem to mind that the entire bridge crew could hear him. "I thought you were assigned to two shifts because Commander Riker had weakened. But he is now back on duty, and you are still on two shifts."

Seated at ops, Data had to glance over his shoulder to see Mengred. "I customarily take two duty shifts."

"Ah . . . it makes sense for your superiors to assign you extra duty since you don't sleep." Mengred sounded pleased. "I suppose that in certain tactical or emergency situations you're ordered to work to all three shifts."

Data turned his chair. "I request an additional duty shift. I am not assigned extra duty."

"No?" Mengred asked slyly. "You must be aware of how they control you."

Data was uncertain how to respond to that comment, so he simply turned back to ops. The Cardassian warship entered the range of their long-range sensors, having disappeared on the other side of the Badlands for the greater part of their survey mission. Data noted their course was set to intercept with the rendezvous coordinates.

Data's display panel was configured to suit his unique computational speed, with updates provided every .02 seconds. Because of that factor, and the special subroutine he had created to search for subspace particle waves, Data noted the spike in tetryon readings. They surged over 1,000 percent above normal, overloading the sensors.

Data was able to detect a disruption in the gravitational field. The gravity on board the *Enterprise* ceased.

As the gravity field inverted, Data noted that the sensors remained off-line. The power conduits in major systems all over the ship went down.

Data braced himself, holding onto his seat with one hand as he rapidly tapped in commands on the panel. He was attempting to locate the directional source for the subspace tetryon wave.

Several crew members let out cries of surprise or pain as they were lofted into the air. Peripherally, Data noted that the ensign at the helm was flailing her legs, sending herself spinning backward.

Data took over control of the helm.

The computer automatically began announcing Red Alert as the warp engines went off line. Since they were under impulse power, Data had to transfer primary systems from the idling warp engines to the impulse generators. At the same time, he brought them out of sublight speed, letting the *Enterprise* come to a halt. His primary concern was the warp core and the overloaded main EPS taps. But since they had not been traveling at warp, the plasma was already being valved off from the warp core.

After 5.4 seconds, gravity recommenced on board the *Enterprise*.

Data evaluated the sensor systems as the bridge officers began to pick themselves up from the deck. After the initial burst of tetryon particles, sensors had been overloaded by a subspace shock wave.

Data initiated a level-one diagnostic of his own systems. It would take two hours to complete, but a high-level diagnostic could provide additional information on what had occurred while the ship's sensors were offline.

"Captain Picard," Data announced. "Please report to the bridge."

Jos Mengred managed to get up, despite the shooting pain in his leg. "What happened?" he demanded.

"Unknown," the android replied.

Mengred shook his head, unable to focus on the android's rapidly moving hands as he controlled the vast starship. The bridge crew staggered back to their panels and tried to orient themselves. Mengred thought it was good proof of the android's capabilities. He hadn't even shifted in his seat—while everyone else on the bridge had been tossed about like bungi beans.

Damage reports were starting to come in. Mengred could hear Data acknowledging each deck officer and giving orders for damage control.

"Status report," Mengred ordered.

The android ignored him, his hands flashing over the panel. Mengred knew the android was deliberately refusing to answer. He had come to expect such a response. Even in the heat of the crisis, the android wouldn't yield command of the bridge. It was quite an admirable creation.

Mengred was sorry he would have to leave the *Enterprise* in a few more hours. But the length of time had been predetermined between Starfleet and the Obsidian Order. Regardless, Mengred had gathered a great deal of valuable information on the crew and their operating systems. One didn't always need to break into a computer padd to gather the right information. All it took were carefully posed questions, never too many to the same individual.

He had discovered these people were astonishingly open. Even the ones who had showed a great deal of animosity toward him had provided valuable information. At first he had considered it another sign of weakness, but gradually he realized it was the result of overwhelming confidence. They were proud to be in

Starfleet, and utterly certain that the Federation would only grow stronger.

Mengred found this attitude refreshing. There was nothing like it in the Cardassian Empire, where no one was sure who was in charge or when a hand would fall on their shoulder with a summons to an investigation. In Cardassia, everyone looked to see who was watching them.

Starfleet was also much more efficient than he had given them credit for, despite their lack of military precision. Only a few moments passed and Captain Picard arrived with Commander Riker right behind him.

Riker stopped short when he saw Mengred. He asked the android, "Was *he* on the bridge when it happened?"

"Aye, sir." The android turned to Captain Picard. "You have the bridge, sir."

"Acknowledged." Picard glanced at Mengred.

For a moment, Mengred thought he would be ordered from the bridge. He settled back in his chair, determined that they would have to drag him off.

Captain Picard sighed. Apparently he decided that it wasn't worth the trouble to eject Mengred. "Status?" the captain asked.

"Warp drive and sensors are off-line. Impulse power at 80 percent, with main systems on auxiliary power. Shields are holding. We are drifting approximately 200,000 kilometers outside of the sensor shadow."

Mengred thought that was the model of a concise report. If only his operatives could be so succinct.

Riker glared at Mengred as he passed by. Mengred

smirked at the commander's shorn, patchy hair. He looked like a wet rabbit.

"Where is the Cardassian warship?" Riker demanded.

"Unknown," the android replied. "The warship was on long-range sensors when the phenomenon occurred."

"Just like before," Riker muttered suspiciously.

"What was it?" Picard asked quietly, standing next to Data at ops.

"Tetryon emissions surged for .02 seconds, sir, before the sensor banks became overloaded. The subspace shock wave disrupted the gravity field for 5.4 seconds."

Picard's tone remained even. "Can you determine the source of the tetryon emissions, Data?"

"Negative, sir. I did not have time to lock on sensors."

"When will sensors be back on-line?"

"We will have limited range momentarily, Captain."

Picard nodded shortly, returning to the command chair. They must have been asleep when the gravity went off, but the captain looked exactly the same as usual, calm and collected despite the emergency. Riker was clearly not as sharp. He was hunched in his seat, glancing at Mengred every now and again, barely restraining signs of his hostility and suspicion.

The rest of the senior bridge crew soon arrived to replace the night shift, including the Bajoran helmsman. She started in surprise when she saw Mengred, then resolutely jerked her chin away. She had refused to speak to him, though Mengred had tried, day after day. It had become quite fun tracking Ro down just so he could sit in her line of view. She was just about ready to snap. He knew the signs, and he was teasing out the last few comments, aware that he should be prepared to defend his life if she finally did attack him.

Worf was much cooler, belying the legendary Kling-on volatility. He took up his tactical station without making eye contact with Mengred. Worf had turned out to be a mystery to Mengred, much to his chagrin. Worf didn't fit the hard-drinking, boastful stereotype of a Klingon warrior. If anything, Worf was more proper and tightly wound than the other Starfleet officers.

When sensors came on line, the android announced that Gul Ocett's warship was still on course for the ren-dezvous coordinates.

"Hail them," Picard ordered.

"Aye, sir," Worf acknowledged.

It was not long before the starfield was replaced with the image of Gul Ocett. The viewscreen was tight on her face. "Yes, what is it?"

Mengred shook his head at her inept bluntness.

"Commander," Picard said, standing up. "The *Enterprise* just encountered a subspace tetryon shock wave. Do you know anything about it?"

Ocett's eyes narrowed. "Another shock wave?"

"Yes," Picard said, more intently. "Didn't your sensors read it?"

Ocett immediately turned away, and Mengred knew she was consulting with the tactical officer. After a moment she returned to the center of the screen. "We read nothing unusual. Only some minor subspace fluctuations."

"Commander . . . ," Picard said doubtfully. "It was strong enough to disrupt our sensors and overload our power conduits. You're telling me that you couldn't detect it?"

"We read nothing unusual," she repeated doggedly.

"She's lying," Riker said flatly. "It's the same thing they did to the *Hawking*. It must be some kind of new weapon. Ask him!" He jerked a thumb in Mengred's direction.

Picard turned thoughtfully. "Yes, Jos Mengred, tell Gul Ocett what happened."

He lifted the fingers of one hand. "The gravity went off."

"For 5.4 seconds," the android added helpfully.

Ocett looked highly suspicious. "We didn't detect anything. Perhaps it was a malfunction in your systems."

"A likely story," Riker muttered.

Picard held up one hand. "Data?"

"Negative, sir. The phenomenon was external to the ship's systems."

Picard turned back to Ocett. "You see why we are suspicious."

"*We* should be suspicious," Ocett retorted. "Twice you have claimed we have damaged you, and both times our sensors have detected nothing. Perhaps you look for a reason to fight. . . ."

"That's absurd!" Riker exclaimed in disdain.

Mengred watched the interplay carefully. He was uncertain of whom to trust. Could the android have caused the malfunction? It was certainly possible. His ability to stay seated when everyone else was flung into the air indicated he may have had prior knowledge of what was about to happen.

Then again, Gul Ocett could be testing a new military weapon. It was known to happen, that Central Command kept innovations secret from the Obsidian Order. But the Order always found out. How convenient for him to be on the *Enterprise* when Ocett used the weapon . . . he didn't doubt her willingness to do so.

Captain Picard caught his eye, and he seemed just as uncertain for a moment. Then his mask of command slid into place.

"We aren't going to start a fight," Picard told Ocett. "But we are going to find out what happened. Picard out."

The captain ordered damage teams to complete their repairs. The crew rushed to comply as Picard waited patiently for their reports.

"What about him?" Riker asked, not bothering to lower his voice.

"He's here to observe," Picard pointed out. "Let him observe."

Mengred counted himself lucky that Picard was so free with their information. Picard's genuine concern indicated that it was not a ruse on their part, though Mengred wouldn't put it past Commander Riker to stage an "attack."

So he tried to be unobtrusive, sitting very still. They all seemed to believe they were dealing with a real threat to the safety of the ship. Fear couldn't be faked, and though these people were trained professionals, he could hear it in their voices, that deadly uncertainty.

Counselor Troi came onto the bridge, and her furrowed brow revealed the empathic tension she was under. Mengred had discovered that Troi was an accurate barometer of the ship's crew.

Mengred was already considering ways he could contact Enabran Tain to ask whether it was possible that Central Command had developed a subspace weapon. Then he noticed that Ensign Ro was swaying in her seat. She stopped herself by leaning forward with a jolt, supporting herself on her elbows.

Data glanced over as she buried her face in her hands. "Is something wrong, Ensign?"

"No . . . ," she mumbled, rubbing her eyes. "Just sleepy, I guess."

Ro tried to sit up straighter, blinking and shaking her head. Her dark hair flared out for a moment.

Data reached out to support her elbow as she started to lean too far to one side. "Ensign Ro!"

She grabbed wildly, trying to catch herself. Data held onto her arm, keeping her seated.

Picard sat forward, "What's wrong, Ensign?"

"M'dizzy . . . ," she mumbled.

"Help her," Picard ordered.

One of other the ensigns moved in from the science station to help Ro. She got up and staggered a few feet. Her pale sweaty face was alarming.

Data performed an interior scan aimed at Ensign Ro. "Sir, it appears she is suffering from tetryon radiation."

"Is that possible?" Picard asked incredulously.

"Accessing," Data said. "I can find no other instance in which tetryon radiation has been detected outside of laboratory tests."

The captain immediately tapped his communicator. "Picard to sickbay, we have a medical emergency on the bridge."

"Crusher here. Captain, I'm getting calls from all over the ship. People are passing out, with severe nausea. I'm reading radiation exposure up to 400 rads on some of these people. What happened?"

"It appears to be tetryon radiation," Picard informed her.

"What?! How can that be? It's only a theory. . . ."

"We'll keep you informed," Picard assured the doctor.

Ro groaned as she was helped up the ramp to the turbolift. Mengred stood up, astonished. How could someone get that ill so quickly? Her eyes were red and watery and she looked miserable as they reached the beam-out point. She was hardly able to stand up as she was transported away, presumably to sickbay.

Mengred realized his mouth was open. He snapped it shut, shuddering at the thought of what Enabran Tain would say about such a display of weakness.

He sat back down. After that, two more of the numerous bridge crew members fell ill right before his eyes. It was loathsome, he who rarely had seen sickness, to be surrounded by people falling over in their tracks. It was as if the very air was poisoned, killing them at their posts.

When Captain Picard began to sweat, to shift uneasily in his chair, Mengred felt an uncharacteristic tremor in his neck ridge. This was not an act. Something was happening to the *Enterprise.*

"Are you all right, sir?" Commander Riker asked the captain.

"I appear to be . . . suffering from the same . . . ," Picard started to say. He placed his hand across his eyes, bending his head forward.

Riker hit his comm badge, "Bridge to sickbay. Captain Picard is not feeling well."

"Beam him down immediately. He should get cellular regeneration now before the damage progresses."

"Acknowledged," Riker replied. He helped Picard stand up. For a moment it looked as if the captain would walk to the beam-out point, but then he faltered.

Riker tapped Picard's comm badge on the upper left chest of his uniform. "One to beam to sickbay," he ordered the computer.

"You have the bridge, Number One," the captain whispered.

As the captain was beamed from the bridge, Riker took command. And Mengred was almost relieved when he was summarily ordered from the bridge.

"Take him back to his quarters," Riker told the security guard. "Make sure the other one stays there, too."

Mengred hurried from the bridge back to his quarters, ignoring the guard who accompanied him. He needed to get a message to Enabran Tain to find out if Central Command was testing a biological weapon carried by a subspace shock wave. Now was the time to use the subspace transmitter he carried in his thumbnail. The problem was that it would take some time for a message to reach Tain and return. He hoped there was enough time to stop Gul Ocett from killing them all.

Chapter Nine

KEIKO O'BRIEN felt a twisting in her stomach, but it was just the baby moving again. She was seven months pregnant and wanted it to be over already. She couldn't wait to get her own body back.

Luckily, she had been in bed asleep when the gravity was displaced. The thick mat had cushioned her fall, so she wasn't hurt. Her botany samples were another thing.

She was down on her hands and knees, having trouble working around the bulge in her abdomen while trying to pick up the sample dishes containing baby Selca trees. Then she had trouble sitting up. Standing up seemed like an impossibility.

Sighing, she swiped a dirty hand across her forehead. The botanical lab was a disaster area because of the gravity failure. An occasional jolt or two was expected, but not a total loss of gravity. Sample dishes had cracked open, spilling tender saplings and buds on the floor, and moist soil was stuck everywhere—on the ceiling, the walls, and all over her.

Everyone else was on emergency duty, but Keiko had been placed on light duty only by Dr. Crusher last week. So she was frantically picking up plants like it mattered, because there was nothing else she could do. After Miles had hurried down to engineering to help repair the circuitry, she couldn't stand to wait alone in their quarters.

Sitting back on her heels, she realized how useless she felt. Her back also hurt.

She was staring right at the bulkhead between the lab and the arboretum, but it took a few seconds for her to realize that it was glowing. It was beautiful, sparkling with colors and silver light.

Lurching to her feet, she grabbed her tricorder from the table. Her hands were shaking as she aimed it at the wall.

The affected area was the secondary layer of stressed tritanium fabric, underneath the microfoam duranium filaments. The tritanium was irradiated, reading an exposure of 462 rads.

She pulled away immediately, backing up until she reached the door. She pressed the control to close it, still looking at the patch of hull that sparkled with inner light.

But irradiation was impossible—the hull had radiation attenuation provided by a thick layer of monocrystal beryllium silicate. How could a patch of the bulkhead, only a small section of the structural element, get exposed to radiation?

Clutching the tricorder, holding her stomach with the other hand, she hurried to sickbay. The corridors were busy with people rushing around. In the turbolift, she was standing next to Ensign Oliver when he doubled over. She had to help him stand up.

"I keep feeling the gravity fail," he told her, his eyes desperately fastened on her, as she supported him. "That drop in the pit of my stomach. I keep thinking it's happening again."

"Breathe slowly and deeply," she advised. "We'll be in sickbay in a minute."

"Am I hurting you?" he asked, giving her a worried glance. But he couldn't keep his balance without her help.

"No, I'm fine," she assured him, hoping that was true. Four hundred and fifty rads would make someone like Ensign Oliver feel very ill, but it could kill a developing baby.

She was glad to pass Ensign Oliver over to a medical technician. Every bed was taken, with more patients leaning against the walls or seated on low replicated cots. She kept having to protect her protruding stomach from people hurrying through sickbay. All the connecting doors were open, and those wards were full too. She noticed Ensign Ro was groaning on a nearby bed.

"Keiko!" Dr. Crusher exclaimed. "Are you all right? I was going to call to check on you, but . . ." She glanced around, letting the tumult speak for itself. Pulling out the medical tricorder, she scanned Keiko, then her stomach. It seemed to take longer than usual.

"Is something wrong?" Keiko asked. "The bulkhead,

it was irradiated, 420 rads. I don't know if I was exposed or how—"

"Don't worry," Dr. Crusher assured her. "You've received a low level of radiation exposure—below 150 rads."

"What will it do to the baby?"

Crusher patted her on the shoulder, already passing the cellular regenerator over her. "The baby is insulated by you. You should go to your quarters and rest. Radiation exposure has been known to bring on early labor. But the full effects take a few weeks to manifest, and by then you'll be eight months along."

Keiko was panicked, but she knew the doctor had other concerns. Crusher was already looking around the sickbay with a worried expression.

"Are you sure it will be okay?" she asked.

Dr. Crusher handed Keiko the regenerator. "Take this and use it once an hour for the next twelve hours. That should neutralize the bulk of the free radicals in your system."

With another pat on the shoulder, Crusher was gone. Keiko stood with her back to the wall, holding the regenerator and her tricorder, watching the medical emergency with wide eyes. She couldn't move.

Then she saw a medical technician clear the pad for an emergency transport to sickbay. A person began to materialize, hunched over, one arm hanging slackly. A red uniform, meaning another command officer was sick.

When the particles coalesced, it was Captain Picard. The medical technician quickly helped him just like he was any other patient, but Keiko felt her throat tighten. The captain! Sick! No. . . .

As Picard was helped through sickbay, even the groans were stifled as everyone realized who it was. Keiko wanted to follow after him, but his eyes were reddened and he glanced at her so piteously as he passed, she couldn't speak.

Keiko rushed from sickbay, running through the corridors, trying to get home as fast as possible. She knew it made no sense, but all she could think about was burrowing into bed where she could feel safe until Miles returned.

Commander Riker sat down in the captain's chair. Now that the Cardassian was off the bridge, he could speak freely.

"Data, what's our status?" Riker asked.

"Warp drive is off-line; it will take another thirty minutes to complete the power-up sequence. Sensors are operational, but our range is limited. The main power conduits have been repaired and we are operating on impulse."

"Weapons?" Riker asked Worf.

"Phaser banks charged and ready, sir." Worf nodded in approval from the tactical station as Riker sat down.

"Full-impulse power," Riker ordered. "Proceed on course."

"Full impulse," helm acknowledged.

Riker quickly consulted the arm panel to assess the situation. Nearly one-quarter of those on board had received exposure to the tetryon radiation, capable of piercing their shields without alerting the biological warning system. The dispersal pattern was erratic, with interior portions of the ship irradiated while large areas adjacent to the hull were unaffected.

He had known the Cardassians did something to him. Now everyone knew. It was not some crippling disease—it was an attack. The Cardassians must have launched their biological weapon on the subspace carrier wave toward the *Hawking*. They had also denied him medical treatment to give the tetryon radiation a chance to do as much damage as possible, while the initial free radicals were absorbed by his system. Very neatly done.

"Sir!" Worf was accessing information. "On-board sensors report a transmission coming from inside the *Enterprise*."

"Source?" Riker demanded.

"Triangulating," Data acknowledged. "It appears to be coming from deck 5—"

"The Cardassians?" Riker interrupted.

Worf contacted security. "Security alert! Unauthorized transmission from Jos Mengred's quarters."

"Transmission has ceased," Data informed Riker.

Riker stood up and just looked at Worf. "Have security take both of them to the brig. I want any recording or transmitting devices they've got."

"With pleasure, sir!" Worf's eyes were hard as he gave the orders.

"Red alert," Riker announced, sitting back down.

"Red alert," Data confirmed as the red warning lights came on. "I have the Cardassian warship on sensors, sir."

"Change course to intercept," Riker ordered.

"Changing course," helm confirmed.

Riker narrowed his yes, softly adding, "Let's see how serious they are about starting a war."

The tension on the bridge was high. None of them wanted to think about Captain Picard falling sick with tetryon radiation poisoning . . . Riker noted that several key stations were now manned by secondary personnel. Not the best tactical situation for a confrontation, but it would have to do.

"Commander," Worf said. "The Cardassians are in the brig. Two transmission devices were discovered under their thumbnails. Jos Mengred has several additional implants in his fingers and a cranial implant that would have to be surgically removed."

"We don't have time for that," Riker said. He wished they did. Carving into Mengred's skull wouldn't be such a bad thing. The Cardassian had spent a week dropping comments about Riker's physical "weakness" to anyone who would listen.

The *Enterprise* closed on the Cardassian warship at full impulse.

"The Cardassians are charging their plasma banks," Data reported.

Riker nodded. If he saw a fully shielded starship accelerating towards him, he would take defensive measures, too. The warship was changing course to evade.

"Stay on them," he ordered.

"Aye, sir."

Worf reported, "Commander, Gul Ocett is hailing us."

Riker stood up. "Open frequency."

"What are you doing?" Ocett demanded. "Where is Captain Picard?"

Riker noted that she split her attention between him and the small data screen on her headset. "Captain Picard is suffering from your earlier attack. We are defending ourselves."

"Again you falsely accuse us of attack!"

Riker raised his voice. "You can deny it all you want, Captain, but we know what's going on here. The *Enterprise* has been hit with tetryon radiation, sent on a subspace carrier wave—"

"That is not my concern," Ocett exclaimed. "If you people are too weak to survive in space, then I would recommend you return to your planets."

The transmission ceased abruptly. The *Galor*-class warship turned.

"They are changing course, Commander," Data announced. It only took a few seconds for the ship to grow larger.

"The warship is approaching in an attack posture, sir," Worf announced.

"Would she fire on the *Enterprise* with Mengred and Pakat on board?" Riker thought it must be a bluff, to see if they would back down.

Data turned. "Sir, it has been observed that the Obsidian Order and Central Command have been at odds in both their goals and methods of execution."

"Nice," Riker said dryly. Just when you thought you knew who the enemy was. . . .

"Approaching at 200,000 kilometers," Data reported.

He slowly counted down their approach, as Riker forced himself to wait. "One hundred fifty thousand kilometers. Entering weapons range—"

"Evasive maneuvers," Riker ordered. "Delta sequence—"

"She's firing weapons!" Worf exclaimed.

The ship dropped in a spiraling maneuver that took them out of the target window. But as the *Enterprise* came around, she shuddered under the impact of two more plasma beams shot from the warship.

"Direct hit on our port nacelle," Worf reported. "Shields holding at 74 percent."

"Warship closing at 100,000 kilometers," Data announced steadily.

"Bring us around to attack," Riker ordered.

Data was preparing for the battle when his self-diagnostic completed. A rare form of tetryon neutrinos had passed through his systems, ionizing molecules in a way that mimicked radiation exposure. Over the past few hours, the diagnostic had automatically run a comparison with Starfleet's database, producing an incident that was similar in terms of mechanical and biological effects. The same thing had happened nearly a hundred years before to the original *Enterprise,* when they had discovered the Badlands.

"Sir!" Data interrupted. "I believe the Cardassians are not responsible for the tetryon radiation."

Commander Riker was in battle mode and he clearly thought he didn't hear Data correctly. "The Cardassians *are* responsible," Riker insisted.

"No, sir, I believe not."

"Why not?" the commander demanded.

"A similar phenomenon affected the crew of the *Enterprise* under command of Captain James T. Kirk in 2268, shortly after reaching the Badlands." Data quickly ran through the physical symptoms that had affected both *Enterprise* crews and their starships. "Commander Spock correctly ascertained that gamma radiation was associated with the phenomenon, but standard sensor sweeps at that time would not have been able to detect the tetryon particles."

Worf announced, "The warship is coming around."

"Evasive maneuvers," Riker ordered. "Get us away from that ship, helmsman!"

Riker came towards Data, his expression intent. "Are you certain about this, Data?"

"Affirmative. It is apparently the same phenomenon that damaged the *Yosemite* and the *Hawking*, though in those instances it was a much weaker, briefer occurrence that took place while the vessels were inside the sensor shadow. Nevertheless, there were apparently enough tetryons to penetrate the shields. That is what caused your illness, Commander, not Myers disease."

"I knew it wasn't Myers disease," Riker said slowly. "Why didn't the sensors on the *Hawking* pick up these tetryon neutrinos?"

"Tetryons can exist only in subspace and are highly unstable in normal space. They move at speeds over warp 9, which makes them invisible unless sensors are specifically calibrated to search for that type of subspace particle." Data reminded him, "Our work on the sensor grid enabled the *Enterprise* to detect the tetryons a microsecond prior to the subspace shockwave, which subsequently overloaded our sensor banks."

"Why wasn't everyone affected by the tetryon radiation?" Worf demanded.

"Tetryons interact erratically with matter, due to the radioactive force they exert on particles," Data informed him. "The situation was identical the first time this phenomenon was recorded by the *Enterprise*, one hundred years ago."

Riker considered the situation for a moment, watching the warship on the viewscreen. "So it happened once before."

"At least three times prior to this incident," Data corrected. "When the original *Enterprise* was affected, 43 percent of the crew were seriously injured. The second shock wave lasted longer than our most recent incident. Except for one death, the crew members recovered with little or no permanent damage when they were treated with cellular regeneration."

"Commander! We are being hailed by Gul Ocett," Worf informed Riker.

"On screen," Riker ordered.

Gul Ocett was livid. "Is this a declaration of war by the Federation?"

"You fired on us," Riker pointed out. "We did not return fire."

"Your behavior has been aggressive," Ocett snapped. "I will complain to Central Command—"

"Could you take back your operatives, first?" Riker

asked mildly. "Oh, and we're returning them minus their subspace transmission devices."

"Transmission devices . . . ?"

"Jos Mengred and Pakat are currently in our brig, having sent a transmission which sparked our . . . aggressive maneuvers."

Data thought Ocett's reaction was fascinating. Her anger and concern were mixed in equal parts, as she clearly wondered what Mengred had been doing without her knowledge.

"So if you could lower your shields," Riker told her. "We'll beam them back to you."

Ocett hesitated. "I would be foolish to lower my shields after your display."

Riker actually laughed, and the tension on the bridge eased somewhat. "If you're worried, we'll shuttle them back to you."

His offer sounded like a taunt. Gul Ocett grew angrier. "You will comply with our original agreement!"

Once again the screen went abruptly dark.

Riker slyly commented, "She isn't big on goodbyes, is she?"

The rest of the bridge crew laughed, while Data wished he could participate in their merriment.

"That *was* a close one," Riker admitted.

"Aye, sir," Data said. "Less than 60,000 kilometers."

Everyone on the bridge laughed again. Data was pleased he had made a joke, even if he hadn't intended to. He smiled at everyone. All he wanted was to join in.

Chapter Ten

Jos Mengred was waiting in the brig, with Pakat glumly sitting beside him, when a strange feeling passed through him. He shuddered, flexing his tingling hands.

Suspiciously he glanced at the guard, but she was seated at the control/display panel apparently monitoring security activity. Mengred shivered again. This time his entire body shook.

Pakat was looking at him strangely. Mengred ignored his aide, blinking rapidly to try to clear his vision. His neck ridges kept trembling, and though he clenched his fists, silently ordering himself to maintain control, there was nothing he could do to stop the tremors.

He kept wondering what sort of biological weapon could be carried on a subspace carrier wave. It would require a wide range in order to affect the many different humanoids in the Federation. Could it affect Cardassians, as well?

Certainly if Central Command was developing a biological weapon that could affect Cardassians, then the Obsidian Order would have discovered its existence—wouldn't they?

Pakat eased away slightly. "What is it, sir?"

Mengred realized his legs were visibly shaking. He tried to still them with his hands, but he could not control them. "I don't understand. . . ."

Pakat's eyes were wide, and he got up, backing away toward the forcefield.

"What is happening?" Mengred raised his hands, which no longer seemed to be his own.

The security guard was alerted and she stood up behind the console, one finger ready to call for backup. "What are you doing in there?"

Pakat whirled, blurting out, "Get me out of here!"

Mengred tried to stand, but his knees would not support him. He felt as if he was floating, looking down on his failing body. He stumbled and fell to the floor.

He could hear the commotion as he raised his head. The security guard was too well-trained to leave her post, even though Pakat was clamoring to be let out.

Mengred managed to pull himself back up on the bench, bracing himself against the wall, unable to sit up straight. He was hearing each heartbeat suddenly amplified. It sounded like blood was gushing through his ears with each beat.

After far too long, more red-uniformed guards entered the brig, holding phaser rifles ready.

Worf appeared next to the forcefield. "Do you have a problem?"

"Let me out of here," Pakat demanded. "Something is wrong with him."

Mengred raised his head, breathing heavily as he tried to focus on Worf. Obviously, something had gone seriously wrong with him. He didn't know what else to say so he remained silent.

"You first," Worf ordered Pakat, pointing to the adjourning bay. "Step out and go in there."

There was a precise procedure for lowering the forcefield. Mengred wished he could take advantage of it somehow, just because they seemed to expect it. But he could hardly hold himself up at the moment.

The next thing he knew, the doctor had arrived. Mengred glanced at her warily as she pulled out her tricorder. "Are you sure you know what you're doing?"

Worf stiffened. "Dr. Crusher is the senior medical officer on board the *Enterprise*."

Dr. Crusher smiled down at him as she ran the medical scanner through the air in front of him. "I know enough about Cardassian physiology to say you've gotten a radiation dose of 300 rads. Congratulations."

"Radiation poisoning . . . ," he said softly. "Is it life-threatening—"

"You'll feel terrible for a few days, but you should recover completely." She injected him with something, and he clapped his hand over the spot on his neck, gaping up at her. He usually checked anything that went into his body.

She began to pass a cellular regenerator over him.

He was outraged at the liberties she was taking, but reluctant to stop her. His own people would have done far less to ensure his health.

"You'll be returning to your own ship soon," Dr. Crusher added, packing away her gear. "Better have your own doctor examine you."

He shook his head, his mouth open.

"Or not . . . ," she said doubtfully. "Anyway, getting your first treatment quickly makes all the difference. It's likely your hair won't fall out like Riker's. Then again. . . ."

Mengred weakly touched his slicked-back hair, appalled by the idea. He wanted to ask if the radiation was caused by a Cardassian weapon, but the very thought of being so open was absurd. He resolutely shut his mouth, knowing that he couldn't trust himself in this moment of supreme weakness. If only Pakat had not seen it happen . . . his authority over his aide was probably undermined beyond repair.

He shut his eyes, concentrating on getting his strength back. He could not allow Gul Ocett to see him this way. It would destroy everything he had worked for, all those months of building blocks of dissension and covert alliances among the crew. He could not afford to lose his power base at this time.

When the Cardassian warship finally proceeded to the rendezvous point, the *Enterprise* cautiously followed along behind.

Data took advantage of the forty-three minutes remaining to complete local scans for tetryon neutrinos.

Tetryon traces could usually be found only through specific byproducts, such as the gamma radiation that was produced when the tetryons passed through the plasma of the Badlands. Data conjectured that the original *Enterprise* had experienced this complex radiation both times, which had contributed to the delay in determining that they were dealing with the same phenomenon.

Data was uncertain as to the source of the tetryons. The subspace shockwave could have emanated from the Badlands, but his simulations indicated that the fast-scattering tetryons would only sustain a shockwave up to 5 million kilometers away from the source. In several instances that it had occurred, the afflicted vessel had been further than that from the plasma storms.

In fact, nothing they had discovered could explain such a phenomenon. Data was pleased to have such a challenging problem to work on.

"Time for our guests to go home," Commander Riker announced. "Data, you can transport them in shuttlecraft 9. I don't want to risk sending the *Hawking* again. They may have broken the command codes."

Data shut down his computations, rerouting them to his quarters. It would take many hours of studying the sensor readings of the Badlands and the on-board scans and diagnostics to reach a theory. Meanwhile, he logged his science report, which designated the Badlands sector as biologically hazardous, with a recommendation for all Starfleet vessels to avoid the sector.

"Do you intend to warn the Cardassians about the subspace tetryon wave?" Data inquired.

"I'll let Starfleet Command make that decision," Commander Riker replied.

Data nodded in acknowledgment, then left the bridge. He went directly to the shuttle bay, knowing Worf and a security team would escort the Cardassians to the hangar.

Data prepared the shuttle for departure while he waited for the Cardassians to arrive. Shuttlecraft 9 was technically a shuttlepod, a much smaller version of a shuttlecraft. He approved Riker's choice, preferring not to take the *Hawking* after the Cardassians had been at liberty to examine her systems.

Worf arrived with Mengred and Pakat, surrounded by half a dozen guards. Data had seen Dr. Crusher's report as it passed through his operations panel to Commander Riker. She had treated Jos Mengred and reported that he would recover with no serious side effects. No new patients had arrived, and she believed the worst was over. The entire *Enterprise* crew had received at least one cellular regeneration treatment to counteract any exposure to the elusive tetryons. A total of two hundred and forty of the one thousand crew members had been placed on medical leave, and would be unable to resume duty for at least one to three days.

Data knew that as soon as he returned from delivering the Cardassians, the *Enterprise* would have to depart the Badlands sector. They were ordered to pick up personnel for the Melona IV colonization project.

Jos Mengred climbed stiffly on board the shuttlepod, with help from two Starfleet security guards. His skin was chalky and distinctly yellow, whereas Pakat was a healthy flush green color. Mengred fell into the chair next to Data, breathing rapidly through his open mouth. Pakat huddled as far away as he could in the rear.

"So, it is over," Mengred said to Data.

Data was still not accustomed to the way Mengred looked at him so closely. "Preparing for departure," Data reported, closing the hatch.

The *Enterprise* cleared them, and Riker ordered, voice-only, "*Make it fast, Data, we have a deadline to meet on Melona IV.*"

"Aye, sir," Data replied. "Shuttlecraft 9 out."

Data swung the little shuttlecraft up and out of the hanger. For a moment they drifted over the glossy white hull of the *Enterprise*, near the sparkling windows. Data noted the lack of tiny figures in the rear observation decks. Usually children gathered to watch shuttlecraft take off, but now too many of them were sick or had sick parents.

"I felt the phaser hits," Mengred said. "Gul Ocett fired on you. Who fired first?"

"The *Enterprise* did not fire on the warship." Data circled the ship and headed toward the Cardassian warship.

"You didn't?" Mengred wondered, almost as if to himself. "Why not? I've been all over this ship. I've seen the power grids. You could have destroyed the warship."

"That is not our objective," Data informed him.

"She fired on you . . . it was the perfect opportunity. Why didn't Commander Riker return fire?"

"I do not question my superior officers," Data said

evenly. "However, I suspect Commander Riker did not want to start a war."

The warship was growing larger on the screen. Data maneuvered around the rear, sinking toward the open hanger.

"You're curious about Cardassians, aren't you?" Mengred asked. He gestured toward the ship. "Would you like to stay on a while? Observe us?"

"That is not part of my duties." Data was indeed curious, but he was glad he wouldn't be ordered to observe the Cardassians.

"It could be arranged." Mengred's voice lowered, as if to keep Pakat from hearing him. "You could work for me."

"I must complete my current assignment on board the *Enterprise*," Data said diplomatically.

Mengred's eyes narrowed, and he hissed, "I could make you stay."

Data met his eyes, realizing that the Cardassian meant it. "The *Enterprise* would not allow that."

Mengred considered him. "They would fight to get you back? You say they backed down before."

Data deliberately did not reply until he had landed the shuttlepod on the deck and put the systems on hold.

Then he turned to Mengred, telling him, "The *Enterprise* would not allow you to keep me prisoner." He opened the door and gestured politely. "And I suspect that Gul Ocett also does not wish to start a war to procure you an aide."

Pakat heard as he left through the door, trying to get

away from Mengred. Mengred hesitated, then slowly stood up. "Your talents are being wasted there."

"Perhaps it is not I who should consider leaving, Jos Mengred. Perhaps it is yourself."

Mengred gave Data a startled look, but refrained from answering.

Data waited until Mengred reluctantly stepped outside, then he closed the hatch. The Cardassian dispatch officer cleared him, and he lifted from the deck. It wasn't until the forcefield dropped and he was back out in space that he was certain Mengred wasn't about to try to keep him on board the warship.

Data could see the swirling plasma storms of the Badlands beyond the *Enterprise*. He decided to retain the image for one of his next paintings. The white ship looked exceptionally sleek against the blurry red and gold plasma clouds.

With his report, Data had already ensured the Badlands sector would be treated with the utmost respect and caution in the future. But for the remainder of the few minutes it took for him to return to the *Enterprise*, Data continued to scan the Badlands, trying to gather every bit of information he could.

He was certain that analysis of the data would fill many of his future leisure hours as he wrestled with the puzzle of the tetryon shock wave. The Badlands was a fascinating phenomenon, worthy of a great deal more scientific study.

OUR FIRST SERIAL NOVEL!

Presenting, one chapter per month . . .

The very beginning of the Starfleet Adventure . . .

STARFLEET: YEAR ONE

A Novel in Twelve Parts

**by
Michael Jan Friedman**

Chapter Five

Presenting one chapter per month...

The very beginning of the Starfleet
Michael Jan Friedman

Chapter Five

Daniel Hagedorn yawned and stretched. Then he pushed his wheeled chair back from his monitor and the blue-and-gold ship schematics displayed on it.

True, the captain and his colleagues had submitted their recommendations regarding the *Daedalus* earlier in the day. But that didn't mean their responsibility to Director Abute was fully discharged—at least not from Hagedorn's point of view.

He meant to come up with further recommendations. A whole slew of them, in fact. By the time he set foot on the bridge of the *Daedalus* or one of her sister ships, he would know he had done everything he could to make that vessel a dead-sure success.

Abruptly, a red message box appeared against the blue-and-gold background. It was from Abute, advising each of his six captains that they would begin interviewing prospective officers the following day.

Hagedorn nodded. He had been wondering when the process would get underway.

There were to be a few rules, however. For instance,

Abute wanted each vessel to reflect the variety of species represented in the Federation, so no captain could bring aboard more than a hundred human crewmen.

Also, Hagedorn couldn't draw on established military officers for more than half his command team. Clearly, the director wanted both the defense and research camps represented on each vessel's bridge.

The captain grunted. They could keep their *Christopher* crews intact after all, but only if some of their officers were willing to accept a demotion. Clearly, practicality would be taking a backseat to politics in this new Starfleet—not that he was surprised, given the other developments he had seen up to that point.

On the other hand, no one would be foisted on him—neither alien nor Earthman. That was one point on which Hagedorn wouldn't have given in, even if Abute had handed the *Daedalus* to him on a silver platter.

After all, the lives of the captain and his crew might one day depend on a particular ensign or junior-grade lieutenant. He wanted that individual to be someone who had earned his way aboard, not a down payment in some interplanetary quid pro quo.

With a tap of his keyboard, Hagedorn acknowledged receipt of the director's message. Then he stored the *Daedalus*'s schematics and accessed the list of officer candidates Abute had compiled.

Frowning, the captain began to set up an efficient interview schedule. He promised himself that by noon the following day he would know every bridge officer under his command.

Cobaryn was relaxing in his quarters, reading Rigelian triple-metered verse from an electronic book, when he heard the sound of chimes.

It took him a moment to remember what it meant—that there was someone in the corridor outside who wished to see him. Getting up from his chair, the captain crossed the room and pressed a pad on the bulkhead. A moment later, the doors slid apart.

Cobaryn was surprised to see Connor Dane standing there. "Can I help you?" the Rigelian asked.

The Cochrane jockey frowned. "You drink?" he asked.

Cobaryn looked at him. "You mean . . . do I partake of alcoholic beverages? In a public house?"

Dane's frown deepened. "Do you?"

"In fact," the Rigelian replied, "I do. That is to say, I have. But why are you inquiring about—?"

The human held up a hand for silence. "Don't ask, all right? Not where we're going, or why—or anything. Just put the damned book down and let's get a move on."

Cobaryn's curiosity had been piqued. How could he decline? "All right," he said. Then he put the book down on the nearest table, straightened his clothing, and accompanied Dane to their mysterious destination.

Dane tossed back a shot of tequila, felt the ensuing rush of warmth, and plunked his glass down on the bar.

The Afterburner's bartender, a man with a bulbous nose and a thick brush of gray hair, noticed the gesture. "Another?" he growled.

"Another," Dane confirmed.

He turned to Cobaryn, who was sitting on a stool alongside him. The Rigelian was nursing a nut-flavored liqueur and studying the human with his bright red eyes. They were asking a question.

"I know," said Dane, scowling. "You still don't understand why I asked you to come along."

Cobaryn smiled sympathetically. "I confess I don't."

"Especially since I never said a word to you the whole way from Rigel to Earth Base Fourteen."

"That does compound my curiosity, yes," the Rigelian admitted. "And even after our battle with the Romulans—"

"I sat in the bar by myself," Dane said, finishing Cobaryn's thought.

He watched the bartender replace his empty shot glass with a full one. Picking it up, he gazed into its pale-green depths.

"Why do I need company all of a sudden?" the human asked himself. "Because I'm out of my element here, that's why." He looked around the Afterburner. "Because I have no business trying to be a starfleet captain."

The Rigelian shrugged. "From where I stand, it seems you would make an excellent captain. You have demonstrated intelligence, determination, the courage to speak your mind. . . ."

"You mean at that meeting this morning?" Dane dismissed the notion with a wave of his hand. "That wasn't courage, pal. That was me losing my patience. I got hacked off at the idea of a bunch of lab coats telling me what I could and couldn't have."

"Nonetheless," Cobaryn insisted, "you said what no one else would have thought to say. You saw a danger to your crew and you did not hold back. Is that not one of the qualities one should look for in a captain?"

The human chuckled humorlessly. "Anyone can open a big mouth. You don't have to be captain material to do that."

"Perhaps not," the Rigelian conceded. His mouth pulled up the corners. "But it does not hurt."

Dane hadn't expected Cobaryn to make a joke. He found himself smiling back at his companion. "No," he had to allow, "I guess it doesn't."

Cobaryn's grin faded a little. "And what about me?"

The human looked at him askance. "What *about* you?"

"I am hardly the obvious choice for a captaincy in Starfleet. The only vaguely heroic action I ever undertook was to ram my ship into that Romulan back at Earth Base Fourteen—and that was only after I had determined with a high degree of certainty that I could beam away in time to save myself."

Dane was starting to feel the effects of the tequila. "Listen," he said, leaning closer to the Rigelian, "they didn't pick you for your courage, Cobaryn. They may have picked you for a whole lot of reasons, but believe me . . . courage wasn't one of them."

The Rigelian looked at him thoughtfully. "You are referring to my ability to command a vessel in deep space?"

"Maybe that's part of it," the human conceded, "but not all of it. Just think for a second, all right? This United Federation of Planets they're building . . . it's not just about Earth. Technically, we humans are only supposed to be a small part of the picture."

"A small part . . . yes," said Cobaryn. His bony, silver brow furrowed a bit. "That is why Director Abute imposed a quota on the number of humans who can serve under us."

Dane pointed at him. "Exactly. And if they're encouraging us to include nonhumans in our crews and command staffs. . . ."

For the first time, the Rigelian actually frowned in his presence. "You are saying I was picked to be a captain because I am an alien?"

"Hey," said Dane, "you're better than that. You're an alien who's demonstrated that he can work alongside humans—who's demonstrated that he actually *likes* to work alongside humans. Do you have any idea how many people fit that particular description?"

"Only a few, I imagine."

"A few?" The Earthman sat back on his stool. "You may be the only one in the whole galaxy! To the mooks who are engineering the Federation and its Starfleet, you're as good as having another human in the center seat—which is what they'd *really* like."

Cobaryn weighed the comment. "So I am a concession

to the nonhuman species in the Federation? A token appointment, so they will not feel they have been ignored in the selection process?"

"Hey," said Dane, "it seems pretty clear to *me*. But maybe that's just the cynic in me talking."

The Rigelian didn't say anything for a while, though the muscles writhed in his ridged temples. Finally, he turned to his companion again. "I take it a human would resent the situation as you have described it?"

"Most would," Dane confirmed.

A knot of silver flesh gathered at the bridge of Cobaryn's nose. "And yet," he said, "I find I do *not* resent it. After all, Earth's pilots clearly have more tactical experience than the pilots of any other world. And if a nonhuman is to work with them, why not choose one who has already shown himself capable of doing so?"

Dane drummed his fingertips on the mahogany surface of the bar. "You can find the bright side of anything, can't you?"

"So I have been told," the Rigelian conceded.

The human shook his head. "Pretty amazing."

Cobaryn smiled at him again—or rather, did his best impression of a smile. "Amazing for a human, yes. But as you will recall, I am a Rigelian. Among my people, everyone looks on the bright side."

Dane rolled his eyes. "Remind me not to stop at any drinking establishments on your planet."

The Rigelian looked as if he were about to tender a response to the human's comment. But before he could do that, someone bellowed a curse at the other end of the bar.

In Dane's experience, people bellowed curses all the time, almost always for reasons that didn't concern him. Unimpressed, he threw back his tequila and felt it soak into him. But before long he heard another bellow.

This time, it seemed to come from a lot closer.

Turning his head, the Cochrane jockey saw a big, balding fellow in black-and-gold Earth Command togs headed his way. And judging by the ugly, pop-eyed expression on the man's face, he was looking for trouble.

"You!" he said, pointing a big, blunt finger directly at Dane. "And you!" he growled, turning the same finger on Cobaryn. "Who do you think you are to imitate space captains?"

"I beg your pardon?" said the Rigelian, his tone flawlessly polite.

"You heard me!" roared the big man, pushing his way through the crowd to get even closer. "It's because of you two butterfly catchers that I wasn't picked to command a Starfleet vessel!"

Cobaryn looked at Dane, his face a question. "Butterfly catchers?"

Keeping an eye on their antagonist, who was obviously more than a little drunk, the Cochrane jockey made a sound of derision. "It's what Stiles and the other military types call us."

Call you, he corrected himself inwardly. He had never had an urge to do a stitch of research in his life.

"Well?" the balding man blared at them. "Nothing to say to Big Andre? Or are you just too scared to pipe up?"

By then, he was almost within arm's reach of his targets. Seeing that there would be no easy way out of this, Dane got up from his seat and met "Big Andre" halfway.

"Ah," grated the balding man, his eyes popping out even further. "So the butterfly catcher has some guts after all!"

"Actually," said Dane, "I was going to ask you if I could buy you a drink. A big guy like you must get awful thirsty."

Big Andre looked at him for a moment, his brow furrowing down the middle. Then he reached out with lightning speed and grabbed the Cochrane jockey by the front of his uniform shirt.

"I don't need any of your charity," the big man snarled, his breath stinking of liquor as he drew Dane's face closer to his. "You think you can take away what is mine and buy a lousy drink to make up for it?" He lifted his fist and the smaller man's shirt tightened uncomfortably. "Is that what you think, butterfly catcher?"

Dane had had enough. Grabbing his antagonist's wrist, he dug his fingers into the spaces between the bones and the tendons and twisted.

With a cry of pain and rage, Big Andre released him and pulled his wrist back. Then the expression on his meaty face turned positively murderous. "You want to fight me? All right—we'll fight!"

"No," said Cobaryn, positioning himself between Dane and the balding man. "That will not be necessary." He glanced meaningfully at his companion. "Captain Dane and I were about to leave . . . were we not?"

"I don't think so," said a sandy-haired civilian, who was half a head shorter than Big Andre but just as broad. "You'll leave when Captain Beschta gives you permission to leave."

"That's right," said a man with a thick, dark mustache, also dressed in civilian garb. "And I didn't hear him give you permission."

Dane saw that there were three other men standing behind them, all of them glowering at the Starfleet captains. Obviously, more of Big Andre's friends. Six against three, the Cochrane jockey mused. Not exactly the best odds in the world—and as far as he knew, the Rigelian might be useless in a fight.

"You want to leave?" the big man asked of Cobaryn, his expression more twisted with hatred than ever. "You can leave, all right—when they carry you out of here!"

And with remarkable quickness, he launched his massive, knob-knuckled fist at the Rigelian's face.

Dane couldn't help wincing. Big Andre looked big and strong enough to crack every bone in the Rigelian's open, trusting countenance.

But to Dane's surprise, Big Andre's blow never landed. Moving his head to one side, Cobaryn eluded it—and sent his antagonist stumbling into the press of patrons that had gathered around them.

Big Andre roared in anger and came at the Rigelian a second time. Dane tried to intervene, tried to keep his new-found friend from getting hurt, but he found himself pulled back by a swarm of strong arms.

Fortunately for Cobaryn, he was able to duck Big Andre's second attack almost as neatly as he had the first. Again, the human went hurtling into an unbroken wall of customers.

But Big Andre's friends were showing up in droves and pushing their way toward the altercation. Some of them, like Big Andre himself, wore the black and gold of Earth Command. Others were clearly civilians. But they all had one trait in common—a rabid desire to see Dane and the Rigelian pounded into something resembling pulp.

"Surround them!" one man called out.

"Don't let 'em get away!" barked another.

Dane tried to wriggle free of his captors. But before he could make any headway, he felt someone's boot explode in his belly. It knocked the wind out of him, forcing him to draw in great, moaning gulps of air.

Then he felt it a second time. And a third.

When his vision cleared, he could see Big Andre advancing on Cobaryn all over again. The man's hands were balled into hammerlike fists, his nostrils flaring like an angry bull's.

"I'll make you sorry you ever heard of Starfleet!" Big Andre thundered.

"That's enough!" called a voice, cutting through the buzz of the crowd the way a laser might cut an unshielded hull.

Everyone turned—Dane, Cobaryn, the big man and everybody else in the place. And what they saw was the commanding figure of Dan Hagedorn, flanked by Hiro Matsura and Jake Stiles.

Hagedorn eyed his former wingmate. "Leave it alone," he told Beschta.

The big man turned to him, his eyes sunken and red-rimmed with too much alcohol. "Hagedorn?" he snapped.

"It's me," the captain confirmed. "And I'm asking you to stop this before someone gets hurt."

Beschta laughed a cruel laugh. "Did they not hurt *me?*" he groaned, pointing at Dane and Cobaryn with a big accusing finger. "Did they not take what should rightfully have been mine?"

"Damned right!" roared a civilian whom Hagedorn had never seen before in his life.

A handful of other men cheered the sentiment. The captain had never seen them before either. Apparently, Beschta had picked up a few new friends in the last couple of weeks.

If the big man had been the only problem facing him, Hagedorn would have felt confident enough handling it on his own. But if he was going to have to confront an unknown number of adversaries, he wanted to make sure he had some help—and to that end, he glanced at his companions.

First he looked at Stiles, who knew exactly what was being asked of him. But Stiles shook his head from side to side. "This isn't any of our business," he said in a low voice.

"Like hell it isn't," Hagedorn returned. Then he turned the other way and regarded Matsura.

The younger man seemed to waver for a moment. Then his eyes met Stiles's and he shook his head as well. "I can't fight Beschta," he whispered, though he didn't seem entirely proud of his choice.

Hagedorn nodded, less than pleased with his comrades' responses but forced to accept them. "All right, then. I'll do this myself."

Turning sideways to make his way through the crowd, the captain tried to get between Beschta and his intended victim. But some of Beschta's new friends didn't like the idea.

"Where do you think you're going?" asked one of them, a swarthy man with a thick neck and broad shoulders.

Hagedorn didn't answer the question. Instead, he drove the heel of his hand into the man's nose, breaking it. Then, as the man recoiled from the attack, blood reddening his face, the captain collapsed him with a closed-handed blow to the gut.

If anyone else had had intentions of standing in Hagedorn's way, the incident changed their mind. Little by little, Hagedorn approached Beschta, who didn't look like he was in any mood to be reasoned with.

"Don't come near me!" the big man rumbled.

The captain kept coming. "That's not what you said when I saved your hide at Aldebaran."

"I'm warning you!" Beschta snarled, his eyes wide with fury.

"You won't hit me," Hagedorn told him with something less than complete confidence. "You can't. It would be like hitting yourself."

"Stay away!" the big man bellowed at him, his voice trembling with anger and pain.

"No," said the captain. "I won't."

For an uncomfortable fraction of a second, he thought Beschta was going to take a swing at him after all. He tensed inside, ready for anything. Then his former comrade made a sound of disgust.

"I thought you were my friend," Beschta spat.

"I am," Hagedorn assured him.

"They turned me away," the big man complained. "The bastards rejected me. *Me*, Andre Beschta."

"They were wrong," said the captain. "They were stupid. But don't take it out on these . . . " With an effort, he kept himself from using the term *butterfly catchers,* " . . . gentlemen."

Beschta scowled at Cobaryn and Dane, who was still in the grip of some of his allies. "You're lucky," he said. "Had Captain Hagedorn not come along, you would have been stains on the floor."

The Cochrane jockey had the good sense not to answer. Hagedorn was happy about that, at least.

The big man indicated Dane with a lift of his chin. "Let him go. He's not worth our sweat."

The men holding Dane hesitated for a moment. Then they thrust him toward Hagedorn. The Cochrane jockey stumbled for a step or two, but caught himself before anyone else had to catch him.

Off to the side, Beschta's friends were picking up the man Hagedorn had leveled. He looked like he needed medical attention—though that wasn't the captain's concern.

"Come on," he told Dane and Cobaryn. "Let's get out of here."

As they headed for the exit, the Rigelian turned to Hagedorn. "Thank you," he said with obvious sincerity.

"You're welcome," Hagedorn replied.

As he left the place, he shot a look back over his shoulder at Stiles and Matsura. They were guiding the hulking Beschta to a table, taking care of their old wingmate.

A part of Hagedorn wished he could have done the same.

Hiro Matsura felt more torn over what he had seen than he cared to admit. In the heat of the moment, he had taken the side of one trusted colleague over another. And on reflection, he wasn't at all sure that he had settled on the right decision.

Soberly, he watched Hagedorn and the two butterfly

catchers leave the Afterburner. Then he negotiated a course to the bar.

"What'll it be?" asked the bartender.

"Brazilian coffee," said Matsura. "Black."

The bartender smiled. "For Beschta?"

Matsura nodded. Obviously, his friend had made a name for himself. "Sorry about the brawl."

The bartender dismissed the apology with a gesture and went to pour out some coffee. "It's okay," he said. "We haven't had a good knock-down-drag-out in weeks." Then he laid a hot, steaming mug on the wooden bar.

Picking up the coffee, Matsura paid the bartender and made his way back to Beschta's table. Stiles had pulled out a chair opposite the big man and was trying to calm him down.

"Listen," the captain was saying, "how long do you think those butterfly catchers are going to last? A month, Andre? Two, maybe? And when they're gone, who do you think they're going to call for a replacement?"

Beschta shook his head stubbornly. "Don't patronize me, Aaron. I may be drunk, but I'm not an imbecile. I have no chance. Zero."

"Here," said Matsura, placing the mug of coffee in front of the big man. "This will make you feel better."

Beschta glared at him for a moment, bristling with the same kind of indignation he had shown earlier. Then, unexpectedly, a tired smile spread across his face. "Some example I'm setting for you, eh, Hiro?"

Matsura didn't know what to say to that. A couple of days ago, he had still thought of himself as Beschta's protégé. Now, he was beginning to feel that he might be more than that. "Drink your coffee," was all he could come up with.

The big man nodded judiciously. "That's a good idea. I'll drink my coffee. Then I'll go home and sleep for a week or two."

"Now you're talking," said Stiles.

Seeing that Beschta was all right for the moment, he clapped him on his broad back and went over to Matsura. "Hagedorn was out of line," he said in a low voice.

"You think so?" asked the younger man.

Stiles looked at him with narrow-eyed suspicion. "Don't *you?*"

Matsura folded his arms across his chest. "The more I think about it, the more I wonder. I mean, Dane and Cobaryn could have gotten hurt. What would that have proved?"

Stiles looked like a man who was trying his best to exercise patience. "Listen," he said, "I didn't want to see people injured any more than you. But this is war, Hiro, and those two butterfly catchers are the enemy."

Matsura considered his colleague's position. "If it's a war, I'll do my best to help win it. You know that. But standing there while Dane and Cobaryn needed our help . . . it was just wrong."

His colleague considered him for a while longer. "You know," he said at last, "I disagree with you a hundred percent. If I had to do it over again, I'd do exactly the same thing."

Matsura started to protest, but Stiles held up a hand to show that he wasn't finished yet.

"Nonetheless," the older man continued. "this is no time for us to be arguing. We've got to be on the same page if we're going to get the kind of fleet we're aiming for."

Stiles was right about that, Matsura told himself—even if he was wrong about everything else. "Acknowledged."

His colleague smiled a little. "Come on. Let's get Beschta home."

Matsura agreed that that would be a good idea.

Look for STAR TREK Fiction from Pocket Books

Star Trek®: The Original Series

Star Trek: The Next Generation®

Encounter at Farpoint • David Gerrold
Unification • Jeri Taylor
Relics • Michael Jan Friedman
Descent • Diane Carey
All Good Things • Michael Jan Friedman
Star Trek: Klingon • Dean W. Smith & Kristine K. Rusch
Star Trek VII: Generations • J. M. Dillard
Metamorphosis • Jean Lorrah
Vendetta • Peter David
Reunion • Michael Jan Friedman
Imzadi • Peter David
The Devil's Heart • Carmen Carter
Dark Mirror • Diane Duane
Q-Squared • Peter David
Crossover • Michael Jan Friedman
Kahless • Michael Jan Friedman
Star Trek: First Contact • J. M. Dillard
Star Trek: Insurrection • Diane Carey
The Best and the Brightest • Susan Wright
Planet X • Michael Jan Friedman
Ship of the Line • Diane Carey
Imzadi II • Peter David

Star Trek: Deep Space Nine®

Star Trek®: Voyager™

Star Trek®: New Frontier

Star Trek®: Day of Honor

Book One: *Ancient Blood* • Diane Carey
Book Two: *Armageddon Sky* • L. A. Graf
Book Three: *Her Klingon Soul* • Michael Jan Friedman
Book Four: *Treaty's Law* • Dean W. Smith & Kristine K. Rusch
The Television Episode • Michael Jan Friedman

Star Trek®: The Captain's Table

Book One: *War Dragons* • L. A. Graf
Book Two: *Dujonian's Hoard* • Michael Jan Friedman
Book Three: *The Mist* • Dean W. Smith & Kristine K. Rusch
Book Four: *Fire Ship* • Diane Carey
Book Five: *Once Burned* • Peter David
Book Six: *Where Sea Meets Sky* • Jerry Oltion

Star Trek®: The Dominion War

Book 1: *Behind Enemy Lines* • John Vornholt
Book 2: *Call to Arms . . .* • Diane Carey
Book 3: *Tunnel Through the Stars* • John Vornholt
Book 4: *. . . Sacrifice of Angels* • Diane Carey

Star Trek®: The Badlands

Book One: Susan Wright
Book Two: Susan Wright

Star Trek: *Strange New Worlds* • Edited by Dean Wesley Smith
Star Trek: *Strange New Worlds II* • Edited by Dean Wesley Smith

STAR TREK
THE EXPERIENCE
LAS VEGAS HILTON

Be a part of the most exciting deep space adventure in the galaxy as you beam aboard the U.S.S. Enterprise. Explore the evolution of Star Trek - from television to movies in the "History of the Future Museum," the planet's largest collection of authentic Star Trek memorabilia. Then, visit distant galaxies on the "Voyage Through Space." This 22-minute action packed adventure will capture your senses with the latest in motion simulator technology. After your mission, shop in the Deep Space Nine Promenade and enjoy 24th Century cuisine in Quark's Bar & Restaurant.

- -

Save up to $30

Present this coupon at the STAR TREK: The Experience ticket office at the Las Vegas Hilton and save $6 off each attraction admission (limit 5).

Not valid in conjunction with any other offer or promotional discount. Management reserves all rights. No cash value. For more information, call 1-888-GOBOLDLY or visit **www.startrekexp.com**. Private Parties Available.

CODE: 1007   EXPIRES 12/31/00.